HELSINKI HOMICIDE:
AGAINST THE WALL

JARKKO SIPILA

Translated by
Peter Ylitalo Leppa

Ice Cold Crime LLC

Originally published in Finnish as
Seinää Vasten by Gummerus, Helsinki, Finland. 2008.

Translated by Peter Ylitalo Leppa

Published by
Ice Cold Crime LLC
5780 Providence Curve
Independence, MN 55359

Printed in the United States of America

Cover by Ella Tontti

Ice Cold Crime LLC gratefully acknowledges the financial assistance of:

FINNISH LITERATURE EXCHANGE

Library of Congress Control Number: 2009929421

ISBN-13: 978-0-9824449-0-0
ISBN-10: 0-9824449-0-7

CAST OF CHARACTERS

Kari Takamäki – Detective Lieutenant, Helsinki Police Violent Crimes Unit

Suhonen / Suikkanen – Undercover Detective

Anna Joutsamo – Detective

Mikko Kulta – Detective

Kirsi Kohonen – Detective

Kannas – Chief of Forensics

Tapani Larsson – #2 in the Skulls

Tapio Korpela – member of the Skulls

Markus "Bogeyman" Markkanen – thug

Kalevi Lindström – businessman

Juha Saarnikangas – junkie

Jerry Eriksson – con man

Ilari Lydman – small time criminal, bouncer

Eero Salmela – Suhonen's friend, now doing time

Jorma Raitio – Salmela's former accomplice

Jouko Nyholm – Customs Inspector

Leif Snellman – Assistant Director, Customs

PROLOGUE
EARLY AUGUST, 2008

Suhonen settled into a white leather sofa and stretched his back. He surveyed the apartment, a four-room flat in Ruoholahti on the west side of Helsinki. The door to the balcony was open and a warm evening breeze swept through the room.

"Wanna beer?" asked the blonde. Without waiting for an answer she set it on the end table. Her tanned breasts strained at the opening of her white V-neck top. Obviously not real, but so what.

"Suikkanen," she cooed, sliding onto the couch next to him. "I like guys from Lahti. I've always had a lot of fun in Särkänniemi." Suhonen grinned. Särkänniemi, Finland's version of Disneyland, was actually in Tampere, about 130 kilometers from Lahti.

She walked her fingers across the undercover officer's chest. The blonde's name was Sara Lehto. Suhonen knew that she had appeared in several low-budget Finnish porn films. The creamy white, simplified interior of the apartment made him think of a porn set.

Suhonen wasn't interested in Lehto. He was after her boyfriend, Tapani Larsson. He was the number two man in the Skulls, a Finnish biker gang.

A week ago, a small pub at the old Kannelmäki shopping center had burned down and the owner had made the mistake of pointing his finger at the Skulls. The gang had demanded money in exchange for protection, but the owner had refused. In later interviews, the owner changed his story and claimed to have absentmindedly emptied an ashtray into a wastebasket.

Suhonen didn't know where Larsson lived, but had been told that Lehto and Larsson lived together. The tip had brought him here to Ruoholahti. After four hours of staking out the subway station, Sara finally breezed through the sliding doors.

Suhonen had followed the blonde to an outdoor patio bar, where she stopped for a Strongbow cider. A few minutes later, she wandered from the bar to Suhonen's table.

Suhonen had introduced himself as "Suikkanen" from Lahti. As an undercover officer for the Helsinki Violent Crimes Unit he had used this alias many times. After another cider, Sara Lehto had checked that her boyfriend wouldn't be home for another couple of hours and invited him back to her place.

Now she gave his pipes a squeeze, sliding her hand into the sleeve of his T-shirt. Suhonen took a cold swig. He was satisfied he'd gotten Larsson's home address. The ex-con's rap sheet was long and violent. Now he could be found if needed and it'd be easy to get Larsson's cell number from Sara's phone.

Sara smiled, closed her eyes and kissed Suhonen on the neck. His arm rested on her shoulder.

Larsson was not your average criminal. Unlike many, he hadn't grown up in reform schools, but had graduated high school with top honors. Though he came from a good family, he had been attracted to gangs in college. He was ruthless, and he rose quickly within the criminal ranks.

Suhonen took another sip. From the hall, he heard an unexpected noise. Before he could turn his head, he heard a man's voice.

"Who the hell is drinking my beer?"

Suhonen cursed to himself. He turned to see Tapani Larsson standing in the hallway. The thug leveled a Czech CZ pistol at Suhonen's head. How come he hadn't heard the door open?

Sara Lehto got up quickly, went to Larsson and wrapped her arms around him. His muscles rippled under a black T-shirt. His arms were covered in tattoos and ink flames climbed his neck. His head was shaved and the four studs in his left ear were connected by a thin, jeweled chain.

Suhonen noticed that his face seemed thinner than it did in the mug shots. Hollow cheeks only made his eyes more piercing.

"He followed me," she accused. "He's probably a Pistolero."

Try Los Sheriffos, Suhonen thought. How am I gonna get out of this? His badge would only be a liability at this point.

"Talk!" he barked. "Who are you?"

"Suikkanen."

"Who the hell is Suikkanen?"

"Suikkanen. No first name." Suhonen said. He held onto his beer, just in case he needed something to throw. His gun was in the pocket of his leather jacket, draped over the back of the couch a couple of yards away.

"Pat him down," Larsson commanded. "And you, Suikkanen, put the beer on the table and get up."

Suhonen stood up and let the blonde check him out. Her rose-scented perfume filled his nostrils. He had left his wallet in the glove box of his car, which was parked near the subway station. His badge was in the small inside pocket of his jacket. She wouldn't find that either, but that wouldn't buy him much time.

Sara rifled through the jacket. "Shit, he's packing," she said, and pulled out a Glock 26.

Larsson laughed. "And that's a surprise?"

She handed the pistol to Larsson and he stuffed it in the waistband of his pants. He directed Suhonen to sit, then came around and sat opposite him. A narrow coffee table stood between them. Sara remained standing behind Larsson.

"Who do you run with? Pistoleros?

"What are Pistoleros?" Suhonen played dumb. Though the Skulls and Pistoleros were not currently in open warfare, Suhonen knew very well the tensions between the two gangs.

Larsson struck Suhonen on the cheek with the barrel of his pistol. Not very hard, but it hurt. The taste of blood filled his mouth. He felt around with his tongue, wondering if he had broken a tooth.

"What the…"

"There's more where that came from. Talk."

"If I tell you, can I go?"

Larsson nodded.

"Alright, alright…I ain't got nothin' to hide. I was sitting at the Corner Pub in Kallio when this guy comes up and offers me a hundred euros if I can find out where this blonde lives. He figured it'd be somewhere in Ruoholahti, so I waited around at the Metro station till I spotted her. And here she is." Suhonen gestured toward Sara.

Larsson stared at Suhonen with suspicion. "Why did he want her address?"

"He said he saw her in some porn flick, and he just wanted to know…Hey, can I go now?"

"Kill him," Sara said. "He wanted to bang me."

Larsson glared at her. "Listen, what good does it do if we kill him. Nothing. Then again, I don't care…if you want him dead, then…"

Suhonen acted worried. "Listen, I have money. Let me go and it's yours."

Larsson laughed. "How much?"

Suhonen glanced at his jacket, then back at Larsson, who nodded, indicating that he could look through the pockets. Suhonen counted his money onto the table briskly.

"Uh…forty-two euros."

Larsson laughed out loud. "Uh…forty-two euros. Heh-heh… Listen, Suikkanen. Ten will do."

"Just ten," he said, though he knew very well what Larsson meant. Suhonen slid a single wrinkled bill onto the table and stuffed the rest back into his pocket.

"Moron! Ten thousand euros."

Suhonen gaped at him. "I don't have that kind of…"

"Well, figure something out or this bloodthirsty blonde will have her way with you."

Suhonen shook his head. "Uhh…right, I think I can raise it. If I sell my motorcycle."

"You have an hour."

"An hour?" Suhonen looked pained. "That's impossible."

Larsson nodded. "Call somebody. I don't care what you do. It's your debt now."

"Ten grand," Suhonen protested. Larsson just waved his pistol.

Suhonen thought for a second, though he knew exactly who he would call. He dug his cell phone out of his pocket.

"Put it on speakerphone," Larsson demanded.

"Alright, alright," Suhonen said and scrolled down the list to Anna's number. Hopefully she'd know to play along. The phone rang a couple times.

"Hello," answered Detective Anna Joutsamo, slightly riled. "Where in the…"

Suhonen interrupted quickly.

"Listen, Suikkanen here," he began, hoping she would catch the alias and know it was an act.

"I'm in a bit of a jam here and need your help."

"Suikkanen, hell! What's this all about?" Joutsamo snapped.

"Look, I've got a little problem," Suhonen continued. "I need a favor. I got this situation where I owe ten grand to a pretty unhappy customer, and he wants it right now."

"Ha, how'd you end up in that kind of debt?"

"Well…that's the story of my life. You know, debt sneaks up pretty quick," Suhonen persisted.

"OK," Joutsamo said in a voice that signaled she had gotten the message. "Well, what do I have to do?"

"You gotta sell my bike for ten grand. You could call Turunen—he asked about it last spring. But I need the money right away. You can bring it…" Suhonen looked inquiringly at Larsson. "Where?"

"The Hietalahti market."

Suhonen turned back to the phone. "You hear that? The Hietalahti market in one hour."

"And what if Turunen's not around?"

"No, he's around. I saw him this morning. He's got the money, too."

"OK. I'll be in the parking lot in my blue van."

"Thanks," Suhonen said.

"You're a piece of work Suikkanen," Joutsamo barked and hung up the phone.

Larsson looked at Suhonen. "Your girl?"

"Nah...my little sis." Suhonen chuckled. "Do you think the wife would've agreed to that? She'd have said, 'shoot him three times to be sure. Once in the nuts and twice in the head.'"

Larsson cracked a smile.

* * *

The market was still; even the gulls were quiet. It was just before 10:00 P.M., though it was still light out. Helsinki summer nights were as light as the winter afternoons were black. The parking lot was largely empty, as most locals had fled to their summer cabins.

Larsson kept his right hand in the pocket of his leather coat. "Don't do anything stupid, or you're the first to go."

Sara kept to the other side of Larsson, hanging back a bit. They walked in a line towards the south side of the market. Old Market Hall on the far left was another reminder of Helsinki's Russian past. The one-story brick building was a former stable, built in 1903 for Czar Nicholas II's cavalry. The Russians had left Helsinki in 1917, but returned during the Second World War in bombers. Fifty years later they controlled the marketplace, as it had become the main hub for cash seeking Russians selling cheap vodka and cigarettes.

Suhonen spotted the blue van in the middle of the parking lot.

"That's my sister's van. She's probably waiting in the front seat."

Larsson nodded. He could make out a dark-haired woman sitting in the driver's seat about fifty yards away.

"What does she do?"

"Look at the van," Suhonen answered. A sign on the sliding door said, "Vesala Electric," in big white letters. "Just a small business, but she does alright."

Larsson seemed satisfied and nodded. They walked on in silence. When they came within five meters of the van, Larsson gave brief instructions. "Get the money from your sister and give it to Sara. If it's all there, you're off the hook. If you go to the cops, I'll kill your sister first, then you."

"Yeah," Suhonen said, and pulled to the front of the line. Larsson and Sara slowed down. Joutsamo rolled down the window.

"Evening," she said gravely.

"Hey sis. You got the money?"

"Yup. But Turunen wouldn't pay more than nine Gs for the bike. I made up the difference myself; you can pay me later. This better be important."

"Thanks."

Larsson started to fidget. "The money," he snarled.

"Where is it?" Suhonen asked.

Joutsamo made steady eye contact as she extended a thick envelope out the window. Suhonen grabbed it and handed it to Sara.

Sara tore it open and cursed. Larsson turned to look: nothing but newspaper clippings. Suddenly, the sliding door on the van flew open. Three S.W.A.T.

officers pointed MP5 submachine guns at the pair. "FREEZE! POLICE!"

Joutsamo slid out of the van and leveled her pistol at Larsson.

"Don't move!"

"Damn snitch!" Larsson hissed at Suhonen, glaring helplessly at the S.W.A.T. team. The submachine guns stared back.

Suhonen stepped behind Larsson, slapped the cuffs on him and took back his Glock and Larsson's CZ. Joutsamo put Sara in cuffs and ordered one of the S.W.A.T. officers to check the pair for weapons.

"Goddammit. You're a cop. This was a trap!" Larsson uttered as the truth finally dawned. Sara Lehto's face was pinched as she burst into tears.

**MONDAY
NOVEMBER 24**

CHAPTER 1
THE PAKILA TEBOIL STATION,
HELSINKI
MONDAY, 9:55 P.M.

A man in a hooded jacket strode past, his gait restless and jumpy. To Juha Saarnikangas, there was something familiar about him, but he couldn't put his finger on it.

Saarnikangas sat in a dumpy gas station coffee shop and stared out the window into the darkness. He watched as the man drew slowly away, continuing north on Pakila Street. The window was sorely in need of washing; in the armpit of Beltway One it would have to be done weekly. On the northern side of the Beltway, the apartment buildings gave way to townhomes and single-family houses.

The man in the hooded jacket paused beneath the yellow glow of a streetlamp. The dim lighting altered the colors, but he guessed that the man's jacket was either blue or green. Beneath his broad hood, he could make out the visor of a baseball cap, which darted nervously this way and that.

The pavement was wet, though it wasn't raining anymore.

Juha was sure the man had done time. Somehow, it was easy to spot a fellow criminal.

"You reading this?" A bald man in a leather jacket pointed to a tabloid on the table.

"Go ahead," Juha said, and the man took it. He was probably the driver of the blue Volvo taxi, which sat in the parking lot of the gas station. It was parked next to Saarnikangas' decrepit Fiat Ducato. The taxi gleamed in metallic colors, while Juha's van was consumed with rust.

Juha reached instinctively for his coffee cup, but it was empty. He had a narrow face and greasy brown hair that reached the collar of his green U.S. Army jacket. His thoughts whirled as he looked out the window. A blue pickup truck roared down the road. The bald man had disappeared.

Saarnikangas wondered if this hooded character was connected to his job. He didn't know exactly what the job was. He had been given a new phone and orders to wait at the Pakila Teboil at 10:00 P.M. There was nothing to do but wait.

Juha regretted that he had given away that newspaper. Sitting here alone would seem more natural if he had something to browse through. He tried to avoid any suspicious movements, but inevitably his right foot began to bounce the moment he lost concentration.

What the hell was he waiting for anyway? He couldn't afford to turn down this job.

* * *

A dense grove of firs flanked the dirt road on both sides. Street lights were few and far between, and Jerry Eriksson pulled back his hood. Dark hair emerged from the band of his cap, just brushing the tops of his ears. A couple beads of sweat trickled down his spine and soaked into the elastic band of his boxers.

Eriksson cursed. Walking was Vallu Kononen's specialty, not his. He remembered watching Kononen's world-championship winning walk on TV sometime in the mid-nineties. Eriksson wasn't sure on the exact year; he had watched it at hockey camp, a place where he spent plenty of time in his youth. That was then and this was now, but brashness and toughness had served him well in hockey, as they still did.

Now he had to hoof it. With four beers in his system he didn't dare to drive. He wasn't one to take stupid risks. He had taken a taxi as far as Oulunkylä, a bedroom community in northeastern Helsinki, and set out from Pirjo's Tavern on foot. Though the walk was a couple kilometers, it wouldn't have been smart to take a cab all the way.

To hell with this. This guy better have some valuable info. On the phone, he had been promised key intel for his next gig. He had no choice but to believe it. The caller had told him that the meeting spot had to be absolutely secluded so nobody could see them together.

Eriksson glanced around again: no people. It seemed that at any moment, a moose might emerge from the tree line. Jesus. Was this really Helsinki? He liked places where the trees grew through the pavement. *Common - disconnected w/ nature*

The damp forest smelled of earth. Eriksson could detect the sweet, penetrating scent of pine needles. It reminded him of the air-freshener that used to hang from the rear-view mirror of his first car.

Near a bend in the road, a red plastic mailbox emerged from the darkness. Eriksson could make out

15

the number "8" painted in white. From there, a narrow driveway led to a clearing in the middle of the woods. Eriksson patted the FN pistol in his right pocket. He smiled to himself. Was he really this uneasy about a little walk in the woods?

The meeting would probably be quick and easy—he'd be back in the bar in no time for a few more beers.

There was no name on the mailbox, not that he expected one. The light from a streetlamp stretched about fifty meters into the darkness where the driveway curved right. The tire tracks were worn deep, and in the middle, a strip of grass was readying itself for winter.

Eriksson kept going till he was sheltered by darkness. He paused to let his eyes adjust, then continued on warily. At the end of the wooded drive, he could barely make out a tiny single-story house, and beside it, a small dark building. Probably a garage or shed, he reasoned. After another brief pause, he took a step into the darkness.

* * *

Saarnikangas paid the young blonde behind the counter for another coffee. The name tag on her blouse said "Leena." Saarnikangas considered how easy it would be to rob the place. He'd probably net more here than at the kiosks. Even if most people paid for gas with plastic, the register was still filled with hundreds of euros.

The heat from the coffee warmed his hands. If he threatened to throw it in her face, she'd hand over the money. That would be more effective than waving a knife at her from across the counter.

Saarnikangas opted for a "thanks," and the girl responded with an uneasy smile. She was pretty, but Saarnikangas had kept his lips shut. Heroin had destroyed his teeth.

Right now, Saarnikangas was clean. The last fix he had had was eight days ago. The clean streak had started out of necessity when he ran out of money and his credit dried up. He had lain on the floor of his apartment in Pihlajamäki for three agonizing days. Now he was feeling better.

He had gotten the call about this job in the morning. The man had asked if he was clean. Juha had been drowsy, but he assured the caller that he'd take care of it. The gig would reduce his debt by five hundred, plus two hundred in cash. Or so he was told.

* * *

Eriksson's eyes had adjusted to the dark. Now he could see that the smaller building was a garage, and behind it was a run-down wooden rambler. Though he couldn't see for sure, some of the windows seemed broken. The walls were covered in graffiti. Firs encircled the yard, where stood a lone swing cobbled together with metal tubing.

Nobody in sight.

Eriksson continued towards the garage, the supposed meeting place. Spray-painted tags plastered the walls of the garage. To Eriksson, they were just gibberish; he couldn't even read them. Aside from the muffled roar of distant traffic, it was utterly quiet.

Garbage littered the yard: wooden planks, what looked like the remains of a sofa and other junk.

As he neared the garage, it occurred to him for the first time that this might not be so smart. To come knocking at a place like this in the dark? Still no one around. He'd done things like this before. He wasn't afraid of the dark either; it was a criminal's best friend. He remembered how his hockey coach had always told the goalies to hug the goal posts; they were a goalie's best friends. Now he was hugging the darkness. Eriksson chuckled nervously.

He instinctively checked his pocket to make sure his gun was still there.

Reaching the far side of the garage, he peeked carefully around the corner. Nobody. What appeared to be an old stove and washing machine lay in the darkness between the garage and the house.

A service door led into the garage. It was ajar.

Eriksson weaved through the scrap wood on the ground and walked quietly toward the door. His stride had changed from fidgety to furtive. Shit, what if this was some kind of a setup. Maybe someone just wanted to get him away from the bar so they could steal his girl.

He opened the door. Immediately, he was blinded by the glare of a flashlight in his eyes.

"Eriksson?" a man's nasal voice asked from somewhere inside.

"Yeah," Eriksson answered, trying to shield his eyes with the bill of his cap. The light moved lower, hindering his attempts.

"Put that light out."

"Come inside," the voice said stiffly.

The light was trained on his face and his eyes hurt. Eriksson took a couple steps forward and felt the grass change to concrete. Sand scraped on the floor beneath his shifting feet. With his free hand, he groped in the darkness so he wouldn't bump into anything.

"That's far enough," the voice said.

"Put that light out," Eriksson said again.

The man didn't respond.

Jerry Eriksson was still blinded by the light, so he didn't see the flash from the gun barrel. He heard a muffled thump, but never had time to comprehend what it was. The bullet hit him in the middle of the forehead and he crumpled to the ground. His body flopped over and his head struck the concrete floor with a thud.

* * *

Saarnikangas drove his van along a wooded road.

A couple of minutes earlier, he had received a call to confirm he was at the gas station. Then he had been given directions to a house nearby. The man hadn't said what was in store—just told him to drive carefully.

Juha chewed his gum, but the taste was already gone. What kind of job was this anyway? There was probably a stash of drugs nearby that he had to deliver. Maybe he could help himself to some of it, too. A small amount wouldn't be missed. And if it was amphetamines, it would be easy to cut without anybody noticing. Selling some of his take would definitely improve his financial situation.

Juha spotted the red mailbox where he was supposed to turn. He had been told to park by the garage, and that the man on the phone would be waiting inside.

The headlights of the Fiat illuminated the graffiti-covered garage and the house behind it. Juha stopped in front of the garage as directed and got out.

Nobody. Juha wondered if he should call out, then chose not to. His orders had been to wait. He spit out his gum.

Suddenly, the garage door creaked and rose. Juha startled. He saw a dark figure hoisting up the door.

"Back up to the door."

Juha got back in the van, turned it around and backed up.

The man giving orders stood behind the van so that Juha couldn't see him in the mirrors. The interior walls of the garage were also covered with tags.

"Stop," the man called out. Juha stopped the van, killed the motor and engaged the emergency brake. "Come here."

The garage was narrow, but Juha managed to squeeze between the door frame and the side of the van. He was initially blinded by the glare of a flashlight in the far corner, but the light shifted to the floor and Juha saw the corpse. Jesus Christ, he thought to himself, then said it aloud.

"Shut up. Just listen," said the voice. Saarnikangas couldn't see the man, only that he had on a black ski mask and blue overalls. "Gimme your phone."

He fished the cell phone out of the pocket of his jacket and handed it over. The man took it, gave him a pistol with a silencer, and pointed at the body with the flashlight. Juha couldn't see the face.

"Get rid of the body and the gun. Dump it someplace where he won't be found. Ever. If they find him, you'll end up in the same spot."

"How in the…"

"Shut up. Just do it," he snapped.

Juha took a closer look at the man lying on the floor and noticed a familiar-looking jacket with a broad hood, now hanging from the victim's neck. It was the same guy he had seen strolling down the street about twenty minutes ago.

"Where should I…"

The shadowy figure shut off his flashlight. "Use your imagination. And don't fuck up. This asshole was a Customs' nark." Then he slipped out and disappeared behind the van.

Juha was alone now. Unable to move, he just stood next to the body, looking at the gun in his hand. What the hell should he do now?

CHAPTER 2
DINING CAR ON THE PENDOLINO TRAIN
MONDAY, 10:20 P.M.

Suhonen was sitting on the rearmost bench of the dining car on the Pendolino express. His back against the wall, he took a sip from his pint. The undercover detective wore his trademark leather jacket. It was pitch dark outside and the windows reflected the interior of the train like a mirror.

Suhonen's stubbly, street-worn reflection stared back at him. His dark hair, once in a ponytail, had recently been cut short. Now forty, Suhonen had been a cop for half his life, first patrolling the streets of Helsinki then working undercover in Narcotics. Detective Lieutenant Kari Takamäki had recruited him to the Violent Crimes Unit to obtain more intel from the streets. Suhonen got more valuable info than most because he treated his informants like human beings, not like tools of the trade.

Over the years, Suhonen and Takamäki had grown to be close friends. While Takamäki appreciated Suhonen's rampant enthusiasm for catching criminals, at times he had to rein him in. Suhonen's methods would never be found in any police manual, but they got results.

A couple of drunks in front of the bar were providing the entertainment. One of them, a man in

22

his mid-thirties with a stocking cap, had brought two glasses, which the other one filled from a bottle hidden in his bag. The friends had boarded the train in Jyväskylä and had obviously already had a few.

"Want some more?" the one with the bottle asked.

"Drink what you got first," the one with the stocking cap shot back. The glasses were still half full.

"Shit, you sound like my old lady," he said. In plain view, he dug the bottle out of his bag and filled his own glass to the very top.

Suhonen was returning from a three-day training course at Lake Naarajärvi, near Pieksämäki in Eastern Finland. The course had been on high speed pursuits, and the training on the practice track had included various obstacle courses and emergency braking procedures. Suhonen had gone on the trip with some doubts, but at least he had had fun. Instructors had been pissed when Suhonen spun a few unauthorized donuts; the other cops had just laughed. *man's mah*

On the way there, he had hung out with a couple of familiar traffic cops from the Helsinki Police. They had stayed a few more days for a course on Police escorts, but Suhonen had been permitted to return to Helsinki.

The dispute between the two drunks was getting louder, and a couple of women from a neighboring table got up and left.

The conductor stepped into the car and the noise died down.

Suhonen's cell phone rang and he pulled it out of his breast pocket. The caller appeared on the display: Takamäki.

"Hello," Suhonen answered.

"Vacation over already?" the detective lieutenant ribbed in his deep voice.

Suhonen glanced at the advertisements near the ceiling of the train car. One of them was for the Pendolino dining car, in which he now sat. It showed a photo of Venice or something like that and the text read, "Pendolino—a piece of Italy wherever you are." Pieksämäki, a not so picturesque part of Finland, sure hadn't felt like Italy. The small town had once been voted the ugliest place in the country.

"What could be better? Speed and danger." Suhonen said.

"I suppose you guys got to know the local bars."

"Yep, that too," Suhonen smiled. Actually, their daily saunas had included just one beer. Who says Finns can't draw the line at one? Otherwise, everything had been pretty low-key. Combine a cop with a car, and booze just doesn't fit the equation.

"What's up in Helsinki?"

"Nothing much. Mostly routine stuff," Takamäki replied.

Suhonen knew that "routine stuff" often meant brutal assaults, arsons and other violent crimes that were part of a homicide cop's daily diet. Though Kari Takamäki's group was officially known as the Violent Crimes Unit, or VCU for short, the old name of 'Homicide Squad' still stuck, even though their job description went beyond catching murderers.

"So you didn't miss me then."

"Not really," Takamäki said. "I actually just called to ask if you're coming in tomorrow. Or are you taking the day off?"

"Not sure," said Suhonen. He had a morning meeting at the Helsinki Prison that was high priority.

"Actually, I'll stop by at least. I have to go to the gym, too."

"Let's go get a cup of coffee at some point tomorrow. Can't wait to hear about all the latest pursuit tricks."

The conversation ended and Suhonen looked up towards the ceiling, where a monitor displayed the train's current speed. Though it didn't feel like the train was accelerating, the numbers on the display changed every few seconds: 236 km/h, 303 km/h, 327 km/h, 367 km/h, 414 km/h...

"Pendolino – a piece of Italian technology wherever you are," Suhonen thought, and hoped the train would make it all the way to Helsinki.

dig at Italy..

crime is routine

TUESDAY
NOVEMBER 25

CHAPTER 3
LINDSTRÖM'S APARTMENT,
TEHDAS STREET, HELSINKI
TUESDAY, 8:30 A.M.

Kalevi Lindström sat on the rowing machine. The front of his white tank top was stained with sweat and Lindström was pleased. The sixty-year old man didn't care much for jogging, so he had converted one of the bedrooms into a fitness room.

In addition to the rowing machine, he had a stationary bike, a stepper, and a punching bag. The floor was covered by a black padded mat. A large television sat in the corner, the screen dark. A pull-up bar hung from the high ceiling and Lindström approached it. His movements were stiff and awkward.

He wasn't muscular, but wiry. His short hair had turned grey and he had often wondered if he should dye it back to black, but had decided instead to embrace it. He believed it made him look more sophisticated.

Markus Markkanen leaned against the wall, watching Lindström's workout with some amusement. Lindström was still paying a fitness instructor to come on Fridays. In Markkanen's opinion, he was tossing money down the drain—

unless, of course, he was banging her too—but he didn't intend to say anything about it to his boss.

If Lindström evoked an image of the elderly Roger Moore, Markkanen was more like a plain version of Sean Connery in *Dr. No*.

It bothered him that the gym didn't smell like sweat, just some citrus-scented air-freshener that either Lindström or the house-cleaner sprayed everywhere.

"You seen Eriksson?" Lindström asked. From a little stool, he hopped onto the pull-up bar.

Markkanen knew that Lindström would make it to four before giving out. "No. He said he was going to the bar last night and he'd call me in the morning. He hasn't called."

"Count out loud," the older man commanded.

Markkanen clenched his chiseled hands into fists, but Lindström didn't notice. A tall, muscular man, Markkanen wore jeans and a grey sweatshirt. He was required to leave his shoes in the entryway, and had learned to always wear nice socks so the old man couldn't tease him.

Markus Markkanen's face was flat and featureless. His brown hair was straight and closely cropped around the ears.

The first chin-up was easy. "One," Markkanen said in a bored voice. His thoughts wandered elsewhere. His son had been slapped with a D-minus on his math test and it worried him.

"Count louder!" Lindström snapped.

In good form, he completely straightened his arms, then pulled himself up again.

"Two," Markkanen said with a little more pep.

Same thing again. So far so good.

"Three!"

30

Lindström lowered himself somewhat, but this time he didn't straighten his arms. He wrestled his chin over the bar anyway.

"Four."

"One more," Lindström panted.

This time he only let his arms go to ninety degrees before starting to pull himself up again. His face was bright red, and his chin barely squeaked over the bar. Markkanen couldn't have cared less had a blood vessel popped in the man's brain.

"Five," Markkanen counted.

Lindström hopped down. "Five! A new record, and good form too. I should make you go the gym more often. It'd do that paunch of yours some good!"

What paunch, Markkanen thought, but didn't say anything. He was six foot three and weighed just under 220 pounds. Maybe his stomach had gotten a little softer in the last year, but as far as he was concerned, he was still in very good shape. He had gotten his body as a youth, street fighting and running from the cops. It had been perfect training for a career on the street collecting debts. He had met Lindström about five years ago and started working for him. Since then, his job description had changed. He didn't have to beat the shit out of junkies any more. That morning, Markkanen had used a scanning device to check the apartment for any microphones or taps. As usual, he hadn't found any.

Kalevi Lindström's background was a whole different story: a good family, MBA, and now, a few businesses operating on the very fringes of the law— some on the wrong side.

Markkanen wasn't in the loop about everything, nor was it his place to ask.

"Go ahead!" said Lindström, challenging him.

31

"Five chin-ups, bet you a ten-spot."

Markkanen hopped up to the bar. He knew he could do at least ten, but after two, he let his hands tremble and rose only halfway.

"Ha! I knew you'd choke."

Markkanen fished a rumpled ten euro note out of his black pants and set it on the bench of the rowing machine.

Lindström sat on an exercise mat and stretched his hamstrings. "You should be doing this, too. Feels good in the... I gotta talk to Eriksson."

"I don't know where he is. His phone goes straight to voicemail."

"Shit! Go find him," Lindström snorted. "Tell him to get over here."

"Is it something I can help out with?"

"No."

Geezer, Markkanen thought as he slipped quietly out of the room.

* * *

Juha Saarnikangas' eyes were clouded. He was waiting at a red light near the Ruskeasuo Teboil station, heading downtown. The worn-out wipers struggled to clear the rain off the windshield, only succeeding in smearing the dirt.

Juha hadn't slept at all last night. The events at the garage seemed like a bad dream. At first, he had intended to load the body into the van, but had decided that it wasn't his kind of work.

There was a limit to what he would do. Stolen goods and drugs were his turf, not bodies.

Saarnikangas had shut the rear doors, jumped into the van, and had made it to Beltway One before he started to shake. He had to go back. Had to get rid of the body. He had no choice; they'd find him for sure.

Juha's hands wouldn't obey his head, nor the other way around. He hadn't gone back. Instead, he had driven the 170 kilometers north to Tampere and from there, another hundred kilometers further. In the early morning he had stopped for gas at an unmanned Parkano ABC, then decided to turn back to Helsinki.

Lydman had gotten him into this. That shit-face had a lot to answer for. As he neared Tampere, Saarnikangas wondered if he should use the gun. With the barrel of a gun at his temple, Lydman would have plenty of answers. Luckily his better instincts prevailed. He was no hit man, just a small-time junkie in a tight spot.

At the Valkeakoski interchange, he had turned off onto a side road to throw the gun into a lake.

He had tried to sleep in the van a bit, but nothing came of it. He had to do something with the body. Bury it? Throw it in a lake? He had no idea; this wasn't his thing. He thought about the body, still lying dead on the concrete floor. He didn't even know who the guy was. This had nothing to do with him at all.

The red light changed to green, though Juha didn't notice it till the car behind him honked. He turned right towards Pikku-Huopalahti. The new suburb was built in the '90s and dubbed "Legoland" because of the apartment buildings in pastel shades of pink, turquoise and violet. Architecturally, it was meant to counterbalance the abundance of concrete grey housing developments from the seventies.

It wasn't worth it to go up against Lydman, he'd have to figure out something else. Still, the guy didn't have the right to send these kinds of shit jobs his way.

A streetcar turned suddenly in front of him, and Saarnikangas had to jam on the brakes.

He kept both his hands on the steering wheel. Having something to hold onto kept them from trembling.

Now flanked on both sides by five-story apartment buildings, he turned left onto Tilkka Street and continued another hundred yards. The lower half of the apartment building was brick-red, while the upper half had been painted pink.

There was a small clearing in front of the building, surrounded by bushes, where he parked the van. A mother pushing a baby carriage scowled at him, but didn't say anything. Juha hurried to the door.

It was barely 9:00 in the morning. Lydman would definitely be home.

Saarnikangas bounded up the stairs two at a time to the third floor. Though the sign on the door said "Nurmi," Lydman had lived there a long time already. He had been busted for a series of three bank robberies in the early part of the '90s and had spent several years in the slammer. The contacts he made in prison had helped the now forty-something man find his true colors. He had also served a couple of other short stints in jail.

Juha pressed the doorbell and heard it ring.

A dog barked loudly, reminding him that Lydman had a huge Rottweiler.

The door opened an inch and Juha saw that the security chain was engaged. He tried to jam his foot in the doorway; it didn't work. Lydman just kicked it out.

"Shit."

"What now?" Lydman growled. His naked upper body was heavily tattooed. He had short, sandy brown hair and a crooked nose, broken in a fight. All he had on was a pair of black jeans.

"What kind of a job you send me out on, for chrissakes?"

"I don't know anything about it, and I don't want to either."

"But I..."

"I said I don't wanna know anything about it," Lydman persisted.

"This was your deal."

Saarnikangas heard a woman asking who was at the door. "Nobody," Lydman said. The Rottweiler stood behind him, growling.

"Stay," Lydman commanded. Saarnikangas stiffened.

"I need your advice..."

"Hey, Saarnikangas! You took the job. That was your choice. If you got problems, they're yours," he said and pulled a couple wrinkled 100 euro notes from his pocket. He shoved them through the opening. "There's your money. The other five will go towards your debt, assuming the job was done right."

"It was," Juha said, looking the man in the eyes.

Lydman's gaze fell for a second, then rose again.

"Good. Do as you're told, and nothing bad will happen. The less we know about anything, the better."

"But I want..."

"What you want doesn't mean shit. This is no game. These are vicious people."

Juha was puzzled and couldn't think of anything else to say.

Two girls, probably first-graders, came down the stairs. Both of them wore bright red jackets and were chattering loudly. Saarnikangas heard them say something about knitting.

Lydman slammed the door shut, leaving Saarnikangas alone on the landing. He made the mistake of smiling at the girls, who hurried down the stairs. "Gross! Did you see his teeth!" he heard one of them sneer.

Saarnikangas waited for a couple of minutes before going down the stairs. He didn't want anyone to think he was following the girls.

By the time he got out the door, they were already out of sight. He stumbled back to the van, wondering what to do. Both of his hands were trembling, probably from lack of sleep. He would have liked to sleep, but he could barely close his eyes. Some downers would help, except he didn't have any. He did have money, though. Shit.

Saarnikangas imagined himself lying in bed. He could just lie there, and nothing would matter. That shithead could say whatever he wanted about vicious people this, that and the other, but it wouldn't matter to him.

The Ducato roared to life. He had to get back to the garage. He had to think. Enough blundering.

CHAPTER 4
HELSINKI PRISON
TUESDAY, 10:03 A.M.

so far most characters are men in their 40s — any women other than named Sgra* briefly Anna

Saku Ainola, Warden of the Helsinki Prison, was wearing his old, grey suit. Suhonen was sure he had been in the same shabby clothes for at least ten years. A dreary man in his forties, Ainola stood waiting for Suhonen to pass through the metal detector at the entrance. Suhonen had left his change, phone and Glock 26 in a locker, so he made it through without a hitch.

The drawn-looking guard at the gate was utterly expressionless. He had seen people of every stripe pass through, and this guy in a leather jacket was just one of them. Though Suhonen looked more like one of the inmates than a visitor, the guard had seen his police-issue Glock and guessed correctly that he was a cop.

"Hello," Ainola said dryly, offering his hand. Both men had firm handshakes. Ainola had a long history at the prison: he had started as a guard, and in his spare time, studied to earn a law degree.

Ainola flashed his ID card, unlocking the door of the gatehouse. He opened it and led the way. The gatehouse was part of the prison's perimeter wall, some twenty yards from the brick-walled, 19th century central building. Helsinki Prison housed mainly high-risk repeat offenders.

Suhonen dodged the puddles in the flagstone yard. His cross-trainers were water-resistant, but not waterproof. A steady drizzle fell from the grey sky.

"Thanks for arranging this," said Suhonen.

"No problem."

Suhonen had specifically requested that Ainola personally arrange the meeting so that no inadvertent rumors would spread.

Ainola swiped his card and pulled open the door to the main building. He led Suhonen to the basement level where a room had been reserved for police interrogations. "Call me when you're ready," Ainola said and slipped out. The door clanged shut and Suhonen heard the lock engage.

The room reminded him of the interrogation rooms at the Police Headquarters in Pasila. Grey walls, a beige table, a phone on the wall and a couple of chairs. Eero Salmela sat at the table. He was wearing dark-grey prison-issue pants, a white T-shirt and a blue hooded sweatshirt. He appeared to have lost weight. His hair was straight and close-cropped, his cheeks sunken, and his eyes were set deeper than before. He looked at Suhonen gravely, his mouth a thin crack. Prison wasn't easy on a man.

"Hey there," Suhonen said. He shrugged off his coat and draped it over the back of the chair. The room was cool, and Suhonen kept his sweater on.

"What's new in the big city?"

Suhonen was tempted to point out that the prison was well within city limits, only about four kilometers from downtown Helsinki. From the nearby tough streets of Kallio, a tennis ball full of amphetamines could almost be thrown into the prison yard. But Salmela didn't seem to be in the mood for jokes. Suhonen sat down. "Been in Pieksämäki a few days, so I can't really call that the big city."

"Naarajärvi prison? What's so interesting over there? Or should I say who?"

"No, no. It was a mandatory police driving course. Nothing you need to worry about."

"Chase tactics, huh?" Salmela wore a skeptical expression, then shrugged his shoulders.

Suhonen and Salmela had known each other since childhood. Chance had dealt the criminal card to Salmela and the cop card to Suhonen. It could have been the other way around, but Suhonen had stayed home with a fever one night when Salmela and a couple other punks from Lahti were busted for breaking and entering.

Salmela, Suhonen's part-time informant, had always provided valuable intel. On his end, Suhonen had helped Salmela out of a few minor legal jams.

A couple of years ago, Salmela's son had been shot dead when a drug deal went bad. Up to that point, Salmela had been a small-time thief and black market dealer, but the loss of his son had turned him to more serious crimes.

"How's your woman?" Salmela asked.

"You mean Raija?" Suhonen laughed. He had managed to live with her for just one year, before they broke up. "A month ago she finally got fed up and packed her bags."

"That hurts."

"A little."

"You're lying," Salmela said.

"You're right. Didn't bother me at all."

Salmela was quiet for a moment. "You're a terrible liar. Did you bring the cake?"

"Baked it myself. Forgot to put the file in," Suhonen chuckled. Salmela had been the one to request the meeting. He was serving a four year sentence for drug trafficking. He had been involved with a gang that was planning a string of armed robberies. Their intent had been to use the stolen money to pay for a large shipment of drugs. Salmela's role was to help plan and execute the robberies. District Court had viewed him as a full co-conspirator, and he was sent away for trafficking along with the other major players.

The scheme unraveled a year ago when Suhonen, working on another case, had tagged along with a S.W.A.T. team on a raid in an apartment in West Harbor. Salmela and a couple other men were arrested along with a stash of weapons and a detailed plan of the armed robberies. The National Bureau of Investigation, the Finnish version of the FBI, had handled the drug investigation.

"Who ratted on us?" Salmela turned serious again.

"I already told you. It was a fluke. We were looking for another guy, checking any suspect apartments in the database. Just tough luck."

"I don't believe you," Salmela said, leaning forward. "But that doesn't matter now. Appeals Court put me in a shitty spot."

"Oh, it's the court's fault now?"

Salmela nodded.

"If you remember, the court gave me four years and Raitio four and a half."

Jorma Raitio was another of the major players in the scheme.

Salmela continued, "Nothing wrong with that. The prosecution was able to link him to a lot more than me. Fair enough. But a week ago, the Appeals Court screwed me."

"How?"

"They jacked up Raitio's sentence to six years, and shortened mine to three. They didn't have enough evidence to tie me to the drugs."

"A shortened sentence? That sounds nice."

"Sounds nice, but it ain't. Now everybody here is wondering, 'How did Salmela get such a cozy deal? And just as Raitio gets a shittier one?' Rumor has it that I've been squealing to the cops so they'd put in a good word for me in appeals court."

"But that's not true?"

"It sure as hell isn't. I know that. But try telling that to the goons in here. Anyone rumored to be friendly with the cops isn't very popular."

"What can I do?" Suhonen asked.

"Tell me who it was and I'll take care of it my way."

"Listen to me," said Suhonen. "I'm not shitting you. It was a coincidence."

He wasn't lying. He had been trailing an escaped convict when a druggie had given him the address to a potential hideout. He didn't know why Juha Saarnikangas had led the police to that spot, and under no circumstances would he reveal the name.

Salmela said nothing, just sat in his chair and stared. Suhonen stared back for a while, then cut the silence, "Listen, I'll help you out however I can."

"I don't need your help. You know me, I'm not gonna go into protective custody. I'll find someone else to get my back."

He got up. The message was clear: the meeting was over.

"Don't do anything stupid," said Suhonen. He got up, grabbed the phone off the hook and dialed Ainola's number. The men stood facing one another, not speaking. Suhonen offered a cigarette and Salmela turned it down. They waited four long minutes until Ainola came and escorted Salmela out of the room.

Suhonen wondered how he passed his time in here. Did he have some prison job, was he in rehab or did he just lie around in his cell all day? The whole situation just pissed him off.

* * *

Juha Saarnikangas stopped his van on the dirt road about twenty yards away from the red mailbox. Even in the daylight, the woods were bleak, wet, and grey. He rolled down the window, trying to catch a breath of fresh air, but he couldn't seem to inhale right. His chest felt constricted. He rubbed his face. This wasn't a good spot to be, even if nobody was around. A little further off, a few houses were visible where people could be watching out of the windows.

Juha put the van back in gear and swung into the tree-lined driveway leading to the garage. The van splashed through puddles of water, the tires struggling to grip. If only the body were gone. Maybe the guy with the ski mask had come back to check on things and taken care of it himself. Saarnikangas didn't have a problem with death. He had seen plenty of his junkie friends die from overdoses, but murder was different. And how in the hell do you get rid of a body? Would he even be able to lift it into the van?

He pulled into the yard and backed up to the garage door.

And who was this guy anyway? Saarnikangas remembered watching the victim from the gas station window, his clothes and his bouncy gait. Undoubtedly a younger man. But why? The shooter had seemed like a professional hit man with his blue overalls and gloves. Unless he was on his way to a job at the body shop, Saarnikangas grinned to himself.

He tried to remember if the man had looked Russian or Estonian. He had spoken perfect Finnish, though that didn't mean much. Seemed like a hired hit, though. Juha remembered him saying something about a "Customs' nark." Revenge then. But whose revenge? Did Lydman know the hit man? What about the victim? Or was it true that Lydman didn't know anything about it? Too many questions.

Saarnikangas rounded the corner and pushed open the side door carefully. Don't be there, don't be there, he muttered. Even in the light of day the garage was dark, but Saarnikangas saw the body on the floor in the exact same position where it had been left about 12 hours earlier: on its left side, curled up slightly. The baseball cap was still on, but it was slanted down over the face.

Saarnikangas didn't see where the victim had been shot. On the cement floor next to the body's head was a patch of dark, dried blood. He assumed the bullet had hit him in the head.

He looked around the garage, trying to calm himself down. The walls were covered in graffiti and everything moveable had been taken away. Only a crude table made from rough-sawn planks remained, the sole thing nobody wanted.

Saarnikangas left the service door open so a little light could get inside. He circled the body, keeping his distance. Still not sure what to do, he approached it slowly, occasionally stopping to think.

He bent down next to the body, extended a quivering hand and slid the bill of the man's cap aside. He froze when he recognized the man's face and saw the bullet hole in his forehead.

"Shit," he gasped, springing back to his feet.

CHAPTER 5
POLICE HEADQUARTERS,
PASILA, HELSINKI
TUESDAY, 2:00 P.M.

Detective Mikko Kulta sat at his desk typing out a report at a leisurely pace. Not far off, fellow detectives Anna Joutsamo and Kirsi Kohonen occupied themselves with other police business. Suhonen's chair was empty as usual. Joutsamo had the radio on. Once again, the headlines were about the terrible economy. Layoffs and failing companies had been at the top of the news for months.

Kulta, a muscular man in a loose-fitting blue sweater, was wearing headphones so he missed the depressing newscast.

He yawned, saved his interview transcript with the click of a mouse, and took the headphones off. Then he ran his hands through his short, pale brown hair, stretched his back and cleared his throat.

"You know what?" Kulta said. "Solving these violent crimes is too easy."

Joutsamo and Kohonen looked up from their desks.

"Really," Joutsamo said dryly.

"Yeah," he went on. "Just look at the statistics. About 80-90 percent of all violent crimes are solved, but only 30 percent of property crimes. Then, out of all the thefts in downtown Helsinki, only about 3 percent are ever resolved."

Kohonen and Joutsamo glanced at one another.

"Stats don't lie," Kulta concluded. "Property crimes are more difficult to solve."

Joutsamo snorted. "I can have a chat with Takamäki about moving you to a more challenging position. Hey, maybe you'd like to join the guys over at Itäkeskus." Itäkeskus was an eastern suburb with a giant shopping mall of the same name, notorious for petty thefts and violence.

"I didn't mean that, but just think about the case I've got right now."

"You're talking about Sandberg's assault and battery?" Kohonen asked.

Kulta nodded. "A man calls 911 at two-thirty in the morning asking for help. He says his wife has beaten him with a potato masher and she's got a knife in the other hand. A squad car heads out and takes the drunk woman into custody. They charge her with domestic assault so the case is transferred to us. So I interview the wife and she confesses to everything, complete with a motive. The husband claims he had been out drinking with some friends that night, but the wife could smell perfume on him."

"Because of the smoking ban in bars," the red-haired Kohonen interrupted. "Used to be that you couldn't smell anything but smoke after a night out."

"Now don't go complaining about smells," Kulta remarked. "Every time you go horseback riding, everyone here can tell."

"Oh, and what about your basketball bag…" Kohonen shot back.

"OK, cut it out," Joutsamo interrupted.

It was quiet for a moment, then Kulta continued.

46

"So, case in point. Violent crimes practically solve themselves. Now, what if somebody had broken into Sandberg's garage and taken, say, a set of rims. Almost without question the case would never have been solved. They'd be lucky if a patrol car ever made it out there."

Joutsamo and Kohonen glanced at each other again, shaking their heads. You could never be sure if Kulta was being serious.

"Listen, Mikko," Joutsamo began, "Go ahead and finish your transcript, and while you're at it, you can ponder why it's always you who gets the cases that seem to solve themselves."

Kohonen laughed aloud.

"He who laughs last has the slowest wit." Kulta smiled.

* * *

Markus Markkanen was sitting on the sofa at home, watching billiards on TV. His feet were kicked up on the coffee table and he wondered when he would pick up a pool cue again. As a youngster, he had played quite a bit. Then again, he had been involved in plenty of other things during those years. He wasn't especially proud of his past, but he didn't regret it either. Not even his nickname, "Bogeyman."

His eight year-old son Eetu was doing his homework on the floor. The teachers had given him some additional assignments. If he couldn't master the material, they just threw more work at him. The apartment was in need of cleaning, but that didn't interest Markkanen. Technically, he and his wife were divorced. Nonetheless, the three of them lived together like a regular family. The apartment was in his wife's name. Located in Helsinki's western satellite city Espoo, next to the Big Apple shopping center, it had four rooms with a sauna and a kitchen. Markkanen had pending restitution for old drug charges, so had he shared co-ownership of the apartment, the repo man would've paid a visit. Right now, his "ex"-wife was at some fitness class. She'd probably be better off running around the block, but if this kept her happy, then so be it, he thought.

"Dad, what's fourteen plus seventeen?" Eetu asked.

"Huh?"

"Fourteen plus seventeen. What's that make?"

"I'm not gonna tell you. Do the math."

"Come on…" the boy whined. "This is lame."

"Nobody's gonna hold your hand in the test," Markkanen said.

"This is bullshit."

"Hey, where'd you learn that kind of language?"

The boy didn't respond, Markkanen continued, "You gotta learn to figure things out on your own. Just do it."

Markkanen snatched a bottle of Johnny Walker off the coffee table and poured some whiskey into his empty glass. He gulped down half. Markkanen had had better whiskey, but this was alright. Alcohol helped him think.

"What's twenty minus thirteen?"

"Didn't I just tell you…"

He stopped short when his cell phone rang. The display said 'Lindström' and he got up and walked into the hallway.

"Hello," Markkanen answered coolly.

"Heard anything about Eriksson yet?"

"Nope."

48

"This is very important."

"Well, he hasn't gotten ahold of me," Markkanen said dryly.

"Don't talk back. We've gotta find him."

"I'll let you know right away if he contacts me."

"No, you have to *look* for him," Lindström demanded, "Have you been to his apartment?"

"Is there something he's doing that I could help out with?"

"No," Lindström snapped and hung up.

Markkanen went back into the living room. Eetu had abandoned his homework and was playing some first-person shoot-em-up game on Xbox.

"Eetu, what's 20–13?"

"Seven," he answered, without looking up from his game.

"You did the math yourself?"

"I used the calculator on my cell phone. You said I should learn how to figure things out on my own."

That made him laugh, but he quickly regained his stern expression. Clever kid, maybe he'll become something after all. He thought about watching some more pool, but decided against it. Instead, he poured himself another drink.

"Dad!" the boy exclaimed. "Did you see that shot... From the hip! Here, watch the replay. Right in the forehead!"

CHAPTER 6
DOWNTOWN HELSINKI
TUESDAY, 8:32 P.M.

Juha Saarnikangas' van was parked on the east end of the Boulevard in the heart of Helsinki. Raindrops were falling lazily onto the windshield. Through the blur, the lights and billboards on Erottaja were visible.

The junkie glanced at the clock on his phone: 8:32 P.M. Two minutes late already. He had been agonizing over his problem and now he had a solution, or at least he thought so.

The door swung open suddenly, startling him, and Suhonen slid inside. His leather jacket glistened with rain.

"Nice Ducato. Is it yours?"

"You're late," Saarnikangas snapped.

"Your clock is fast," said Suhonen. The broken dashboard clock showed 1:30.

Saarnikangas forced himself to breathe slowly. Both his hands were on the steering wheel. He knew Suhonen would study his every movement and draw his own conclusions from them.

"So?" Suhonen asked. "You wanted to meet?"

"I have a question for you," Saarnikangas began, still looking out the windshield. He hit the wipers once, so he could see through the glass.

"You see that small brown building up there? If you can tell me what's special about it, I'll tell you something you don't know."

Suhonen studied the plain building at the intersection of Boulevard, Erottaja and Northern Esplanade. It led to the Erottaja parking garage. He recalled that sometime in the early '90s he had received a tip, which had led him to a couple of sport-gambling hustlers who were operating out of the basement of the building. Probably not what Saarnikangas had in mind. Besides, sport hustlers weren't that unusual. It had become a big business.

"Listen Juha," the officer snorted. "Enough of the quiz show. You called me, so let's have it."

"You know, if all you do is stare at the pavement when you walk this city, you'll miss out on all the interesting stuff," Juha said.

Suhonen knew that Saarnikangas had studied art history at the University of Helsinki before drugs had taken over.

"So we're talking about history," Suhonen feigned excitement. "I do remember a story about that building from the '60s or '70s. Narcotics was on a raid and confiscated a whole half an ounce of hash. *Helsingin Sanomat* even ran a story on it that hung on the wall of the office for quite a while. It takes a bit more than half an ounce to get a journalist excited nowadays, although the police are interested in whatever crumbs they can find."

"No, art history! Alright I'll tell you. That building is the first one that Alvar Aalto ever designed in Helsinki. It was finished in 1951, soon to be followed by the Rautatalo, Kulttuuritalo, Finlandia-talo and Enso-Gutzeit's headquarters. This is where it all began."

Junkie Has facts of Helsinki art history.

"Thank you. I've been enlightened," he smirked, though he was actually amazed by this tidbit.

"There's something else."

"I'm waiting."

Saarnikangas continued to stare straight ahead and kept his hands on the wheel. "I heard something that should interest you."

"Oh?"

"Do you know Jerry Eriksson?"

Suhonen thought for a second. "Seems vaguely familiar... Eriksson you say? Wasn't he involved in some internet fraud or something like that?"

"Yeah, that too."

"What about him?" he asked, but was interrupted when his cell phone rang. It was his ex-girlfriend Raija. He pushed the "end call" button and the ringer went dead instantly.

Saarnikangas waited a bit before continuing, "I heard he might be in deep shit."

"How deep?"

"Deep. Maybe six feet under, or at least in danger of it."

Suhonen didn't ask how Saarnikangas knew about this, since he wouldn't have answered anyway. A streetcar rumbled along the Boulevard and sped past the van. It would continue to the Hietalahti Market, then turn around.

Rain was keeping almost everyone indoors. Only a few umbrellas bobbed along the street.

"What do you mean?" Suhonen asked.

"Murdered. Maybe."

"Where? When? Why? And by who?"

"I don't know. Everyone has enemies, but I haven't the slightest clue who Eriksson's are."

Suhonen scowled at the man sitting next to him. Saarnikangas continued to stare out the windshield. "Either you're shitting me or there's something you're not telling me. Which one is it?"

Saarnikangas shifted, keeping his hands on the wheel. He didn't dare look Suhonen in the eyes.

"Aalto would've been better off if he had never designed the Enso headquarters, but otherwise he's a first-class architect." The headquarters of Enso, the largest Finnish paper company, sat on an imposing site on the Helsinki waterfront, about a half a kilometer down the Esplanade from where they were. The modern five-story building was composed of large windows surrounded by white marble squares, and seemed utterly orphaned in its 19th century Art Nouveau surroundings.

"Juha!" Suhonen barked.

Saarnikangas didn't answer.

Suhonen jerked Juha's right hand off the wheel and twisted it, forcing him to make eye contact.

"Listen," Suhonen said quietly, looking him directly in the eyes. "You called me. Eriksson's disappearance is interesting, so if you know anything more about it, speak now."

"Or never," Saarnikangas continued. Suhonen wasn't smiling.

The silence lay heavy. Saarnikangas muttered in a low voice, "Well, there is this one thing. Rumor has it that Eriksson was some sort of Customs' nark and that he was knocked off in some abandoned house or garage."

"What garage? Where?"

"Not sure."

"Talk!"

"Well, uhh, I don't know what garage, but you know the Pakila Teboil, right?"

Suhonen nodded.

"Somewhere close by there. That's all I know."

"Where'd you hear that Eriksson was a Customs' nark?"

Saarnikangas laughed. "I overheard someone talking on the subway."

Suhonen wasn't surprised by his answer.

"OK," Suhonen said, "When did this happen?"

"I'm not really sure. Not long ago. I heard about it today and thought, being an upstanding citizen and all, maybe the authorities would be interested in this," Juha said, almost forgetting one important thing.

"Intel has a price, right?"

"Of course," Suhonen chuckled.

"Five hundred, at least."

"Let's see if we find the body first, then we'll get back to you. You can be sure of that."

"OK," Saarnikangas backed down. "It's just a rumor, not a sure thing or anything."

"I'll get back to you," Suhonen said and got out of the van.

The door slammed shut and Juha watched as the cop crossed the Boulevard and disappeared. He took a deep breath before starting the van. This had gone well. With Suhonen's help, maybe he could wash his hands of the whole thing.

* * *

Suhonen was walking west on the Boulevard toward "Plague Park," nicknamed after the 1710 epidemic. About a thousand people were buried under the park in mass graves. Yellow lights gleamed off the wet cobblestones. He crossed Yrjönkatu, where his car was parked about fifty meters away. The linden trees had dropped their leaves, and through their canopies he could clearly see Helsinki's Old Church, bathed in light.

Jerry Eriksson's name was familiar, but Suhonen couldn't picture his face. A young newcomer, anyhow. But a Customs' nark? Why would Customs be interested in a low-class swindler like him? Or maybe his info on Eriksson was out of date.

As he reached his unmarked Peugeot, Suhonen unlocked the doors with a remote and the blinkers flashed.

He had a murder to solve—if indeed there was one—but no corpse. Yet. The first order of business would be to find Eriksson, dead or alive.

Suhonen started the car and considered organizing a search party.

The Pakila Teboil, he mused. Maybe he'd just go have a look around. Yeah, there were a hell of a lot of houses in that area, but not so many abandoned ones. A few hours of canvassing the neighborhood wouldn't hurt.

His cell phone rang again. It was Raija. For a second, Suhonen considered answering, then hit the red button.

**WEDNESDAY
NOVEMBER 26**

CHAPTER 7
POLICE HEADQUARTERS, PASILA, HELSINKI
WEDNESDAY, 8:50 A.M.

A fluorescent light was flickering in the VCU's windowless conference room at the Pasila Headquarters. Though the room could accommodate up to twenty cops, it was largely empty now: only Mikko Kulta, Anna Joutsamo and Kirsi Kohonen were present. Various documents and newspapers were spread out on the table. In the adjacent kitchenette, the coffee maker purred. Takamäki had called Joutsamo to set up a meeting for 9:00 A.M. sharp.

"Mikko, can you do something about that?" Joutsamo said, pointing at the flickering light.

"You mean call building maintenance?"

"No, like now."

"Of course. Did you know, by the way, that the Minister of the Interior has the objective of making Finland the safest country in Europe," Kulta announced, getting up. "This plan is based on a skilled, helpful, trustworthy, cooperative, and efficiently organized police force."

He climbed up on the table. "So I'll take a bold step towards accomplishing that goal by changing this light bulb."

59

Joutsamo and Kohonen watched their colleague with gaping mouths.

Kulta continued. "You know, this reminds me of that case in Malminkartano. We got a tip about a possible body in an apartment building and went to check it out."

He pried the translucent cover loose. "It was an odd place, the windows had been covered up with black cardboard and all the lights were out. Just one of those dim night-lights in the corner.

A cloud of dust descended from the fixture onto the conference table. "Well, we had our flashlights, but you can't do a proper investigation with those. We did find the decayed corpse of an older woman, though. The ceiling fixtures had no bulbs, so we had to go to the store to buy a couple packs. Once we screwed those bulbs in place, the investigation got underway."

He held the cover in his other hand and worked the bulb loose. The flickering stopped.

"Thank you," Joutsamo said.

"What was the deal with the woman?" Kohonen asked.

"She had some kind of light sensitivity disorder. She had been holed up in that cave for decades. Meals on Wheels had been bringing food to her... Except for them, nobody cared..." Kulta said, fastening the cover back in place.

Kohonen interrupted. "Well, at least the police cared enough to come and figure out the cause of death."

Kulta hopped back onto the floor and set the burnt out bulb onto the table. "I can't remember the cause of death any more, but it's a hell of a sad story."

60 { welfare state, individual, does anyone care? }

"What's a hell of a sad story?" Detective Lieutenant Kari Takamäki asked, stepping into the room. Suhonen was right behind him.

"My paycheck," Kulta said flatly.

"Well, today you can earn every penny," Takamäki replied. "Let's grab some coffee and get started."

A few minutes later, they were back, each with a steaming cup of coffee. The lieutenant sat at the head of the table, as usual. Mikko Kulta, Kirsi Kohonen and Suhonen were on his right side, and Anna Joutsamo on his left. Forty-five year-old Takamäki wore a grey sport coat, blue tie and a white shirt. He had short brown hair, which he combed to the left, an angular face and slightly sunken cheeks. His straight nose was straddled by piercing blue eyes. VCU cops had a saying that seeing a hundred corpses made your eyes callous. Takamäki had doubled that number a while back.

"OK, let's run through the case first, so everyone's on the same page."

Kohonen interrupted, "Just the five of us working on this?"

"Don't you trust my detective prowess?" Kulta joked.

"I don't. This is a homicide, not a property crime," Joutsamo shot back. She had already done some preliminary work. *Anna - no time for jokes*

Takamäki was baffled by the exchange, but steered back on course. "We'll get more help later on in the day. I'll brief them on the case then. Suhonen, you want to start?"

Suhonen nodded. "Yeah... One of our informants brought this to my attention. He told me last night that a certain Jerry Eriksson was rumored to have been killed, and gave me some leads on a possible location."

"How'd he know about it?" Joutsamo asked.

"Good question," Suhonen said. "I asked, but he didn't say."

"OK," Joutsamo jotted down some notes.

"Jerry?" Kulta said, puzzled by the English name. "What Jerry?"

"Baptized as Jerry, toe-tagged as Jerry," Suhonen said, and continued, "Anyway. The coordinates I got were pretty vague. After meeting my informant, I decided to search the area around the Pakila Teboil station. According to the tip, it was supposed to be an abandoned house. It took a few hours, but by about three in the morning, I stumbled on the right garage. There was a body there alright."

"Was it Eriksson?" Kohonen asked.

"Presumably, but no positive ID yet. I only had my flashlight, but I could tell it was a corpse, not a mannequin."

Kulta interjected, "Those flashlights can come in handy."

"What?" Takamäki furrowed his brow.

"Nothing," Kulta said. "Go ahead, Suhonen."

Suhonen took a sip of coffee. "Anyway, the body was there, so I checked to make sure he was dead. I tried not to disturb the area so forensics would have a clean crime scene. I called in for a cruiser to seal off the garage, and Kannas' CSI team got there around six in the morning, right?"

Takamäki nodded.

"What kind of place was it?" Joutsamo asked.

"It's an old abandoned rambler with a separate garage. There's all kinds of junk in the yard and the walls are full of graffiti. I don't know who owns it, but nobody has lived there for a while," Suhonen said.

"Was he killed there in the garage, or moved from someplace else?" Kulta asked.

Suhonen shrugged. "My guess is he was killed there, but forensics will get the facts."

"We have confirmation from Kannas that the guy was dead and that nobody was in the adjacent house." Takamäki pointed out. "He estimated he'd have more info by noon."

"Sounds like they're using a slow approach. Good," Joutsamo remarked. In forensics, a slow approach means that you don't just bolt over to the body. Instead, as investigators approach the body, every inch of the floor is studied systematically so that all evidence in the room is recorded without contamination. *Anna— likes slow, methodical, by the books*

Takamäki let Joutsamo continue.

"OK. For now, we're going to presume that the victim is, in fact, this Jerry Eriksson. I took a look at his record," Joutsamo said.

Joutsamo took several printouts of Eriksson's mug shot from her stack of papers and passed them around. His face was narrow and his hair tousled. His gaze was vacant, as in most police photos.

"This Eriksson has done pretty well for himself. Twenty-seven years old and lived in Helsinki. We even found an address in Kannelmäki, in Northern Helsinki. He was a typical modern scam artist who knew how to use technology to his benefit. Back in 2000 or so, he had his own cluster of companies involved in charity fraud, as well as some other businesses, apparently selling cell phone games and ring tones. In either case, I'm not sure whether Eriksson was fronting for somebody else or if these

63

were actually his own deals. At any rate, the charity frauds earned him a year and a half in the slammer back in the spring of '06."

"That kind of guy usually has plenty of enemies," Kulta interjected.

"I haven't had time to check on any of his known associates yet," Joutsamo added. "In addition to that, we found some older, minor drug charges and fraud convictions. Then there's this tidbit from Suhonen's source about the possibility of Eriksson being a Customs' nark."

"Aha," Kulta uttered.

"That would constitute a motive for murder. He was shot, wasn't he?" Joutsamo looked at Suhonen.

Suhonen nodded. "Bullet hole in the forehead, not sure from how far away. Kannas or one of the medical examiners will give us an estimated time of death. It wasn't a very fresh kill. I'd say two or three days old, max."

"OK," Joutsamo said. "This garage doesn't seem like the kind of place where you end up accidentally. We can assume that at least Eriksson and the shooter were in the garage. Seems reasonable that Eriksson was either lured there on purpose or that a deal went bad somehow."

"How reliable is this 'nark' allegation?" Kulta asked.

"Just word on the street, though it came from the same source that knew about the body."

Kulta nodded. "Why did the killer leave the body there?" he wondered. "Obviously, if you leave it someplace like that, sooner or later someone's going to find it.

"Good point," Takamäki said.

Joutsamo continued, "On top of that, how did word get out so quickly? Maybe the body was supposed to be found, like someone wanted to send a message. Suhonen's source could be complicit in that."

"I don't think so. He's not at that level," said Suhonen.

"Plus, why would he have come to the police himself?" Kulta pointed out.

Takamäki cleared his throat. "Right, we can speculate endlessly on these issues, but first we need some hard facts," he said.

"Never assume," Kulta said, smiling. He had heard that from Takamäki dozens of times.

"Well said, Mikko. You've got the mind of a cop—a traffic cop," the detective lieutenant grinned. "Let's start by digging up everything we can about Eriksson. We'll need a comprehensive background check. Anna, go through his history some more and track down his phones so we can get info on his friends and contacts. Keep in touch with Kannas, too. I would think he'd have had a cell phone on him as well."

"OK," Joutsamo said.

"Mikko, check out Eriksson's apartment in Kannelmäki."

Kulta nodded.

"And Kirsi," Takamäki turned toward Kohonen. "You take Pakila, see if any of the residents or businesses there have seen or heard anything. Suhonen, if you're not too tired, try to figure out who Eriksson has been hanging out with lately."

They stood up.

"I'll go talk to Customs," Takamäki said. "Our next meeting is at 2:00 P.M. By then we should have more information from Kannas, too."

"Kind of a nasty case," Kulta added.

"Naah," Joutsamo grinned. "These murder cases solve themselves. You just wait for a cruiser to drop off the killer for an interrogation."

Usually that wasn't too far from the truth, she thought. Finland was home to one of the top per capita homicide rates in Western Europe, but most slayings were the result of drug and alcohol addicts solving their disputes with whatever weapons they could get their hands on. Sometimes the perpetrators called the police themselves to blubber a confession. At other times, they were too intoxicated to notice the death until morning.

Professional hit men were less likely to call in a confession. They were also good, though rarely perfect, at covering their tracks. Hence, contract hits consumed extraordinary amounts of police time. This case looked like it would be one of those, Joutsamo surmised. *[handwritten: so no comment on state of society - just rational re: expenditure of resources]*

* * *

Jouko Nyholm had a headache. That wasn't especially unusual. He had taken a couple 400 mg capsules of ibuprofen, but this time they didn't seem to be working. *[handwritten: the body]*

Customs Inspector Nyholm sat in his office at the Board of Customs on Erottaja. The building, originally designed by Theodore Höijer in 1891, was known as the Kaleva House, after the life insurance company. The rooms were spacious, but Nyholm felt claustrophobic. He took off his thin-rimmed spectacles to clean the lenses.

The Board of Customs employed nearly four hundred people, of which about seventy were involved in law enforcement. Nyholm belonged to a group that looked for illicit shipments arriving at various entry points throughout the country. They then coordinated the information with customs inspectors on the ground.

Nyholm was perfect for the job because he knew how to bring people and things together. His forte was things, his weakness people. At least when it came to those closest to him.

Forty-five years old, Nyholm had short-cut hair, already turning grey at the temples. Grey was also the color of his business suit, which he wore only for work. He had a pair of them, in case one needed dry cleaning. Amazingly, even after twenty-plus years, his wife continued to wash his shirts, though he wasn't sure how much longer that would last. Beyond laundry, he didn't have much of a relationship with her. Their daughter was already 18, so the inevitable divorce shouldn't cause the kind of undue emotional burden that it would in a younger child. His relationship with Kristiina was not in good shape either. The girl brought her laundry home for washing and sat to eat at dinner, but that was about it. So at least in some sense, father and daughter were cut from the same cloth.

Nyholm knew his work inside and out. Did anything else matter? Hell, this headache mattered. He shouldn't have downed those last couple shots of whiskey last night, but why cry about it now.

He had more work than he could ever want. Over a million semi-trucks passed from Finland to Russia every year. It was impossible to track all the imports and exports. How would Customs know if someone was giving false information? Also, the real owners of the exporting, forwarding, and shipping companies hid behind fronts. The paper trail of these Russian and Finnish import-export companies led to offshore tax havens: the Isle of Man and Guernsey in the UK, and even some obscure island nations in the Caribbean.

The incidents of fraud were numbered in the thousands or tens of thousands, but investigators were numbered in the tens. It helped that the scams were always connected to money. Russian Customs could easily be tricked by double-invoicing for goods. The Russians were given a low value for the imported goods to avoid customs and taxes. Often this method included kickbacks to the Finnish companies willing to double-bill. Another method was to alter the paperwork that specified the contents of a shipment: flat-screen televisions magically turned into socks and laptops into toothbrushes.

Plenty of scammers, only a few watchdogs. According to this equation, the more the watchdogs watch, the more the scammers scam. Nyholm knew he had a shitty job. It was only as good as he was willing to make it, and he was only as good at it as he needed to be. He didn't want to be perfect.

Nyholm got up. He had the sudden urge to wash his face with cold water. Whiskey, the wife, the daughter and the headache were hardly problems at all.

He heard footsteps approaching in the hallway. 270 pounds were enough to shake the piles of paper on Nyholm's desk. He tried to improve his posture, shifting papers to look busy.

powerless
against
larger
forces
of
global
capitalism
+ crime

68

Leif Snellman appeared in the doorway. He was a large man with a crew-cut. His only other outstanding feature was his nose, which was far too small in relation to his broad face.

"Dammit Nyholm," Snellman growled in a low voice. "I need that report from last month for the twelve o'clock meeting. Hurry up," he said and disappeared without waiting for a response.

That didn't bother Nyholm at all. As long as Snellman had left.

CHAPTER 8
KANNELMÄKI SHOPPING CENTER, HELSINKI
WEDNESDAY, 11:20 A.M.

A large, red-brick building sat behind the run-down Kannelmäki shopping center. It was long, with four floors and four entrances leading into separate stairwells. Detective Mikko Kulta shook his head. Had they built it vertically, as in most capitals, the City of Helsinki wouldn't always have to seize more land from its neighbors.

A year ago, he had gone to look at a small studio nearby. But on his salary, it would be impossible to get a mortgage, even for such a small pad. Either he'd have to find a rich woman to marry, or continue to rent.

Kulta had left his unmarked Ford Mondeo next to the strip mall. On the east side, the single-story mall bore the bare aesthetic of the late fifties, and on the south side, the land dipped down, making room for two levels. A cement staircase cut through the center of the mall. In front of a body shop on the lower level were a half-dozen cars, waiting their turn.

Kulta spotted a blue maintenance van in front of staircase B. Though the distance to the door was only thirty yards or so, he pulled up the zipper on his blue fleece jacket. The rain had stopped, but the wind had picked up. Earlier in the morning, the sun had briefly peeked out. Thin clouds skirted swiftly across the sky.

Kulta thought about his upcoming practice for the Police basketball team. He'd have to skip it. Duty would eat up all his free time, as usual. Debris from a tall grove of birches littered the pavement. When he reached the van, the maintenance guy was nowhere in sight, so Kulta banged on the side panel.

A narrow-faced man in his fifties scrambled into the driver's seat. He wore blue overalls and a black cap, from which tufts of messy grey hair stuck out.

Kulta noticed a scar on his left cheek. It had been poorly cared for, making it a very distinctive feature. He wondered what kind of colorful past he might find if he looked into the guy's record.

"Hello," Kulta said, "I'm from the VCU."

"You wanna show me a badge?" the man replied dryly.

Kulta dug his wallet out of his side pocket and removed a small plastic card. It had the same blue and white colors as an ordinary Finnish ID card.

The maintenance man squinted at it for a long time, then nodded. "Alright. Just standard procedure."

"Let's go. Staircase B, second floor."

The front door was unlocked, and Kulta entered first. The stairwell smelled musty. Two strollers were parked at the base of the stairs. Kulta took the stairs two at a time; the maintenance man struggled to keep up.

"What's the hurry?" he panted.

"Just standard procedure," Kulta remarked flatly and pointed to a tan door. The name on the mail slot read Sainio, but according to Kulta's information, it was occupied, or rather had been, by Jerry Eriksson.

In Kulta's pocket was a search warrant signed by Takamäki. Finnish police could search apartments with a Lieutenant's authorization. Phone taps needed court approval.

The maintenance guy sifted through his keys till he found the right one.

"Shouldn't we ring the doorbell first?" he asked.

"What do you mean 'we?' Just open the door," Kulta said. To be on the safe side, he opened the zipper on his jacket. His gun was in the shoulder holster.

* * *

Kirsi Kohonen wore a black wool hat, but that didn't help her freezing toes. I ought to start bringing warmer shoes to work, she thought. These thin-soled running shoes don't cut it anymore. The door opened and a tall, elderly woman appeared. She looked close to seventy, was at least four inches taller than Kohonen, and wore a blue blouse with plain slacks.

A shrill bark came from somewhere inside. The distance from the crime scene was about a hundred yards, but there was no direct line of sight to the abandoned house. Kohonen showed her badge to the woman.

"Detective Kohonen from the VCU."

"Good to hear. That badge is just a big blur to me without my glasses," the woman laughed.

Kohonen put her badge back in her pocket. "We're trying to gather some info on a recent incident and…"

"What incident?"

"Well, actually, I can't say."

"Why?"

"It's confidential. I'm not authorized."

The woman stared at Kohonen. "I see."

"Anyhow… Have you noticed anything unusual in the past few days?"

"Where?"

"Here in your neighborhood."

"Nothing unusual ever happens here. What could I have noticed?"

Kohonen kept a straight face. She had to persist. It was possible the woman didn't know anything, but she couldn't be sure yet. "Have you seen any cars or people recently that seemed suspicious? Either last weekend or the early part of this week?"

"Well, there've been those police cars over there at number 8. They wouldn't let me over there, though," the woman said, pointing towards the red mail box.

"I meant earlier, ma'am."

The woman appeared to think for a moment.

"What does 'suspicious' mean?"

"Any cars or people that you don't normally get in the area."

"I haven't seen anything like that."

"Nothing out of the ordinary?"

"What happened over there? Drugs? Murder? What?"

Kohonen wondered if the woman had been a journalist in her younger days. "I'm not at liberty to say. Sorry."

"Well, I haven't seen anything either. So the score's tied: zip-zip." The woman grinned.

"Are you sure?"

She started to close the door. "Yes."

"What about your husband?"

"Oh," she chuckled, still closing the door. "He hasn't seen anything either. He died a year ago."

"Thank you," Kohonen said to the door. Well, she thought, shaking her head, when it came to dead bodies they were also tied: one-one. This neighborhood was too quiet.

* * *

The maintenance man opened the door cautiously. A pile of junk mail lay on the floor.

"OK," Mikko Kulta said, waving the guy off. "You can go now."

The man turned to leave, but paused on the landing. A dirty look from Kulta was all it took to get him moving again. The man muttered something that Kulta didn't catch. He sifted through the junk mail, looking for a newspaper. There was none. From a detective's standpoint, a newspaper would have been helpful. It made it easy to figure out the last time someone had been in the apartment. Unfortunately, many people were dropping their subscriptions to the dailies.

Kulta stepped inside quietly, his gun holstered but ready. It was dark in the apartment, and the curtains were closed. He flicked on the hallway lights. On his right was a coat rack, and on his left, the door to a bathroom. Five or six jackets hung from the hooks.

Kulta had been in dozens of drug flats, and this didn't seem like one. More like the opposite: an oriental rug in the foyer and furniture that looked middle-class.

He closed the door behind him and glanced into the bathroom. Seemed pretty standard: a bathtub,

74

sink, toilet, and wastebasket. Everything was spotless. This was definitely not a drug hole.

There were two toothbrushes, but no make-up arsenal. A bachelor pad then.

At the end of the hallway, the apartment opened up to the left, revealing a spacious studio. A large window reached to the floor, leading out to a small balcony. The kitchenette was situated behind the bathroom. Kulta checked around: nobody here, breathing or not.

He noted that the room was quite stylish, especially compared to his own flat. A queen-sized bed, sofa, table and flat-screen television were arranged thoughtfully.

Kulta glanced briefly at the entertainment system: Xbox, stereo, games, DVDs and CDs. Apparently, Eriksson had liked rock from the '60s and '70s; his music included Led Zeppelin, The Who, Rolling Stones and others in the same vein. Kulta almost felt a fondness for the guy: at least there was no "gangsta" rap.

A laptop computer rested on the coffee table, just in front of the couch. It was closed. Kulta didn't touch it.

Forensics could go over it with a fine-tooth comb and check for prints. The drug-sniffing dogs would come later. His job was to perform a superficial examination to see if there was anything that could speed up the investigation.

It suddenly occurred to him that this might be the wrong address. This seemed more like one of the apartments of some jet-setting Nokia engineer.

There were no envelopes or bills to reveal the resident's name.

Kulta opened the closet and immediately noticed a photograph on the inside of the door. He knew the spot: the bottom of the big hill on the Särkänniemi Log Chute, one of those automatic photos that you can buy after the ride. Kulta recognized Eriksson. In front of him was a young, blonde woman, leaning back in his arms. Who could that be? The photo was dated August of the previous year. At any rate, now it seemed likely that this was, in fact, Eriksson's apartment.

Kulta slipped on a pair of latex gloves and carefully removed the photo. He'd have to explore more before Forensics arrived. Otherwise, the techies would claim, once again, that homicide detectives just sat behind their desks, waiting for others to do the dirty work.

impressive, forbidding presence here
state

* * *

Lieutenant Takamäki sat at the wheel of his unmarked Volkswagen Golf on Mannerheiminkatu. He was waiting at a red light at the corner of the National Museum, yawning. In the '80s, the Museum had posed as Moscow's Kremlin in the American movie *Gorky Park*. A crane had hoisted a red star to the top of the tower.

Helsinki's main drag ran north-south from downtown. It was named after Field Marshal Mannerheim. An equestrian statue of the revered military and political leader stood a few hundred yards ahead, roughly opposite the stone Parliament House.

Suhonen had called at three in the morning to tell him about the body, and the investigation had started without regard for the time of day. The VCU tackled their cases with dogged efficiency. There was no need to make an art of it. But this murder was clearly trickier than your typical drunken stabbing. The murderer was still on the lam and was enjoying a generous head start.

The trip to the Board of Customs on Erottaja was only about a kilometer, but in this traffic it would probably take twenty minutes.

Takamäki's thoughts were swimming. The manner and location of Jerry's Eriksson's murder seemed to indicate a dispute between professional criminals: a shot to the head in an abandoned garage. His team would probably have to work overtime to solve the case. That didn't matter, although a break every now and then would be nice.

The problem with working in the Violent Crimes Unit was that, no matter how much the team accomplished or how hard they worked, more cases kept pouring in. They never stopped. Every night in Helsinki, someone was arrested for assault and battery or worse. And every morning, Takamäki's team got busy cleaning up the mess.

Takamäki was confident that this case would be solved. He *had* to think that. In numerous other cases, which had dragged on much longer, the press had eventually asked, "Will the perpetrator ever be caught?" In those situations, he had no choice but to answer, "Yes, of course." Still, the cases weren't always solved.

The line of cars lurched forward another twenty yards before brake lights brought everything to a halt again. A giant 140 million-euro Music Center was under construction, and the trucks were blocking traffic.

Takamäki's phone rang and he dug it out of the breast pocket of his blazer. The call was from home. His younger son wanted to know if Dad would be able to take him to hockey practice tonight. Takamäki said he couldn't promise anything and told him to ask Mom just in case. If the detective lieutenant's pay had been better, he'd have spent the twelve grand to buy a microcar for the kid. Though the legal driving age in Finland was eighteen, fifteen-year-olds were allowed to drive these 5.5 horse two-seaters.

The trip to Erottaja took twenty minutes, as he had guessed. Surprisingly, he found a parking spot and made it just in time for his noon meeting.

The security guard in the lobby told him to wait while somebody came down to meet him. Takamäki had only one question, and Assistant Director Leif Snellman was the one to answer it: what did Customs know about Jerry Eriksson?

An aide escorted him through a maze of hallways to Snellman's office. When they arrived, Snellman rose from behind his desk and approached Takamäki. The office was spacious enough for a large walnut bookshelf with glass doors and a conference table made of hardwood with space for six.

"Hello," Snellman said, extending his hand. His handshake was limp.

"Hello," the Lieutenant answered. He had run into Snellman several times at various seminars, but had never actually gotten to know him.

"It's good to cooperate with other agencies like this," Snellman remarked and gestured for Takamäki to sit at the conference table. A thermos of hot coffee and a couple of cups were waiting. "With drug cases it's just not very common and we don't have much expertise in violence."

Takamäki knew that the Helsinki Police and Customs had had their fair share of conflicts in drug investigations. Snellman poured Takamäki a cup of coffee without asking.

"So," Snellman began. "On the phone you mentioned a Jerry Eriksson and wanted some information on his connections to Customs. What kind of a character is this guy?"

Takamäki liked the fact that his host cut right to the chase. He tasted his coffee. It was fresh, clearly better than police coffee.

"Eriksson has been connected to a capital crime," Takamäki hedged. "I can't go into details yet, but we have some information indicating that he might have connections to Customs."

"It was my understanding that he's a criminal, not a civil servant?"

Takamäki nodded, sipping his coffee, "Yeah, from the underworld."

"So not from the upper crust like us," Snellman grunted.

"We searched our various databases—and we have plenty—but we got no hits. Bad news, in other words."

"Tough to say whether that's bad news or good news."

"Seems to me that the real question is whether or not Eriksson is one of our informants."

"Yeah. That's one way to put it."

"You should've put it that way right off, so I'd know where you're coming from," Snellman grumbled and picked up a stack of papers on the table. "Never mind. After we got off the phone, I took a look at our confidential intelligence reports from the last month. These include the names of some informants, but not all."

Takamäki waited in anticipation.

Snellman continued, "Jerry Eriksson isn't mentioned here. That doesn't mean for certain that Eriksson doesn't have some kind of connection to Customs. Our undercover guys have contacts that are never put down on paper. Probably not any different from your agency."

Takamäki was surprised that Customs would document *any* of their informants on paper. Never in his life would Suhonen write down the name of an informant in any report. He wouldn't even write reports.

"Understood. Can I read those reports?"

Snellman shook his broad head. "No can do. We can't give any of these out. Even to a trusted colleague in law enforcement, it's just too risky. But like I said, Eriksson's name doesn't appear here."

"Could he have used another name?" Takamäki suggested.

"Say the name and I'll tell you if it's here."

"Is there a way to dig deeper?"

"Is it that important?" Snellman seemed interested. "We can certainly send out a message to everyone asking for any information about this Jerry Eriksson. His last name is common enough that we'd probably get plenty of bad leads. One thing's for sure, though, a couple hundred agents on the ground will wonder what this is all about."

Takamäki sipped his coffee. This didn't sound promising. "You're right. That might jeopardize the investigation."

"How important is this, really?"

"Important enough for me to come here," he said carefully.

Snellman had seemed pretty helpful. Maybe he could say a little more. "We're dealing with a murder, and any connection to Customs could constitute a motive. We know that Eriksson has a history of fraud, but we don't know what he's been up to lately."

Snellman put the pieces together quickly. "So Eriksson was murdered because he's an informant of ours."

Takamäki nodded. "But that's an unconfirmed rumor."

"Bad news, whether it's true or not. I mean the connection to Customs."

Snellman stood, picked up the intercom off the table and pushed a button. Takamäki was amazed that these still existed.

A crackly voice answered, "Yeah, Nyholm."

"You should be here already," Snellman growled.

"Right," the voice on the other end said.

Takamäki looked at Snellman quizzically.

"Jouko Nyholm, one of our inspectors. Actually, he could be some Chief Inspector by now, but to me he'll always be just an Inspector. Do you know him?"

Takamäki shook his head.

"Well, at any rate, he's a competent man. He knows almost everything about our intelligence operations. I can tell him to ask some of our key agents about this Eriksson. Discreetly, of course."

"Good."

They waited a minute for Nyholm, during which Takamäki got a chance to admire the cushy surroundings that Customs enjoyed. According to Snellman, it paid to be subordinate to the Finance

Ministry. Customs brought money to the state, the opposite of the impoverished Ministry of Interior, which oversees law enforcement. In Snellman's view, being profitable should count for something.

Nyholm knocked on the door and stepped inside.

Takamäki took note of his shabby appearance. The man stood hunched over, as if apologizing in advance.

"Nyholm, this is Detective Lieutenant Takamäki from Homicide," Snellman said, and continued on without bothering with handshakes. "They're working on a case that may involve us."

Nyholm fished a pen and notepad out of the breast pocket of his blazer.

"That's smart. It's good that you take notes," the boss sneered.

Nyholm still didn't say anything, just stood waiting for instructions. Takamäki was amazed by this attitude, even if Snellman wasn't the easiest of bosses.

"According to their intel, an individual by the name of Jerry Eriksson could be connected to the case."

Takamäki detected a slight tick when Snellman mentioned the name.

"Jerry Eriksson?" Nyholm repeated calmly.

"You heard me," Snellman barked, then rattled off Eriksson's social security number. Nyholm confirmed it before Snellman continued, "Find out if any of our undercover agents have heard of this guy."

CHAPTER 9
HELSINKI PRISON
WEDNESDAY, 1:20 P.M.

Eero Salmela knew of him, but didn't know him. Tattooed flames wrapped around the man's neck and his left ear was studded with four earrings, linked by a jeweled chain.

Tapani Larsson usually wore a black, skin-tight T-shirt and black Adidas sweatpants. Now, with the autumn wind howling over the perimeter wall and through the yard, his muscular build was hidden beneath a hooded sweatshirt. The clothes were plain—all gang symbols were banned in prison.

Clouds raced across the sky toward the east.

About twenty inmates were circling the yard. For the past four laps, Larsson and two of his cronies had been closely following Salmela, who was walking alone. In the middle of the yard, a single bench press sat unoccupied.

Three days of rain had turned the track into mud and Salmela's cheap prison-issue shoes were heavy with mud.

Salmela knew that Larsson had been doing time since last summer for extortion. He'd probably be in for a few years. It paid to stay away from gang leaders like him.

Though walking around in a circle wasn't exactly fun, it was one of the only permitted outdoor activities. Salmela had been counting his steps, but had lost track a while back. Counting the days left in your sentence was futile. Numbers had no place in prison.

"You're Salmela, right?"

Salmela was startled by the voice behind him. He stopped short. Larsson and his two buddies had caught up to him.

Salmela could see from Larsson's body language that he didn't mean any harm, at least for now. If they had intended to cut him down, they wouldn't do it here in front of the guards and the surveillance cameras. The situation would be more dire if Larsson weren't there. Gang leaders never got their hands dirty for this sort of thing.

"Yeah."

"Larsson," he introduced himself. He kept his hands in the pockets of his sweatshirt.

"I know."

"Let's take a walk," he ordered.

Salmela got a closer look at his ink: the base of his neck was ringed by a snake, an eagle and a naked woman. The flames rose from there.

"How'd you like your lunch?" Larsson asked with a wry smile.

"You organizing a riot against cabbage soup?"

Larsson laughed dryly. "That was funny, actually."

"It was?"

"Sure. But Jorma Raitio's been saying stuff about you that's not so funny."

"So he's talking about me, huh?" Salmela kept a poker face, but couldn't help wondering what the hell his ex-friend had done now.

"Don't you know?"

"Of course I know," he answered. They were nearing the volleyball court. The four of them walked in pairs, Salmela and Larsson in front, and the other two in the rear.

"He says you're a snitch."

"Bullshit."

"Is it?"

"Yes."

They walked for a dozen yards, then Larsson continued, "He gave me the court papers from your case, asked me to read 'em and do something about it."

"You read 'em?"

"Yeah."

"So what're you gonna do?"

Larsson smiled. "That's what I'm doing right now. I figured I'd talk to you about it first."

"Why?"

"You probably don't know my background, but there was a time when I studied a lot of law. Only later did I get lots of practical experience on criminal law."

"Is that so?" Salmela asked.

"Based on your papers, I can see why you got a shorter sentence. The Appellate Court's decision was based on solid, legal facts."

"Good. I feel the same way."

The men fell silent and walked for another dozen yards. Salmela wondered what this was really all about. Why had the gang taken an interest in him? In his own opinion, he was a middle-level player at the most. He didn't have money, not even hidden on the outside.

"Why aren't you doing anything?" Larsson asked.

"What am I supposed to do?"

"Raitio is spreading bullshit rumors about you and you're just sitting on the fence. A lot of people here would take that as a sign of guilt. Eventually someone's going to take Raitio up on his offer."

"What offer?" said Salmela, then immediately regretted showing his ignorance.

Larsson didn't notice, or didn't care.

"An iron pipe to the knee and the head."

Salmela's expression was grave. "How much is he offering for that?"

"A grand."

Now Salmela understood what this was about. The Skulls were after a counter-offer. "And what's your price?"

"Two."

"I don't have that kind of money in here."

"I don't need it in here. We'll take care of it on the outside."

Salmela wasn't exactly looking forward to doing business with the Skulls. It would lead to trouble sooner or later. On the other hand, taking out a contract for a prison beating wasn't all that risky. The victim would say he fell down some stairs, and the perpetrators would walk away scot-free. It was a code that even the guards knew. Ratting on another inmate would be an affront that would be paid back with interest, compounded at usury rates. If Salmela didn't order the hit, he would end up in the prison hospital himself.

"Two grand, you say?" Salmela wanted to confirm the exact amount.

Larsson nodded.

"Take care of it."

"Good. As a bonus, we'll put the word out that you're OK, and under our protection."

Larsson slowed down, indicating that the deal was done. The three heavies hung back about twenty yards for the rest of the walk. Salmela continued on alone. This protection would cost him dearly, but he had no other feasible alternatives.

Walking felt like a godsend suddenly. The old prison had plenty of staircases.

* * *

Since everyone was already there, the meeting started early. Mikko Kulta had been last to arrive.

"Let's keep it short," Takamäki said from the head of the table. "Everyone is busy."

Anna Joutsamo, Kirsi Kohonen, Suhonen and Kulta had taken their seats on one side of the table. Opposite them were a couple of detectives sent from Lieutenant Ariel Kafka's team, and Kannas, the burly Chief of Forensics.

"Anna," Takamäki said, glancing at Joutsamo. "Anything new on Eriksson?"

Joutsamo shook her head. "Nothing really. I don't think we discussed the parents this morning—both of them are in their fifties. His father, Eero, is an IT salesman, and his mother is a nurse at the university hospital. Neither of them has a record. In addition, he has a younger brother who's a junior in Matinkylä High School."

"OK. Let's not notify the parents yet," Takamäki said, then turned towards Kulta. "What about the pad in Kannelmäki?"

"Well, judging from the apartment, Eriksson hasn't exactly been scraping by. He lived alone and had nice furniture—or at least nicer than my place. Didn't find much concrete info. Forensics is probably turning the place upside down right now. I did a quick search and found this photo," Kulta said, handing out copies of the Log Chute snapshot with the blonde girl in front and Eriksson behind her. His arms were wrapped around the girl.

The detectives examined the photo.

"So far, we have no idea who the girl is, I'm still working on it. From the picture, we can assume that the girl might know something about Eriksson and his friends. But I didn't find anything that would directly explain why he was killed. Of course, we'll probably get plenty of information from his computer: when he last used it, what web pages he's been browsing and so on."

Google maintained records of all searches for the past year and a half. Their log tracks the search term, the day, time and the computer's IP address. In addition, Google drops a cookie for every search, which tracks information about the computer, the browser and the operating system. This information can also be hoovered from the computer itself.

"You didn't come across any bank statements or anything like that?" Joutsamo asked.

"Not that I saw."

"Maybe we'll find some on the computer."

Takamäki nodded. "Good. At least we have a couple leads. The girl and the computer. Kohonen?"

"Kind of quiet on my end," answered Kirsi Kohonen, who had canvassed the houses near the crime scene. "Not a very curious crowd in the neighborhood. Several people noticed the police cars, but that doesn't do us much good. The house has been vacant for several years and there are plans to build some kind of community center on the site, which the neighbors of course have opposed. Decisions about the building have been frozen due to the complaints. Occasionally, some people related to the project have been running in and out of the house, but the neighbors didn't pay much attention. In other words, not much. Nobody saw anything, heard anything, or said anything."

"Said anything?" Takamäki looked skeptical. "Should we have another go at it?"

"It was a figure of speech," Kohonen said, though she didn't have anything against another go-around. It had occasionally paid off in the past.

"Anything else?"

"That's it for now."

Joutsamo interjected. "We've obtained a permit to search the records for the cell phone towers in the area surrounding the crime scene. That should give us some idea of whose phones have been in the area."

"Good," Takamäki said. "Before we get into forensics, I'll talk about my trip to Customs. They didn't have any initial information on Eriksson. In other words, we don't know whether the murder had anything to do with Customs. But they're going take a closer look."

Takamäki waited for a moment. Nobody had questions, so he continued around the table.

"Kannas?"

The imposing, fifty-something man's hair was a bit tousled and his heavy blue sweater seemed awkwardly warm for the stuffy office. Takamäki and Kannas had been friends since the Academy. They had also patrolled together around the Presidential Palace in the eighties.

"Ahem! Sorry, getting over a cold. We did find something at the crime scene. The body."

Nobody laughed.

Kannas decided to cut to the chase. "First off, your assumptions about the body were correct. We ran the fingerprints, and were able to verify that the murder victim is, in fact, Jerry Eriksson. He was shot in the forehead. One interesting detail was that the victim had on a Los Angeles Lakers cap. There's a basketball on the logo, and the bullet entered in the very center of the ball. Any basketball coach would have to admit that's a *pretty good shot*," Kannas quipped, glancing at Kulta, the hoopster. Nobody smiled.

"At any rate, it wasn't from point blank range. The weapon was a hand gun."

"Do we know whether it was a pistol or a revolver?" Kulta asked.

Kannas glared playfully at Kulta. "A machine gun can be a hand gun according to our official manuals. We can rule out cannons and grenade launchers. In other words, it's not yet known whether it was a pistol, a revolver or a rifle. We didn't find any casings, but that doesn't necessarily mean anything. The shooter could have picked them up. Based on the entry hole in his forehead, I would say it was a small-caliber handgun. The coroner should be able to verify that when they dig out the bullet."

"When was he shot?" Joutsamo asked.

"Well, he was pretty chilly. Based on the body we estimate sometime between Sunday and Tuesday morning."

"That's a big range."

"True, but that's the best I can do."

"Shame."

"A little more about the garage. The cement floor was rough enough that it didn't show any prints. The doorknobs had been wiped clean or something, so no prints there either. There's a sandy spot in the yard, just in front of the house, where we took a plaster cast of some tire tracks. They're worn GT Radials, made for vans."

"For a van?" Takamäki asked.

"Yup. You can tell from the size and the tread pattern."

"What make and color was it?" Kulta joked.

"Bring me the van and I'll tell you if the tires match." Kannas shot back. "A couple more things. There were a lot of cigarette butts and a wad of chewing gum in the yard, which we submitted for DNA testing. We put a rush on them, but there's no telling when the results will come back. However, at this time, we don't have anything that would connect those items to the crime."

Kannas continued, "Eriksson didn't have a phone on him. We're not sure if it was taken, or if he didn't have one to begin with."

"These types always have a phone," Kohonen interjected.

"Tell us where it is then." Kulta said.

"Mikko, stick to the case," Takamäki snapped. "If you don't have anything reasonable to say or ask, then let the rest of us think."

Kannas bent over and took a Zip-Loc bag out of the briefcase beside his chair. Inside was an FN pistol. "Instead, we found this in his pocket. I guess it's your job as detectives to draw the conclusions, but from our standpoint, I can say that there were no bullet holes in the walls and we didn't find anybody else's blood. In other words, Eriksson probably didn't have time to use it."

"Kirsi, track down the history on this weapon," Takamäki said.

Kannas handed the plastic bag to Kohonen. "The serial number is intact."

Kannas took another plastic bag out of his briefcase. "These are the contents of Eriksson's pockets. You should go through them when you get a chance. I haven't actually inspected them, but we took photographs of everything."

"Anna, you can take care of that," Takamäki said, and Joutsamo took the bag. At a glance, it contained some tattered papers, candy wrappers, coins, keys and a small black wallet.

* * *

Joutsamo was wearing latex gloves and had spread the contents of Eriksson's pockets out on the conference room table. The others had left. Eriksson had had a single five-euro note and coins that amounted to eight euros and twenty cents. Joutsamo set the money, the papers and a pack of chewing gum aside. She also had a notepad and a green pencil stub to take notes with.

There were four keys: two regular door keys, a deadbolt key and a Saab car key. Joutsamo guessed that one of the ordinary-looking keys and the deadbolt key were for the Kannelmäki apartment. But what was the other door key for? And did Eriksson have a Saab? They'd have to go back to the Kannelmäki apartment and take a look at the parking lot. Or could it possibly be for Eriksson's parents' car? A car would be interesting if it were indeed Eriksson's. They might find something in there that could generate some new leads.

It was clear that Eriksson had been murdered for a reason, though the motive remained a mystery. Based on the facts they had compiled, it was extremely unlikely that Eriksson was the victim of a random killing.

Joutsamo sketched an outline for the murder. In many instances, it was easy to extrapolate a crime from a few basic facts. This murder didn't seem the slightest bit emotional. It was coldly mechanical. The isolated crime scene and the nature of the act pointed to that conclusion.

Because they weren't dealing with a crime of passion, the perpetrator was probably not among the victim's immediate family. Typically, in these kinds of cases, the killer was motivated by money. In addition, the murderer was probably asocial and had a criminal record. Joutsamo recalled some research, which showed that one third of murderers who killed for personal gain had previously been convicted of property crimes.

She didn't have enough facts to draw more detailed conclusions. Joutsamo needed more information. If the police were able to figure out what Eriksson had been doing recently, they might be able to track down some possible motives. Had he met with any friends recently? Would they know of any enemies he might have had?

The big problem was that no cell phone had been found. With a cell phone, it would be a simple matter to establish his circle of friends and business associates, as well as a record of his calls. Naturally, Joutsamo had called directory assistance to see if

Eriksson had any listed numbers. Apparently, he either used a number listed under someone else or a pre-paid card. Did the absence of a cell phone simply mean that the killer had taken it? That would indicate that he had probably been in phone contact with Eriksson.

If this were the case, the calls could be tracked down. With a court order for the phone company's records, all phone calls within a specific area would be disclosed to the police. Sorting through all the calls would be tedious, but if there were no other leads, it would be done.

The rumpled papers from the Zip-loc bag turned out to be receipts. The first one revealed that on Sunday, Eriksson had bought eight cans of beer, a frozen pizza and a brick of coffee from the Alepa grocery store at the Kannelmäki shopping center. The time stamp on the receipt was 8:32 P.M.

Good, Joutsamo thought, and wrote the time down on her note pad. The first clue as to Eriksson's activities. It was also consistent with Kannas' initial estimate of the time of death.

Unfortunately, Eriksson had paid cash. Plastic would have been better, since it could be used to trace Eriksson's other activities. There were no credit or debit cards in the wallet. Maybe he didn't qualify for one. His credit rating was abysmal due to unpaid debts and court-ordered compensation for his frauds.

Joutsamo unfolded the other bundle of paper. The receipt was from the same store, also paid for with cash. A six-pack of beer and two hamburgers. But it was dated Saturday. Joutsamo was disappointed, but she jotted down the information on her notepad. She wondered if he drank the beers alone.

Lastly, Joutsamo picked up the old black wallet, about the size of a passport, and emptied the contents onto the table. The photo on his license was the same one that Joutsamo had seen in the driver's license database. Eriksson looked much more innocent in this photo than in his mug shots. But who owned the apartment in Kannelmäki, Joutsamo wondered. When they had extra time, they'd have to figure that out. The condo association would have some name on record: either a person or a business.

Joutsamo turned back to the wallet. The billfold contained four one-hundred euro notes, two fifties and six twenties. All together, 620 euros. At least that ruled out robbery.

The billfold had two compartments. In one side was the money, in the other some receipts. Joutsamo fished them out and immediately recognized the thin strips as taxi receipts. About half a dozen of them.

The first two were about a week old, but Joutsamo dutifully marked the dates in her pad. She took the third receipt and, as she registered the date and time, felt a shock of revelation. Eriksson had paid €19.20 on Monday evening to ride 10.3 kilometers between 6:34 P.M. and 6:53 P.M. The locations didn't appear on the receipt, but the name of the taxi company did.

This information from Monday narrowed the window of time in which the murder had occurred. The next receipt was even better. The date was the same, but the time was from 9:33 P.M. to 9:46 P.M. The trip was 7.6 kilometers and the tab came to €14.20. The name of the taxi company was Oinonen and the phone number was even printed on the receipt.

Joutsamo was about to call the Oinonen company to ask for more details about the passenger and his destination, but decided to finish examining the wallet first. Minutes didn't matter at this point.

Takamäki popped into the room. "Anything interesting there?"

Joutsamo nodded. "Eriksson's last acts are starting to take shape."

"Good," Takamäki said in a voice that seemed a bit tepid for what she had told him. Her surprise doubled when he added, "Is this going to take much longer?"

"Probably not. A few minutes, but then I'll have to make copies of these."

"Do it later."

"What's going on?"

"Forensics found a list of debts in the Kannelmäki apartment. We have a good candidate for a suspect. He owed Eriksson fourteen grand."

"Who?"

"The list says 'Juha S,'" Takamäki said. "I want you and Suhonen in my office in five. They also found about half an ounce of what appears to be meth."

CHAPTER 10
BOARD OF CUSTOMS,
EROTTAJA, HELSINKI
WEDNESDAY, 2:45 P.M.

Customs Inspector Nyholm sat in his desk chair. Out the window, he could see the courtyard and hotel windows on the Boulevard. Occasionally, some eye candy walked by, but he just stared into space.

Nyholm rubbed his eyes and cursed to himself.

Snellman and that cop hadn't said why he had to look into Jerry Eriksson. Nyholm had actually recognized the detective lieutenant. He had seen Takamäki often on TV and in the newspapers. The policeman's cold eyes had seemed to look right through him.

And now he had to track down Eriksson's connections to Customs. Where would he begin, Nyholm mused, laughing aloud.

He knew where he could start. Exactly where.

"Son of a bitch."

The phone rang and Nyholm inadvertently answered with "bitch." It suited: the caller was his wife, who replied, "Excuse me?" He didn't apologize for his rudeness.

"Stop at the store on your way home."

"I can't. Meetings."

"Again?" she said coldly.

"That's the custom here," Nyholm replied. "How's the girl?"

"Don't know. Haven't seen her."

"Really," he said dryly.

"I'll be better off here alone anyway," she snapped and hung up the phone.

Nyholm groaned. He'd have to stop at the store. She was probably talking about liquor, not groceries. He tried to forget his wife and focus on the matter at hand. He'd have to be sharp.

He picked up his desk phone and pushed speed dial for the head of intelligence in the southern region. He had to get some field agents involved so his efforts would seem adequate. Hopefully nobody knew Eriksson.

* * *

Joutsamo knew she should already be in Takamäki's office, but she had to make the call.

"Oinonen," a man answered in a hurried voice.

"Anna Joutsamo from the Violent Crimes Unit. You have a minute?"

The man on the other end laughed. "Sure. Just waiting for the train here, so nothing to do but talk on the phone and read classics."

Joutsamo drew a picture of the man in her mind. Your typical long-winded cabby. The kind who always had something to say, whether passengers liked it or not.

"I'm calling to check on one of your passengers." Joutsamo had a copy of Eriksson's receipt in her hand.

"Okay, shoot."

"On Monday night, between 9:33 and 9:46 P.M., you gave a ride to a younger guy in a hooded sweatshirt. Do you remember where you took him?"

"Monday, huh? Today's Wednesday, right? Heh, the days just sort of blend together in this job," Oinonen said and thought for a moment. "Guy with a hoodie… Yeah, now I think I remember. He flagged me down on Helsinki Avenue in Kallio. Over there by Tenkka, as I remember".

"The Tenkka Bar?" Joutsamo clarified and jotted the name down in her notepad. Tenkka was one of the few institutions in what was a rough neighborhood. Most of the bars and pubs changed ownership so often that there was no sense of tradition. They just got people drunk on inexpensive beer and cheap vodka.

"That's the one. What's this about?"

"It's a case I'm working on," Joutsamo skirted the issue. "Was he alone?"

"Yep, nobody with him."

"What about before he got in the cab? Anyone else with him?"

"Well, there were others milling around on the street, but this guy with the hoodie was definitely alone. As far as I could tell."

"Good," Joutsamo remarked, though it would've been better had he had a companion. It would've been one more lead to follow up on.

Joutsamo noticed Takamäki standing in the doorway, looking impatient. She nodded.

"How'd the trip go, then?"

"I tried to strike up a conversation, but nothing. The guy didn't say a word. He was kind of in his own world. He didn't seem so drunk or high that he'd have been nodding off. You know, for a cabby at that hour, the night is still young."

"And where was he headed?"

"Yeah. Now that was a little strange. When he first got in, he said to go to Oulunkylä. But then when we got there, he asked me to keep going further north towards Beltway One and Pakila. All of a sudden, when we got to Pirjo's Tavern, he told me to stop and he got out. Seemed to me like the trip was cut short. It wasn't because he didn't have the money, though. He paid with a fifty, if I remember right."

"Do you remember if he had a cell phone? Did he call anyone during the trip?"

"I don't think he called anyone," Oinonen said. "But now that you mention it, he might have been fiddling with a cell phone. It's also possible that it was an iPod or something. It was dark out and the back seat is even darker, so it was tough to see. But I do remember that he really wanted a receipt. He asked for one."

"OK," Joutsamo said and jotted a note on her pad: Why receipt?

Joutsamo continued, "I'm going to have to ask you to come down to the station to make a formal statement. It doesn't have to be right away, but we'll let you know."

"Awright, must be a pretty serious case?"

"I'll let you know when you get here," Joutsamo said, to arouse his curiosity. "And please, don't mention this conversation to anyone."

"OK," the man said, and the call ended.

Takamäki was at the door again. "Any progress?"

"Some. Apparently, at 9:30 P.M., Eriksson took a taxi from Helsinki Avenue to Oulunkylä, just a few kilometers away from the crime scene."

"A taxi?" Takamäki wondered. "Well, let's go to my office. Suhonen's waiting for us."

Joutsamo was still thinking about the conversation. "Damn. I can't remember if there are any security cameras in that area."

"That wouldn't help if he was in the taxi alone."

"No, but it's possible that Eriksson met the killer somewhere else before going to the garage. They could have met at Pirjo's Tavern and gone from there. Maybe the security camera could've caught a glimpse of a potential suspect."

"It's worth a shot, but let's go talk to Suhonen."

* * *

Suhonen was perched on the window sill in Takamäki's small office. As usual, he kept his leather jacket on. The detective lieutenant took his seat behind the desk and Joutsamo took the chair by the door.

A bookshelf against the wall was filled with different colored folders, containing case files. A diploma on the wall proved that Takamäki had participated in an international FBI course on profiling. *Mr. Kari Takamaki*, it read. A couple missing dots over the "a," but at least they hadn't called him *Ms*.

Outside, the morning wind had ushered in another low-pressure system. Beneath the street lamps, the sleet was driven nearly sideways.

Takamäki showed them a letter-sized printout of a photograph. "Forensics found this in Eriksson's apartment. It was taped to the bottom of a desk drawer."

Joutsamo examined what appeared to be a photo of a note. In capital letters, someone had written, "JUHA S. 14,000 DUE NOV 15," followed by a couple of exclamation points.

"In the same drawer, forensics found what they believe to be a bag of amphetamines."

"Was Eriksson dealing?" Joutsamo said, more thinking aloud than asking a question.

Takamäki glanced at Suhonen, who added, "And why would he hide the note in his own home? Was he worried that someone would raid his apartment?"

"All good questions," Takamäki said.

"Were there any prints on the note? When can we get a handwriting analysis?" Joutsamo asked.

"Not sure," Takamäki said. "Kannas will take care of it... Suhonen, tell Anna."

Suhonen was still sitting on the windowsill. "This Juha S. is the informant who told me about the body."

"Wow," Joutsamo let go.

"Right," Takamäki said.

"Let's take him in," Joutsamo said immediately.

"Good idea," Takamäki said.

"Naah," Suhonen stalled.

Joutsamo looked at Suhonen. "I don't suppose Saarnikangas told you that he owed the victim almost fifteen grand?"

"No, he didn't. Nor did he tell me where he heard about the body."

"Right," Joutsamo continued. "Maybe you should have asked him where he saw the body, not where he heard about it. Or maybe even where he killed him."

"Seems like there's probable cause," Takamäki said.

Suhonen raised his hand, gesturing for some quiet. "Then why would he tell me about it?"

"To throw us off track."

"Naah," Suhonen said again. "I know this guy a bit. I can't say *well*, but still... In my view, he's not a killer. He's more like a pawn, though he's not as dumb as most junkies. He's a kind of survivor, who always gets out of trouble by squeezing through some crack."

"So you're saying he's not capable of murder?" Joutsamo asked.

"Everyone's capable of murder in the right circumstances. Still, it seems to me that if Saarnikangas were in debt, he'd try to resolve it somehow, not bury it by shooting the guy."

Joutsamo shook her head. "Seems to me we should take him in and interrogate him. If, like you say, he's some kind of low-class druggie, then he'll talk within three days."

Takamäki turned back to Suhonen.

"I think we should wait for more details from Forensics. The DNA evidence and what not," Suhonen said. "I agree that Juha knows more about this case than he told me. I could try to get it out of him."

"I disagree." Joutsamo said.

"With what exactly?" Takamäki asked.

Joutsamo looked at Suhonen for a moment.

"Alright. This case started with your intel, so let's see where you can go with it. Let's try Suhonen's way, for now at least. But we definitely shouldn't tell him that we know about this debt," Joutsamo said.

"Of course. I thought maybe we should use some old fashioned police work, but blended with a little modern technology?"

"What do you mean?" Takamäki asked.

"Well, a phone tap and a GPS tail."

"A tracking device?"

Suhonen nodded.

Police tracking devices could be easily attached to any automobile. Every twenty seconds or so, they sent out a signal to an officer's computer or even to a cell phone, with the location of the tracking device. Narcotics had used them with great success. The cops no longer needed five units to follow a suspect's vehicle; its location simply arrived automatically. Narcotics had made an art of planting the devices inconspicuously. It only took about twenty seconds, and the device was nearly invisible. It could also be built into any interchangeable car part. A Finnish company had developed the technology, but foreign police forces and various intelligence organizations had taken a keen interest in it. Everything related to this device had been declared a state secret in Finland.

"We'd know where he was at all times. He drives an old Fiat van. Let's watch and listen before we arrest him and show our hand. If Saarnikangas is actually the culprit, I don't think he did it because of the debt."

"Anna?" Takamäki turned to her.

"So he drives an old van, huh? According to Kannas, the tire tracks they found were from a van, and they were worn out... But your way is fine with me. It's not like we have to hurry to prevent a crime or anything. But when you plant the tracking device, check out those tires."

"OK," Takamäki said. "Phone tap and tracking device."

"And the tires," Suhonen added.

CHAPTER 11
MATINKYLÄ, ESPOO
WEDNESDAY, 3:05 P.M.

Markus Markkanen was lounging on the sofa in front of a blaring TV. The sports channel was showing a rerun of an NHL hockey game, but he wasn't watching, just staring past the screen.

His "ex"-wife Riikka was in the kitchen making coffee.

"Want some?" Riikka called.

There was no answer.

"Hey," Riikka called again. "Coffee or not?"

"I don't think so," Markkanen drawled.

He turned his blank stare toward the kitchen. Riikka was measuring coffee into the filter. A shapely woman in her thirties, her perky breasts seemed to stand at attention beneath her white T-shirt. Markus and Riikka had been together, or, more accurately, had been drinking together in the same circles since the late-90s. They quickly took to one another and Riikka had gotten pregnant unexpectedly. Eetu was born in 2000.

Although Markus had spent a year in prison, the marriage had endured. It had ended in name only a few years ago, but the relationship had continued. They told the boy that his daddy had gone to work abroad. The last few years had been better, thanks to money. Since he had been working for Lindström, they had much more of it. Money didn't just soothe the family, it actually created happiness.

"Maybe I will have some," Markkanen said, sitting up on the sofa. He was wearing grey wind pants and a black T-shirt. He surfed through the channels absent-mindedly, but couldn't seem to find anything interesting. Eetu had gone to a friend's house after school.

"You have anything going on today?" Riikka wondered.

"A meeting at four."

"With Lindström?"

"Yeah," Markkanen grumbled. She knew his line of work, but they didn't talk about the details.

"Why do you let him boss you around?"

"He doesn't boss me around," Markkanen snapped.

"Does too. Come here, go there, take care of this, do that. For all that you do, you should be able to run his business yourself."

"Do you remember who paid our bills when I was doing time?" Markkanen asked, though he knew very well that she remembered.

Riikka fell silent and they listened quietly as the coffee maker gurgled. Markkanen had always suspected that Riikka had paid Lindström back with something other than legal tender. They had never talked about that, though. And never would. If something had happened, it was in the past.

"Listen," Riikka said, sliding onto the sofa next to him. "I need some money."

He wanted to ask what she needed it for this time, but he dug out his wallet and counted out three hundred.

"That enough?"

"Yeah," Riikka said. "It's a really gorgeous blouse."

Markkanen laughed silently when she kissed him on the cheek. He'd have to remember to shave before leaving.

"You know, we should go on a vacation somewhere warm," Riikka suggested.

"Again?"

"Yeah, it's so depressingly dark and cold here."

Markkanen stood up. Riikka remained sitting.

"Where you going?"

"To get some coffee."

His cell phone rang in the hallway, and he had to rummage through the pockets of his jacket to find it.

"Hello," Markkanen answered.

The caller was Lindström. He sounded angry. "Where are you?"

"Why?"

"You were supposed to be here at three."

"You said four."

"Shut up! Get over here now."

"OK," Markkanen replied.

Riikka watched him from the sofa, gloating. "No…he doesn't boss me around. No, no…"

"Be quiet," Markkanen said, pulling his jacket on. About to leave, he called out, "Remember to take Eetu to tonight's hockey practice."

The ice-rink was only minutes away from home, but still too far for the kid to walk with a heavy hockey bag.

* * *

It was almost 4:00 P.M. and Suhonen was standing at the turnoff onto Vuolukivi in the Pihlajamäki neighborhood. Pale four- and eight-story towers, built in the '60s, loomed overhead.

Rocky Pihlajamäki was the first Helsinki suburb built in the sixties to be officially preserved by the city. The Finnish Historical Board had also requested protection for it, though Suhonen wondered why. The Historical Board had also worked to preserve the "Sausage House," a monstrosity of a building just across the street from the Helsinki Railway Station, named for the sausage-shaped ring encircling the second floor. For the people of Helsinki, the Sausage House is an institution. For visitors, it's a curiosity.

Suhonen's cell phone buzzed. Raija again. This time he decided to answer it. He wasn't sure what he'd do if she wanted to meet.

"Hi," Suhonen said, trying to sound as friendly as possible.

"Hi," she said back. "Why don't you answer your phone?"

"Been busy at work. You know the drill."

"Yeah. I know," she answered coolly.

Raija was quiet for a moment and Suhonen wondered if she was calling to complain or just to chat.

"Listen, I just called because I left that teapot of mine at your place. I want it back."

"Huh?"

"You know, the one I bought last spring. I forgot it in the rush."

"Oh yeah? That's what you're calling about?"

"Yeah."

"OK. I'll just bring it to your office when I get a chance," he said, feeling his temper flare. "Sorry, gotta go. More work."

He hit "end call" and watched as a couple of pot-bellied men lumbered into a local bar. A gaudy sign in the window advertised free karaoke and billiards. Suhonen felt like joining them. He didn't care for karaoke, but billiards and beer would be just fine. It would soften his stale mood.

But there was no time now. He had gotten ahold of Saarnikangas on the phone and they had arranged to meet in Pihlajamäki. Did Juha live around here nowadays? He wasn't sure. Last he knew, the guy had lived in Itäkeskus, or East City, near the infamous shopping mall. He was now five kilometers northeast of Itäkeskus, next to the Lahti Highway.

Saarnikangas' dirty Fiat sat in the parking lot. Suhonen had swung by the van and installed the tracking device. It hadn't taken more than 25 seconds. While he was at it, he had checked the brand on the tires.

According to the motor vehicle registry, the van was owned by one Krister Vuori. The man was doing three years in Helsinki Prison for drug trafficking.

Suhonen's second phone—the prepaid one—rang.

"Well?"

"Where are you?" Juha asked.

"Out front."

"Come on in. Stairwell B in the long building. Third floor; the door says Teräsvuori."

Suhonen strode through the quiet yard and entered the stairway. The spiral stairs were built into the side of the building and surrounded by glass walls. Suhonen dashed up the stairs two at a time and, reaching the third floor, rang the doorbell.

Saarnikangas was already at the door and he opened it quickly. Suhonen suspected he had been lurking behind the door, peering out the peephole. A black Metallica T-shirt and tattered jeans were draped over his skinny frame. His hair was tangled as usual.

Suhonen stepped past him into the studio, which opened up from the hallway to the left. A beat-up mattress lay on the floor surrounded by a cluttered pile of paperbacks. Next to the balcony door, a TV sat on the floor and a plastic patio table served as a dining table.

"Nice pad," Suhonen said.

"It's practical," Juha remarked. "Not mine, of course."

"What's new with Krister?"

"You mean Vuori?" Juha laughed, but his voice was pinched. The druggie paced around the room, unable to stand still. "Do you know him?"

"I know of him, yeah."

"He's doing time in Sörkka. He left this pad and the van in my care. Apparently, the city hasn't figured out that the tenant is in the slammer, so I've been able to live here."

"Quit trotting around and sit down," said Suhonen, pointing to a white plastic chair. Juha obeyed like a scared puppy. Suhonen remained standing a couple yards away.

"About Eriksson."

"What about him?"

"What do you really know?"

Saarnikangas continued to fidget in the chair.

"Exactly what I told you before. Nothing more. I heard some rumors, so I told you."

"You're in deep shit."

"How so?"

"If you don't talk."

"What the hell are you talking about?" Saarnikangas raised his voice and folded his thin arms across his chest. "I told you everything. I don't know anything more. You have the body, so it's your job to figure out who did it."

"How do you know we have the body?" Suhonen asked with a grim expression.

Juha's chin dropped open for half a second. "Don't you?"

"I haven't said anything about that. You seem to know."

"Stop trying to confuse me. How many times have I helped you cops out... Shiiit..."

"Enough swearing. Pretty soon you'll be helping out in the prison cafeteria."

"Goddamnit," Saarnikangas said, starting to stand up.

"Sit," Suhonen said calmly and Juha obeyed. "Listen to me. We did find the body and the police are looking for someone to skin. We have to find the killer, and fast. The case is hot and we'll find every single morsel of evidence. Now's your chance to help us out, not to mention yourself."

Saarnikangas squirmed in his chair. "But... I honestly don't know anything more about it."

"Do you have a gun?"

"Huh?"

"Do you have a gun?" Suhonen repeated.

"No," he answered hesitantly.

"Good to know."

"Why?"

"Well, we won't have to send the Bear Squad to bring you in when we figure out your role in this case."

Helsinki S.W.A.T was nicknamed the Bear Squad. The Unit had been formed to protect foreign dignitaries for the 1975 U.S.-Soviet summit in Helsinki. The police had chosen a bear as its symbol because in a confrontation, the team would swat like a bear.

"Don't start…"

"I'm serious. You'll be in deep shit if you don't talk now. If you don't have anything to say, then find something out. I'll call you tonight." He turned away.

"Suhonen," Juha said. The detective stopped.

"What?"

"About the swearing. You know where the word 'hell' comes from?"

Suhonen walked away. "I don't have time for your trivia."

"It's Ancient Swedish, derived from the name of 'Hel', the mistress of the netherworld…"

Suhonen closed the door behind him and took out his phone. He made it to the stairs by the time Joutsamo answered.

"Well?"

"I met with Saarnikangas."

"Yeah. You must've been in his apartment," Joutsamo said. "The phone tap is working and we listened in on your little phone conversation."

"Good," Suhonen said. "But going forward, I have to remember to watch what I say to him on the phone. He wriggled and squirmed, but it won't be long before he either calls me or makes a run for it. If anything happens, let me know."

"Yup."

"Oh yeah," Suhonen added. "The tires on his van were GT Radial Maxways."

Joutsamo asked him to repeat the brand again.

"It's a match then," she said.

Suhonen ended the call and opened the police GPS tracking application on his phone. A glowing red dot indicated that the tracking device was in the parking lot on Vuolukivi. All systems go. The battery wouldn't be a problem; these newer models could last up to a few weeks.

CHAPTER 12
LINDSTRÖM'S APARTMENT,
TEHDAS STREET, HELSINKI
WEDNESDAY, 3:55 P.M.

"Bogeyman" Markkanen stepped into Kalevi Lindström's apartment building. Classical music boomed into the stairwell and rose into the vaulted ceilings, seeming to lift the elegant decor with its lilting tempo. Everything was of the highest quality. The walls had been recently painted, complete with an elaborate molding where they met the ceiling. Markkanen knew that the renovation team had used original 1930s photographs of the building as inspiration.

It had taken Markkanen about 40 minutes to drive the 15 kilometers from Espoo to South Helsinki. This was the swankiest part of town. Parking spots were impossible to find, as most of the Art Noveau buildings were from the late 19th or early 20th centuries and had no garages.

Lindström's door was made from solid walnut. The chrome doorbell looked original, though it had been bought at an antique store and installed during the renovation.

He pressed the button. The bell jangled forcefully and he waited. He was forbidden to ring twice. It took Lindström about a minute to come to the door. He wore brown tailored pants and a white dress shirt.

"There you are," Lindström said and let Markkanen inside.

The younger man knew the rules. As usual, he left his black shoes in the foyer and hung his coat on a hanger.

"Let's go to my office," the boss said. The apartment was spacious by Finnish standards, at least 2,000 square feet. In addition to the office and the fitness room, he had a kitchen, a formal dining room, a bedroom and a living room.

Lindström lived alone. As far as Markkanen knew, he wasn't married, probably never had been. Markkanen wasn't sure if he was straight or not. Of course, he had never asked about it; it wasn't relevant. At least the older man had never come on to him.

The office was designed like a library. A laptop and a few stacks of paper rested on a large desk. Dark built-in bookcases encircled the room. Near the door were a low table and two armchairs. The window offered a view of Tehdas Street, but at the moment, brown curtains hid the spectacular view.

Lindström turned on some lights, gestured for Markkanen to sit in one of the armchairs and took a seat opposite him.

"Still haven't heard anything about Eriksson?" Lindström asked.

Markkanen shook his head. "Vanished into thin air."

"Just doesn't make sense. I know he would've told me if he was going on a trip. Do you know if he had any enemies?"

"Who doesn't?" Markkanen remarked. What kind of a question was that, he thought, but said nothing. Everybody had them, some more than others.

Lindström nodded his head. "Right, right... We'll have to figure out who, but right now I have a more pressing matter." The man set his elbows on the armrests of his chair and brought his fingertips together so they mirrored one another. "Markus..." Lindström began.

Markkanen was taken aback to hear his first name. His boss hadn't addressed him that way in a long time, if ever.

"...I've always considered you hired muscle. Don't take this wrong, but your fists have been your best assets."

You should know, Markkanen thought. He hadn't received the "Bogeyman" nickname in his youth for nothing. He kept his expression serious.

"You're good at settling debts and roughing people up. And also organizing things. But now that Eriksson is missing, you're going to have to step into his shoes. At least for a while."

Hmm, Markkanen thought. So now he was supposed to squeeze into that rookie's shoes? So long as the diapers weren't part of the deal. Still, he liked the direction this was headed. "Right," he said as impartially as possible.

"Tomorrow I'll be receiving twenty freight containers of flat-screen TVs. The ship will be docking in the port at Kotka. Each container will have 50-75 units. Altogether, roughly 1,000-1,500 TVs. The TVs will be between forty and seventy inches. Very good quality. Not the cheap stuff you get from clearance sales."

The man leveled a steady gaze at Markkanen. "I'm not going to go into details now, but there's a considerable difference in taxes if the paperwork says 'rubber gloves' rather than 'top-of-the-line electronics.' Understand?"

Markkanen nodded. He knew that one of Lindström's businesses had something to do with import-export. Markkanen had arranged some of the transport logistics himself and also rode shotgun from time to time. Goods that were officially bound for Russia had actually stayed in Finland and were sold onto the black market tax-free.

"Good. The containers are headed for Russia, but we have to disclose their contents to Customs when they arrive here. Russian Customs isn't a problem, but the Finnish side has occasionally been a little sticky. That's where Eriksson has been coming in. He's taken care of any issues with the Finnish Customs."

"I see," Markkanen said. Though he had suspected something like this, he never knew the exact details. "How?"

"He gathers information."

"From where?"

"This is why you've always been the hired muscle," Lindström said with a wry smile. "From Customs, of course. He has a man on the inside. I know his name, but Eriksson never told me what their arrangement was."

A man on the inside. Wow, Markkanen thought. "That's good."

"Right. At first, I thought it was a secretary. But this guy is management."

"Money?"

Lindström smiled. "Yes. It involves money, but there's something else."

"What?"

"Jerry is a clever kid. He's my cousin's son; he knows how to play the game."

Markkanen was shocked. Cousin's son! Eriksson and Lindström were related? This was news to him. And something he definitely should've known. Shit, he thought.

"What is it?" Lindström asked. "You look surprised."

"Well, I just didn't know Eriksson was your relative."

"Yeah, we weren't that close before Jerry came to work with me."

"Right, right," Markkanen said. He should have figured it out beforehand. It was one surprise too many. Maybe the old man was right about him and his abilities. "So what do I have to do?"

"It should be simple, even for you. Just take it easy, at least to begin with. Get in touch with Jouko Nyholm at Customs. Tell him that Eriksson's gone on a trip, and that you're taking care of business for now. We need to know if they're having any surprise inspections, and whether our cargo has raised any red flags." Lindström looked at Markkanen inquiringly.

"So I'm gonna bribe a Customs Officer?"

"Yep. Sounds simple, right?"

"Yeah. And if he resists, I'll threaten to turn him in," Markkanen smirked.

"If at first you don't succeed, use a bigger hammer."

"A big hammer is my tool of choice," Markkanen answered in a serious tone. His thoughts returned to Eriksson. To think he had a management-level informant at the Customs office. Jesus. No wonder he and Lindström were so cozy. And relatives, too. Well, now the job was his. Finally, Markus Markkanen's situation seemed very promising.

CHAPTER 13
EAST EXPRESSWAY
WEDNESDAY, 5:00 P.M.

Juha Saarnikangas was driving at a steady speed along the East Expressway toward downtown Helsinki. The dashboard clock showed 1:30, but that's what it had been showing for the last two months, maybe longer. The evening rush, a long line of lights, was pouring out of the city past him. The battered wipers made a mess of the view.

As he neared the Kulosaari bridge, a rooftop clock broadcast the time in glowing orange numbers: 5:02 P.M. Juha knew Lydman started his bouncer's shift at the Corner Pub door at five. He worked two nights a week, and Juha suspected he was also dealing at the door.

He had to get in touch with Lydman. He had already been to his place in Pikku-Huopalahti once, and didn't want to go there again. The phone wasn't safe. Suhonen's visit had shaken him. Wasn't it enough that he had tipped him off about the body? Why couldn't the police just take care of it themselves so he could be left out of the whole mess.

He could tell Lydman and the others that he hadn't been able to lift the body the first time, and when he came back, the cops had already arrived.

From what Suhonen said, it seemed like he was a murder suspect now. "You're in deep shit," his threat still echoed in his mind. He had asked about a gun and hinted at an encounter with the S.W.A.T. team. The case was hot, then, too hot. Shit.

A taxi blew past a yield sign and cut in front of Saarnikangas. He leaned on the horn, forgetting that it was broken. The highway split into two and he took the route to Kallio. Juha tried to remember if he had left any evidence at the crime scene. Fingerprints? DNA? Bits of thread? The cops always looked for those types of things. He couldn't remember. The events at the garage seemed like a distant nightmare. Except that it was no dream.

It had probably been stupid to tell the police, but at the time it had seemed like a clever move.

Suhonen had the number to his phone, so it was probably under surveillance already. That's why he couldn't just call Lydman. He'd need a new cell phone. On the other hand, he'd have to keep using the old one just enough so Suhonen wouldn't suspect anything.

* * *

Suhonen was looking at a map of Kallio on his cell phone display. The red dot blinked at the corner of Fleming and Aleksis Kivi, then turned onto Fleming. Kallio, or "the Rock," had been a working class area up until the eighties. But as factories moved away from downtown, the population shifted from families to young adults looking for cheap rent. The cheap rents also tended to draw a rougher crowd.

Suhonen stepped on the gas. He was a couple minutes behind.

Based on the map, Saarnikangas was headed somewhere in the heart of Kallio, but where?

Joutsamo was looking at the same map at her desk. She had also informed Suhonen over the phone that Saarnikangas hadn't made a single phone call. The phone was still active, though. She had asked if he needed any backup, but he had assured her he could handle it.

The lights turned green and Suhonen swung onto Kustaa. He passed what was formerly the Hill Mortuary on the left. The brick building was originally built in the 1920s, and a sign above the door read in Latin, "For mortals, only death is eternal."

Suhonen was familiar with the building, but not as a mortuary. The last bodies had been embalmed and loaded onto the "corpse train" bound for the Malmi Cemetery. At its peak, there had been five trains a week, each including two cars for the dead and four for the families. The living were brought back to Kallio.

In the '80s and '90s, a local gang had used the dilapidated building as their headquarters, and Suhonen had been there many times. Now that it was a youth community center, he no longer had any business there.

Suhonen turned right onto Aleksis Kivi and the mortuary receded in the distance. His phone indicated that Saarnikangas was already at Helsinki Avenue. Suhonen sped up.

* * *

Saarnikangas swung the van into the chicane on Helsinki Avenue, on the east end of Brahe Soccer

Field. Brown shabby buildings served as changing rooms and a sign pointed towards the café. One good thing about the van was that he could leave it just about anywhere. Saarnikangas had found a laminated Service Call sign in the glove box, which he displayed inside the windshield. Technically, the Service Call sign would allow him almost limitless parking, at least if the meter maid didn't check the plates. There were no meter maids in sight, and even if there were, it wouldn't have mattered. Neither Saarnikangas nor the owner of the van, in prison already, would pay the ticket.

After locking the doors, he headed toward the Corner Pub. The street was bustling with activity. A streetcar rattled by and turned towards the Sports Center, former home to one of Helsinki's semi-pro basketball teams. During its glory years, the team had drawn a few hundred spectators on a good night, a fraction of the attention local hockey teams received.

Some junkie was arguing with himself under a streetlight. Then again, who would really know if he had an earpiece under that mop. Bright neon lights and signs for cut-rate beer flashed from the bar windows, luring thirsty customers. The Corner Pub was offering a half liter for €2.50.

Saarnikangas cut across to the south side of Helsinki Avenue. The Corner Pub was situated next to an Alepa grocery store. Juha saw a familiar figure standing in front of the entrance, already dragging on a cigarette. He was wearing a black beanie cap and a dark overcoat. A bouncer's ID tag glinted on his chest.

* * *

Suhonen could see from the map that Saarnikangas had left the van at Brahe Soccer Field. He was pretty sure the guy didn't have sports on his mind. A bar or someone's apartment could be nearby. Given the narrow streets, it didn't seem like a good spot for a car-to-car conference.

Nor was he sure whether Saarnikangas intended to meet anyone. His phone had been idle. Maybe the guy just wanted a beer, but if that was the case, there were quite a few bars closer to his apartment in Pihlajamäki—even one just across the road.

Suhonen ran a red light, crossed Helsinki Avenue and headed back up Fleming, which was shadowed by tall apartment buildings. The structures, like most of their kind in this part of the city, were about six stories high, the façades ranging between cement, brick and stucco. The first vacant parking spot was in front of number 14, near a tattoo shop. The nose of his car blocked a third of the gate to the building's courtyard. He didn't care; cars could squeak by and there were no delivery trucks about at this hour.

Suhonen hurried down the hill toward the grocery store on the corner.

"Hey, what's the big hurry," said a man stepping out of a doorway onto the sidewalk.

Suhonen shot a dirty look at the younger man, who was barely half his weight. The man took a step back.

"Well, shit, I guess it's none of my business."

You're damn right, Suhonen thought, but didn't say anything. The air was getting colder and he zipped up his leather jacket, continued on to the corner store and took a quick glance around the corner.

* * *

"Listen," Lydman snarled, a cigarette butt in his hand. "I already told you, I'm not interested. Understand?"

"Well, no," Saarnikangas protested.

Lydman was a good four inches taller and looked threatening in his black coat and beanie cap. He took a drag on his cigarette, and his gaunt cheeks hollowed even further.

"Oh you don't? Maybe all that smack has finally fried your brain cells."

"Not all of 'em. And what do those steroids do to your brain, anyway? Certainly not making it any bigger."

Lydman took a step towards him. "Are you fucking with me?"

Juha felt like laughing. Absolutely he was fucking with him. Was Lydman really that stupid?

A woman well over two hundred pounds stumbled out of the bar. Her makeup was overdone and her smile looked more like a grimace. She extended her hand to Lydman. A few coins clinked as they changed hands.

"Thanks, princess."

The woman waddled off a few yards before Juha said anything, "Princess?"

"It's her nickname," Lydman said and shrugged. "Anything else?"

"Yeah. And try listening this time. You're the genius who sent me to that gas station…"

"I said I don't want to hear it. Not one word! I sent you there because that's what I was told to do."

"Who told you to?"

Lydman didn't answer.

Saarnikangas felt like he was hacking at a brick wall with a spoon. Maybe something more serious was in order. "Hey, you don't know everything."

"Hah," Lydman sneered. "Didn't I just tell you I don't want to?"

"This is different," Juha muttered. Lydman was quiet for a moment. "A narcotics cop has been asking me questions about someone."

"That's your problem."

"Could be yours too."

"You threatening me?" Lydman said quietly.

"No, just trying to explain."

"You're one irritating dick. I'll give you a two-second head start before I kick your ass."

Juha took a deep breath. "I went to that garage and found a dead body. The guy who did it was still there and he told me to ditch it somewhere."

Lydman's expression remained flat, and Saarnikangas guessed that he still needed clarification.

"Say something! *You* got me this job."

"You take care of it?"

"Yeah, yeah. Of course," Saarnikangas said. Yet another of his plans was unraveling because he didn't dare tell the truth.

Lydman studied his face. "You're lying."

"Of course I took care of it," Juha insisted. He stared helplessly at Lydman's cigarette as it burned down toward the filter. When the last bits of tobacco went up in smoke, Lydman would go inside and his time would be up. This hadn't gone the way he had hoped.

"I don't care what it takes, deal with it," Lydman said, taking a couple steps backwards.

"Thanks for your understanding."

Lydman's expression was icy. "You don't understand shit. You truly don't get it, but that's your problem."

Saarnikangas was silent.

"Did you say the pigs were already asking about this guy?"

Saarnikangas nodded.

"If you fucked this up, you better crawl into some hole and shoot yourself. But apparently you'd fuck that up too. Let me be precise. If you say one word to the cops, I'll kill you...slowly." He flicked his cigarette onto the sidewalk.

* * *

Suhonen watched Saarnikangas and an unidentified man chatting in front of the bar. Juha seemed fairly relaxed, but the bigger man's body language betrayed his anger. Seemed like fists could fly at any moment.

The conversation lasted a couple of tense minutes. No bouncer would have acted that way if he were just dealing with a routine customer complaining that he couldn't get in.

In the end, the big guy shoved Saarnikangas, who had the good sense to back down and walk away. The bouncer stayed behind and fished another cigarette out of his pocket despite the sleet, which had just begun to fall.

Looked like Saarnikangas was walking back to his van.

Though he had been to the Corner Pub many times, Suhonen didn't recognize the bouncer. He wanted to get a closer look at his face.

It took him a good minute to get to the entrance of the bar. He walked casually. No hurry nor trouble, just a cheerful guy with a light buzz.

"How ya doin'," Suhonen flashed a smile and gave a quick wave from about five yards off.

The bouncer narrowed his eyes, took a hard drag on his cigarette, and managed a nod.

"Wet and cold, the perfect combo," Suhonen went on.

"It's warmer inside."

Suhonen got a good look at him, but the face wasn't familiar. He took note of the tattoos, which emerged from beneath the collar of his jacket. "A little glögi in here would make it warmer yet." He patted his stomach. Suhonen stepped inside. *This joint should have been listed on the preservation register of historic places*, he thought. The bar had gotten its start during the recession of the early '90s, the first severe one since the Great Depression. The downturn had been triggered by the collapse of the Soviet Union, Finland's key trading partner. At its worst, unemployment had reached almost 25%, leaving plenty of idle customers with unemployment checks to spend. During the recent boom years, business at the Corner Pub had been relatively slow. Now, amidst the new financial crisis, it was picking up again.

The bar was just inside the door, so within three steps you could have a drink in your hand. The wooden tables were covered with cigarette burns, but the familiar clouds of smoke were gone.

The place was almost full and some of the customers still had their coats on. The jukebox crooned out Elvis' "Love Me Tender," but the patrons seemed more focused on their drinks.

Suhonen found room for himself at the counter, and the bartender, a fifty-something man with a bushy mustache, came to take his order.

"Coffee."

The barkeep nodded and shuffled off. In half a minute he brought back a steaming mug.

"One euro."

Suhonen gave him the money. "Is that bouncer new here?"

"What do you mean?"

"Haven't seen him before," Suhonen said, and tasted his coffee. Stale.

The bartender grunted and turned to another customer.

Suhonen looked around to see if there were any familiar faces. He glanced at his phone: the red dot was moving along the East Expressway through Kulosaari. He wondered if Juha was headed back to his apartment in Pihlajamäki. He'd know soon enough.

The bouncer came back inside and snuck behind the bar. Suhonen followed him out of the corner of his eye. Without taking off his jacket, he made a beeline for the employee phone, which was attached to the wall next to the coffeemaker.

Now this was interesting. Why would a guy use a landline if he had his own cell phone? Running out of minutes probably wasn't it.

The man stood in front of the phone, blocking Suhonen's view of the keypad. The call took about three minutes, and Suhonen tried to think of a way to figure out the number. Of course, the easiest way would be the redial button. The number would show up on the screen. In order to do that, though, he'd have to get to the phone somehow.

The bouncer made another call. This one only lasted about fifteen seconds and Suhonen figured he had only done it to clear the previous number from the phone's memory.

Suhonen checked the time: 5:22 P.M. With that information, they'd be able to pinpoint the call in the phone records for the bar, as long as Takamäki and Joutsamo were willing to get a warrant. That wouldn't be a problem, since they had even received warrants for phone booths on lesser grounds.

The bouncer went back to the entryway and stood between the two sets of doors. This guy was definitely an interesting character, Suhonen thought.

CHAPTER 14
TEHDAS STREET, HELSINKI
WEDNESDAY, 5:27 P.M.

Markus Markkanen had called directory assistance with no luck. The number Lindström had given him was either unlisted or prepaid.

Markkanen was sitting in his boxy, blue 300-Series BMW in front of an elegant Art Nouveau building on Tehdas Street. The '90s Beamer was in need of a wash. The sleet had turned to wet snow, though it was barely below freezing.

A police cruiser crept past, heading east toward the Russian embassy.

Markkanen decided to make the call. Now was as good a time as any. He picked up his cell and dialed the number. It rang three times before someone picked up.

"Hello?" a voice said hesitantly.

"Is this Nyholm?" Markkanen asked.

"Who's asking?"

"Mark."

"Mark, huh?"

"Yeah," Markkanen said. "I have some business with you."

"Let's hear it."

"First let's hear if you're Nyholm."

After a brief silence on the other end, he spoke up, "Yes."

"Good," Markkanen said. That Nyholm had revealed his name was a key victory…a glimmer of trust. "Listen, Nyholm. We have a friend in common."

"Oh, yeah?"

"Yeah. Eriksson."

Nyholm's speech quickened. "Eriksson. Right. What about him?"

"He's traveling and asked me to take care of some things in the meantime."

"Where did he go?"

"He didn't say. He left in a bit of a hurry."

"Is he in any trouble?" Nyholm asked.

"I don't know. He didn't say."

"When's he coming back?"

"Don't know that either," Markkanen said. "But back to business…"

"Listen Mark, but how do I know Eriksson sent you?"

Markkanen hesitated a moment. "Because he asked me to contact you."

"So *you're* telling *me*. He didn't say anything to me."

"Probably didn't have time."

Nyholm paused. "Eriksson has a tattoo. He said he only tells his closest friends about it…"

"Right," Markkanen interjected.

"So let me ask you first. What did he have tattooed on his left shoulder?"

Oh shit, what the hell was that ink? They had gone to sauna once with Lindström at the luxurious Palace Hotel Penthouse. Markkanen remembered the hookers, but... Seemed like it was a number. Yeah. That's what it was. "It's a number. Must be an '8.'"

"Correct," Nyholm responded. "And why was Eriksson so pissed off?"

"Aaah... It had something to do with hoops. Some star from Los Angeles had the number 8, but right after Eriksson got the tattoo, the player changed it to something else."

"That's good enough," Nyholm said. "So, you know Eriksson."

"OK," Markkanen said. He wanted to take a deep breath. Skeptical bastard.

"But that doesn't mean anything."

"What do you mean?" The question slipped out before Markkanen realized he should have ignored the comment. He would have rather had this conversation face to face, where at least he could read the other guy's expressions and body language. Street smarts had taught him how to react to get what he wanted.

"I mean just what I said."

"Let's get back to business." Markkanen said. "You know I'm handling Eriksson's stuff. I wouldn't have called you otherwise. I know he had an arrangement with you and all I need is a little information."

There was silence on the other end.
"Why can't Jerry take care of this?"

Markkanen spoke in a calm voice; he knew he had already won. This was Nyholm's last attempt at resistance.

"Jerry's away and I'm taking care of it. Nothing more. Business as usual."

"You said your name was Mark?"

"Yup. Markus actually, but you can call me Mark." Markkanen eased up a little. He was pleased that at least for now, there had been no need for threats. "Listen... I need some info on a few shipments."

"Well... OK," Nyholm relented.

"A ship named 'Colleen' is scheduled to arrive in Kotka tomorrow. Along with some other stuff, it's carrying twenty freight containers of rubber gloves," he said, glancing at the notes Lindström had written for him. "They were sent from China, bound for Russia. I need to know whether the containers are going to be inspected or have shown up in any reports. You know the drill."

"Yeah, I do."

Markkanen read off some code numbers, which would allow them to pinpoint the cargo.

"I'll check, but..."

"But what?" Markkanen asked, already eager to celebrate his victory.

"This isn't a one-sided deal. How much do I get?"

He thought for a moment. Lindström hadn't told him what the going rate was.

"Time for an inflation adjustment", Nyholm said, "I need 25% more, so make it an even 10 Gs a month."

Markkanen considered this. So Eriksson had coughed up eight Gs, and now the guy was demanding ten. It wasn't his money, though. What did he care. "Sounds fair."

"Listen," Nyholm said quietly on the other end. "We're gonna have to keep a low profile for a while, and this can't be happening very often."

"Why?"

"Eriksson seems to be a hot name right now."

"What do you mean?"

"Well, some homicide detective was here today asking questions about him."

Markkanen closed his eyes and felt a shiver run slowly down his spine. He forced a calm voice. "What was he asking about?"

"I don't know the details. They seemed to be interested in his connections to Customs."

Markkanen cursed to himself. "OK. Let's just be careful. How you gonna let me know about the cargo?"

"For tonight only, we can use the prepaid phones. I'll send you a text that'll say 'yes' or 'no'. 'Yes' means that you have a problem. Then I need you to open up a free email account and tell me the username and password. After this, all our exchanges will go through that account. Don't send any emails, though. Just save your messages as drafts. We'll both have access to the account, so we can check the draft messages to communicate."

"Sounds good."

"And cash only. I'll post a draft email on the account telling you where to send it and how," Nyholm instructed.

The call ended.

The job was done. Markkanen thought he had done pretty well, though he felt uneasy hearing about the cops. But he could deal with that too.

He started the car. The wipers struggled to clear the snow off the windshield.

* * *

Eero Salmela was lying on the bottom bunk in his cell. The junkie on the top bunk was asleep, breathing heavily. At one end of the cell was a small window. The bright lights from the yard cast an outline of the window onto the ceiling. The bars were sharply defined.

Salmela couldn't sleep, and he looked at his watch. The glowing hands read a quarter after ten.

At dinner, Salmela had heard about Raitio's tumble down the stairs. Apparently, his left knee was in rough shape. So far, the prison hospital had been caring for him, but surgery was inevitable. According to the rumors, his knee would never recover and he'd limp for the rest of his life.

Shitty deal, Salmela thought. But shit was part of the job description, and always had been. Even that had its limits, of course. Once again, his thoughts returned to his own son, who was shot dead over a drug deal two years ago. That wasn't fair. A petty dispute that cost a young man his life. Of course, Lauri had chosen his own path, but why hadn't he at least taught the kid some street smarts. Back when he was twelve, Eero had shown his son a few slick kicks on the soccer field. In the same way, he had taught him to whittle without cutting his own fingers.

Before his sentencing, and also after, Salmela had spent many dark nights reminding himself that he hadn't wanted to give the boy advice on how to be a criminal. But the thought always came back to haunt him: since the kid had one foot in this life already, he *should* have taught him.

Regret was futile, though.

Salmela closed his eyes and pulled up the covers. As if government sheets could shield him from his own guilt. They didn't help, but neither did beating himself up. Whatever was done or not done was in the past. He had to live with the consequences. It was that simple.

This was his life. He had to look out for himself; anything else was pointless. That's why Salmela was pleased that Raitio was lying on a hospital bed with a wrecked knee, and not himself. True, it had cost him, but he would always be able to scrape up some money in one way or another.

Besides, Raitio had been stupid to go around spreading baseless rumors. Unless he was damn sure, he had no right to make those accusations. Of course, Salmela understood very well that his past chats with Suhonen could've been construed as working with the cops, though Suhonen would never reveal that to anyone. Plus, this wasn't a one-sided deal. It was a quid pro quo arrangement that benefited both sides. There was no shame in that. Anyway, nobody knew about his association with Suhonen. Or so he hoped.

It was no different with the so-called purists of the criminal class, either. They assure you that honor is the most important thing. But when times get tough, your pals are the first ones to betray you. They take your money, your stash, your woman, rat to the pigs...who knows what else.

Anyway, Raitio didn't have it so bad. Sure, his knee was shattered, but they were pumping him full of pain killers. He probably got to sleep on a softer cot than anyone else.

His thoughts were stuck in a loop, and one kept coming back. Salmela had tried to steer clear of the gangs, but now he was flying the colors of the Skulls: black and white.

At some point, payback time would come, and it wouldn't be just a matter of money.

Snow collected on the window ledge, and the silhouette on the ceiling appeared to shrink slowly.

* * *

Two inches of snow covered the ground, enough to soften the bleak surroundings on Helsinki Avenue. Suhonen was sitting in his Peugeot a few hundred yards away from the Corner Pub. It was just past 2:00 AM and the bustle on the street was beginning to pick up. The Tenkka Bar, where Eriksson had hailed the taxi, was across the street. A sign promised karaoke every night.

He had been watching the bouncer at the Corner Pub for a few hours, then had moved his stake-out to a window table at a nearby cafe. He couldn't drink coffee alone endlessly without making people wonder, so now he was back in the car.

The bouncer was in and out. At times, it seemed like people would come to meet him. A few words were exchanged, but as far as Suhonen could tell, the guy wasn't dealing.

He had called in a request for Narcotics to photograph the man. By 10:00 P.M. with the help of an "electric company" van, it was done. While the bouncer stood outside, the van approached, stopped at a red light, and an officer in the back took eight photos. At first glance, Narcotics hadn't recognized the man, but at least now they had pictures. Suhonen wanted a name and address.

A few guys emerged from the bar and one got excited about the snow. He scraped up a snowball and hurled it at his buddy's back. The buddy, visibly upset, scooped up some snow and shoved it into his laughing friend's face. Just as it looked like it would come to blows, the third guy broke it up. Soon, they all calmed down.

The bouncer stepped outside again. This time, he didn't stand around by the door, but walked straight towards Suhonen.

Suhonen started the car and made a quick phone call.

The bouncer turned the corner by the Alepa and headed up Fleming toward the spot where Suhonen's car had been parked earlier.

Suhonen accelerated westward on Helsinki Avenue toward the intersection. Luckily, his tires had studs. Turning onto Fleming, he saw an old Mazda 626 leaving its parking spot.

The Mazda climbed the hill and turned right. Suhonen followed and they made another right near the Central Fire Station. Now they were headed north.

They came to a T by the Brahe Soccer Field and the Mazda had two choices: east or west on Helsinki Avenue. Suhonen didn't dare follow him anymore, but he waited to see which turn lane the Mazda got into.

He hung a left westward towards the Sports Center. Suhonen made another call to report the car's direction, then turned right.

* * *

"OK, he's coming this way," Officer Tero Partio said. The forty-something Partio was sitting behind the wheel. His younger partner, Esa Nieminen, was riding shotgun. Their cruiser was parked on the western end of Helsinki Avenue near the Linnanmäki amusement park.

"Let's do it here," Partio said, flicking on the cherries. He was wearing the standard yellow safety vest over his blue uniform. The sturdy Partio and skinny Nieminen both got out of the car.

The Mazda came toward them. Partio held up his right hand, and the car slowed to a stop. In his other hand, he held a breathalyzer and some straws.

The Officer peered in at the driver and noticed that he matched the description.

"Good evening. Driver's license and registration," Partio said.

The man dug his wallet out of his back pocket and displayed his license. Partio looked at the name: Ilari Lydman. He also memorized the birth date on the license.

Lydman rifled through his glove box, found his rumpled registration form and warily handed it to Partio.

Partio looked at it briefly. The car had been due for inspection last summer. "You're a bit past due for an inspection. Get it done," he scolded.

Lydman shrugged.

Ordinarily, Partio would have taken the car off the road, but this time he had other orders. Once they had the ID, they were to let him continue.

"Now I just need you to blow in here."

Lydman blew into the straw.

"Says zero. Drive safely." Partio said, waving him onward.

Nieminen was already up the road waving down another car. Partio heard him asking for the driver's license and registration. Hell, they were only supposed to stop the Mazda. At least he'd make them blow in the Breathalyzer too, so the Mazda driver wouldn't suspect anything.

Partio took his phone and called Suhonen.

"Hey," Partio said.

"Well?"

"The driver was Ilari Petteri Lydman." He recited the birth date.

"Nice work. Where was he heading?"

"West towards Mannerheiminkatu."

"Thanks."

Partio turned to Nieminen, who had just finished checking the second car. "Sooo, this driver's name was Jukka Wallander."

"Super," Partio remarked. "Now get back in the car."

Nieminen peered up the street. "Hey, here comes another car. Looks like a taxi."

"Get in the car!" Partio barked.

THURSDAY
NOVEMBER 27

CHAPTER 15
DEPARTMENT OF FORENSIC MEDICINE
THURSDAY, 9:05 A.M.

Takamäki left his vehicle next to the Department's red-brick building in a spot reserved for the police, though he was driving his own Toyota station wagon. Well, it was the driver of the vehicle that mattered, he thought.

The complex was located near the "Legoland-district," but these buildings had no pastel colors.

He hurried toward the entrance. Two inches of fresh wet snow lay on the ground. The temperature was barely freezing.

The Lieutenant signed in. The receptionist, in her forties, smiled and told him that Dr. Nyman would be down in a few minutes. Tuija Nyman, a specialist in forensic medicine, had called him the previous evening and promised the results of Eriksson's autopsy by morning.

A few minutes later, Takamäki and Nyman sat in her crowded office. Both had coffee. Takamäki had always thought that the thin fifty-something woman looked Greek somehow. Her hair was a shimmering black and she had a slender, attractive face. Only her hard eyes, which had seen it all, betrayed her profession.

"How's jogging?" Nyman asked with a smile. For Takamäki, that smile was reason enough to be there in person. Nyman could have given him the information over the phone. The Department of Forensic Medicine was part of the University of Helsinki, but its Medical Examiners handled all law-enforcement related medical investigations from DUIs to autopsies.

"Jog—you'll die healthier... Lately I've been doing seven, eight kilometers."

"Could I talk you into a marathon?"

"Not even you..." Takamäki smiled.

Nyman took several papers out of a plastic file folder.

"I opened up Eriksson yesterday... The cause of death was pretty clear. A bullet in the head, and here it is in Latin. Interested?"

"Well, I could've figured out the Finnish version from the crime scene photos and I've heard the Latin version a few times."

Nyman smiled again. "The weapon was a .22 caliber, and the bullet was somewhat flattened. I'm guessing it'll be good enough for comparison. You're probably interested in the time of death?"

Takamäki nodded.

"Judging from the combination of air and body temperatures and other signs in the corpse, I would estimate that he was shot sometime between Monday evening and Tuesday morning. As you know, that's only an estimate."

Takamäki wrote the information on his notepad, though he already had a better estimate based on the taxi receipts.

"I extracted the DNA and sent it along with hair samples to the lab for analysis. Eriksson's blood alcohol level was .07. We didn't find any unusual medical conditions, but the corpse wasn't exactly in tip-top shape. His lifestyle was beginning to show. No surprise, then, that his stomach contained the remains of pepper steak, fries and red wine. He probably ate a few hours earlier."

"Sounds like a death row inmate's last meal," Takamäki said. Though he hadn't learned anything particularly new, he didn't mind. It was always nice to visit the coroner.

* * *

Joutsamo stood in front of a timeline she had drawn on the white board and filled in the information with a black marker. This particular conference room had been reserved for the Eriksson case.

The time was listed above; below that were known activities.

There were about ten items on the timeline. At the end of the line was the Medical Examiner's estimated time of death, which Takamäki had called in. The timeline for Monday went like this:

6:53 P.M. Taxi to Kallio

Dinner. Where?

9:33 P.M. Hailed a taxi in front of Tenkka

9:46 P.M. Gets out at Pirjo's Tavern

Time of murder? By Tue Morning.

The next item was from Wednesday around 3:00 A.M.: Suhonen finds body.

Takamäki and Joutsamo studied the diagram.

"Based on what the M.E. found in his stomach, their working assumption was that Eriksson was killed fairly soon after his taxi ride to Oulunkylä.

That would put the time of death sometime between ten and eleven o'clock."

"Unless he had the steak at Pirjo's Tavern or somewhere else later on," Takamäki speculated.

"We should find out if Eriksson went straight from Pirjo's Tavern to the garage, or if he stopped somewhere in between. It would help if we could get a more specific time of death." Joutsamo said.

Joutsamo had also started a diagram for Saarnikangas. At this point, it only had one item: "Tuesday 8:30 P.M. – Meets Suhonen on Boulevard."

"Saarnikangas' phone records will be here around noon, so we should know more about his activities then."

"Assuming he had the phone with him," Takamäki said. The police had had many cases where criminals had changed phones to throw the cops off or to create an alibi for themselves.

"What about the phone records for the Pakila cell tower?"

"That'll come around noon as well. Apparently, between Monday evening and Tuesday morning, about 5,000 calls were logged."

"A hell of a lot," Takamäki remarked.

"That's because all the cell phone traffic from Beltway One gets routed through that tower."

"Hmm," said the Lieutenant, then changed the subject. "Did Kohonen find anything on Eriksson's handgun?"

"It was reported stolen from a Turku gun shop in the spring of '01. Doesn't help us much. It didn't show up in any other database."

"So that doesn't get us anywhere," Takamäki said. "What about his activities between Pirjo's Tavern and the garage. Did you get a chance to find out if there were any security cameras?"

"No. But as they say, I'm working on it."

Takamäki nodded. The team had to prioritize. Only a few years ago, the Violent Crimes Unit had almost eighty officers, but because of budget cuts, that number had been reduced to sixty. Police work had become like any other business, with the goal of optimizing results. They had no time for finer strokes. Arrests had to be made as quickly and as efficiently as possible, so they could move on to the next case. That also meant the VCU had to limit their cases to only the most serious ones.

"What about phone taps?"

Joutsamo shook her head. "We were all over it last night when Suhonen was trailing Saarnikangas, but he didn't call anyone. We recorded the line overnight, but still nothing."

"And Suhonen?"

"He saw Saarnikangas talking with some bouncer. Up until about ten Suhonen was shadowing the bouncer, but then I went home. I haven't talked with him this morning."

Takamäki thought for a moment. "So, same status. Pretty much the same info as yesterday, but we have a little better idea on the time of death."

"The case is at a standstill," Joutsamo said. "Saarnikangas is our only real suspect."

Her phone rang. "It's the front desk," Joutsamo said, puzzled.

"VCU, Joutsamo," she answered in a crisp voice.

"Hi, this is Kyrölä from downstairs," a man drawled. The front desk of the Pasila Police Headquarters was on the ground floor. Joutsamo recalled a fifty-something man from there. They had occasionally eaten at the same table in the cafeteria.

In his time, Vesku Kyrölä had been one of Helsinki's toughest K-9 cops. That was before a junkie had flayed his German Shepherd "Miska" with an axe. The incident landed Kyrölä on sick leave, and then behind the front desk.

"What's up?" Joutsamo asked.

"Glad you answered. We have a report of a missing person."

"Listen, we're working on another case here. I don't have time. Could you call the main number to the VCU and someone will help you?"

"Really?" Kyrölä asked.

"Yup," Joutsamo answered curtly, shrugging at Takamäki.

Kyrölä didn't seem bothered on the other end. "OK. Just thought I should give you a call since the computer says any information or inquiries about this person should go to you."

Joutsamo raised her eyebrows. "Who's missing?"

"I would think you'd know," Kyrölä said, more seriously now. "Jerry Eriksson."

"Hold on," Joutsamo perked up. "So someone is there reporting Eriksson as a missing person?"

"That's what I said."

"Are they with you right now, or…"

"Of course not. I'm calling you from the back room. She's sitting at the front desk."

"Who is she?"

"I don't know her name. A young woman. Very pretty."

"So she's there?"

Kyrölä paused for a while before continuing, "Did someone smack you on the head with a baseball bat, or why are you so slow?"

"Be right there. Tell her the VCU is handling all missing persons reports, and I'm on my way."

Kyrölä laughed. "That's how it always works."

"Of course, but don't give her the impression there's anything out of the ordinary."

"So there's something out of the ordinary," Kyrölä concluded. "Come on down. I'll make sure the lady doesn't go anywhere."

* * *

The elevator clunked to a stop on the fourth floor and Joutsamo gestured for the girl to proceed. From the elevator, a door on the left took them into the hallway. The walls were light grey, the floor a darker shade. The building had been used heavily since the '80s and it showed. A major renovation had been due for some years now, but budget cuts had pushed it back.

"And another left here," Joutsamo directed.

The detective had immediately recognized her as the girl from the photo in Eriksson's apartment. Joutsamo had asked the young woman to follow her upstairs. Both had on jeans, but the younger one wore a tighter fit.

Fear showed in her eyes when she saw the white sign on the glass door: Violent Crimes Unit. "What happened?"

Joutsamo tried to smile. "Probably nothing. All reports of missing persons go through the VCU. We get dozens of these cases every year and the vast majority have a happy ending."

The pair stopped at the door of a small interview room. Joutsamo peeked inside to make sure it was empty, then escorted the woman inside. The room was just large enough to accommodate a table, computer and three old office chairs. A large map of Helsinki hung on the wall.

"Have a seat there," Joutsamo directed. She took her own seat behind the computer, but didn't turn it on.

The blonde girl's face was thin, and her eyes red from crying.

"Tell me what happened," Joutsamo began. She wanted to hear the story as candidly as possible before even checking the woman's ID.

"Well, I haven't heard anything from Jerry for a couple of days. He hasn't called or answered any of my calls. I'm afraid that something happened."

"What could have happened?" Joutsamo asked calmly.

"I really don't know, but he hung out with some strange guys sometimes..." she left the thought hanging.

"And what?"

"I really don't know. Some of them are just weird, like, you know," she said and swept her hair back.

"And Jerry Eriksson is your boyfriend?" Joutsamo asked.

"Yeah. He's my boyfriend. He's never done anything like this."

"When did you see each other last?"

"On Monday night we went out to eat at Tenkka Bar and Jerry got a call around nine. He left pretty soon after that to meet someone..."

"Who?" Joutsamo interrupted.

"I don't know. He doesn't tell me about that stuff."

"Was it just the two of you at the restaurant?"

"Of course there were other customers, but we sat by ourselves. One of his friends had recommended it and Jerry wanted to try the place."

"Did he seem worried when he left?"

"Not that I could tell. More like excited, somehow. He said it would probably take a couple hours and he'd call me afterwards, but he never called," she said. A tear rolled down her cheek.

"There was nothing unusual about that?"

"Well, no. Every now and then he takes off somewhere, but he always calls. Later that night, we were supposed to go to a bar with some of his friends. I got tired of waiting and went home at about midnight."

"What friends?"

"I don't know."

"Do you live with Jerry?" Joutsamo asked, intentionally using the present tense. She knew the girl didn't live in the Kannelmäki apartment.

"Not really. Jerry has an apartment in Kannelmäki next to the mall. I stay there sometimes, but he's never given me a key."

"How well do you know Jerry's friends?"

"Not very well. I know who they are, but they're not my friends."

To Joutsamo, the young woman didn't seem like a criminal, just genuinely distressed. And for good reason, but the detective wasn't about to tell her that.

Joutsamo switched on the computer. "Do you have any ID so I can take down your information?" Joutsamo entered her password and searched for the missing persons form.

At least Eriksson's activities were taking shape and the police would get his phone number from her. He probably had several phones, but even one was valuable, since the warrant for the phone records enabled them to search for any other numbers he could have used.

The blonde pulled a driver's license out of her purse and handed it to Joutsamo. Her name was indeed Kristiina Nyholm, as she had announced downstairs.

Jouko Nyholm sat in his Erottaja office, cursing the fact that he hadn't bought the Thailand vacation package advertised in the window across the street. A couple weeks in the sun would do him good. It would probably help his headache too, or at least he could treat it first thing in the morning with a bottle of hooch.

Nyholm knew his irritation was pointless. He could always walk over to the travel agency, right now if he wanted, but he knew he wouldn't.

Still, it was a good day: last night when he got home, his wife had already been asleep, and this morning she had left for work before he woke up.

His desk phone crackled and Snellman's voice came over the speakerphone, "Get over here."

Nyholm swore again and got up.

The boss was sitting behind his desk and Nyholm took a chair opposite him. The legs on Nyholm's chair were short so he had to look up in order to make eye contact.

"Did you find anything on this Jerry Eriksson that we can tell the police?"

Nyholm shook his head. "No. I made some calls, but nobody's heard of him."

"So we're telling him we got nothin'."

"That's right," Nyholm answered calmly.

"Do we have anything else going on?"

Nyholm shook his head again. "Nothing out of the ordinary. Some phone taps and normal undercover ops on a few drug cases, but otherwise no."

* * *

The digital speedometer displayed 88 kilometers per hour. It was over the limit, but not by much.

The landscape along Route Six between Kotka and Kouvola was numbingly grey. There was no traffic to speak of.

That morning, Markus Markkanen had received confirmation from the Kotka harbor that the TV containers had been unloaded and transferred onto semi-trucks.

There had been no issues with Customs or otherwise. The majority of the ship's cargo was headed directly for the Russian border, save for two, which were sent to Kouvola, a town of about 90,000 just north of Kotka. Markkanen had booked a warehouse in an industrial park, where the cargo could be unloaded and the crates filled with rubber gloves, as the packing list stated. The containers were then bound for Russia. The same gloves had been back and forth over the border half a dozen times, doing the same job.

The TVs already had a buyer, though Markkanen only had a fictitious name and a phone number. Each container had room for 50 to 70 large flat-screen

TVs. On the show room floor, each would sell for between 8,000 and 15,000 euros.

Only 30 more kilometers to go.

Over the past year, the news had been reporting that Russians were buying land in Eastern Finland. Markkanen wondered if these TVs were bound for their summer villas or intended for retail. It was none of his business. His job was to ensure that the transfer at the warehouse went smoothly, and to collect the money.

His speed had climbed over 90 and Markkanen eased his foot off the gas.

* * *

Suhonen's phone beeped. He bolted awake and snatched it off the nightstand. That's when he realized it wasn't a call. It was his alarm. The room was dark; the curtains blocked out the sunlight.

He flopped onto his back and scratched his side. An old stab wound itched from time to time, begging for lotion.

Suhonen stretched his arms and legs. He'd have to make it to the gym today. That and wash the dishes, do laundry and vacuum. His two-bedroom in Kallio wasn't exactly tidy.

After Suhonen's "marriage candidate" had moved out, Kulta proposed that they room together. If they pooled their money, they could save enough for a flat-screen TV and a housekeeper. The stove and dishwasher were dispensable, since the pizza guy would bring the food. If you brought a girlfriend to the pad, you'd have to fill the fridge with beer. The housecleaner could be paid with deposit returns from all the empty bottles and cans.

Suhonen had promised himself to eat more healthily. But once again, the night had ended with a meat pie doused in ketchup & mayo and a pint of milk from an all-night grill stand, which he had pounded at four in the morning.

Should, should, should. He should get in the shower now.

Suhonen grabbed his phone off the table and squinted at it. The clock said 9:31 A.M. He checked the GPS tracker for Saarnikangas' van. It was still at the apartment in Pihlajamäki and hadn't moved all night.

He selected another vehicle from the drop-down menu. This one had sat in Pikku-Huopalahti overnight. The previous evening, he had caught up to Ilari Lydman's Mazda, followed it, and installed a tracking device in the parking lot.

Suhonen stood up, took off his boxers and headed for the shower.

He stopped at the bedroom door and took turns stretching his quads.

CHAPTER 17
POLICE HEADQUARTERS,
PASILA, HELSINKI
THURSDAY, 10:30 A.M.

"Good to see everyone made it," Lieutenant Takamäki said to start off the meeting. He had arranged it on short notice. Mikko Kulta, Kirsi Kohonen and Anna Joutsamo sat on one side of the conference room, Takamäki and Suhonen on the other. Kannas, the Head of Forensics was at the end of the table behind a stack of papers.

Sergeant Maija Laakso from the Financial Crimes Unit sat a couple chairs further down. Earlier, Suhonen had wondered aloud why she was attending, but Joutsamo said Laakso was representing the computer nerds. Apparently, they had found something on Jerry's laptop.

Suhonen tasted his coffee. He could have gone for some pastries too, but thanks to budget cuts, they were bound by a coffee-only policy. He studied Joutsamo's timeline on the wall. Eriksson's movements on Monday evening were beginning to come together.

"Let's get started," Takamäki continued, glancing at Kannas.

"OK," the big man growled. "Some of the evidence from the crime scene has been analyzed. We found a decent amount of hair and fibers, but we haven't been able to go through them all yet. We do know that someone with blue overalls and a black wool hat has been at the scene. Of course, we're waiting for you to bring us more samples for comparison."

The detectives nodded.

"We found a wad of chewing gum and some cigarette butts in the yard. There were plenty of those, but we focused on the fresh ones. The most interesting piece of evidence was the gum, which gave us a DNA sample. We compared it to the DNA database this morning and found a match," Kannas paused. "In other words, we have a possible suspect."

"Wow," Kulta exclaimed.

Kannas slid a document toward the detectives. Joutsamo snatched it first and glanced at Suhonen. "Juha Saarnikangas."

Suhonen's face was expressionless.

"It's difficult to determine how old the gum is, but we can probably try some further analysis at the lab. I would think they could tell from the composition whether it's relatively fresh or ancient, but I don't actually know. However, it's clear that Saarnikangas has been at the crime scene. We can confirm that he's been there recently by analyzing the tires on his van. The tire tracks at the scene were left by GT Radials, and, according to Joutsamo, Saarnikangas has a matching set on his van. If we make a direct comparison, we can easily prove whether it was the same van."

Takamäki nodded. "So Saarnikangas is a strong suspect. You all remember, of course, that Saarnikangas owed Eriksson a rather large sum of money. I should also mention that according to the

Board of Customs, the tip about Eriksson being a Customs nark isn't true."

Joutsamo interjected. "In other words, Saarnikangas had an apparent motive and we've linked him to the crime scene. His criminal record is another strike."

Takamäki interrupted Joutsamo. "Before we make any conclusions... Maija, why don't you tell us what you found on the computer."

Laakso had dark hair, a round face and heavy build, and she wore glasses. Suhonen figured she hadn't attended the police academy, but was hired from some IT firm.

"Right," Laakso said. "The computer was a typical laptop—cost about a thousand euros. The internet service provider was Wizard. We haven't received the broadband service reports from the ISP, so for now we're just relying on the data from the laptop."

Laakso glanced at the others, but nobody said anything.

"So... We found Jerry Eriksson's fingerprints on the keyboard, along with somebody else's," she said, glancing at Joutsamo. "Based on an initial comparison, the second person was probably Kristiina Nyholm."

Joutsamo cut in. "This Kristiina was here this morning to report Eriksson as missing and I interviewed her. She told me about the events of the evening, and also gave me Eriksson's cell phone number. We've filed a warrant for the phone records. Just in case, I took her fingerprints and had a look at them with a magnifying glass. They appear to match those found on the laptop."

"Did you have the legal authority to take her prints?" Kulta asked.

"I asked her and she agreed," Joutsamo answered.

"I don't suppose you told her that her lost property had been found already."

"No."

"Cruel," Kulta scolded.

Before Joutsamo could say anything, Takamäki interjected, "Anna and I agreed on that strategy. Go on, Maija."

Kulta shrugged.

"He had your typical Windows software, but we didn't find any interesting documents. There was some photo-editing software and what not, but no photos on the hard drive. Because of kiddie-porn cases, we have excellent programs for finding photos anywhere on the hard drive. Nor did we find any Word or Excel documents. The email application had never been used."

"What we found on the internet side was much more interesting. Apparently, he used the computer for banking. Here's the account number," Laakso said, passing a sheet of paper to Takamäki.

"Whose is it?"

"It belongs to a fronting company. We haven't requested the official account information since that requires a Lieutenant's authorization."

"Consider it done," Takamäki said, handing the paper to Joutsamo.

"The computer has also been used to access a couple of free email servers. Here are the user names and passwords," she said, and gave the paper straight to Joutsamo. "We found a few fragments of text, which are included on that document."

Joutsamo glanced at the page. The text was a lot of sports talk, but more importantly, the recipient's email address was included. It was unlikely that

Eriksson would jabber on about hockey games with his killer, but if need be, the address would allow them to learn more about his circle of friends. At this point, that was unnecessary: Saarnikangas' DNA had been found at the crime scene. That was strong evidence.

"In addition, I have a list of the web pages he visited recently. To an outsider's eye, it looks like fairly ordinary internet activity, but since I don't know the details of the investigation, I'll leave that to you. But there are, for example, Google searches for 'police' and he's also been reading about criminal law."

"A civilized criminal," Kulta said.

"Thank you, Maija," Takamäki said.

Laakso stood up. "Let me know if you need anything else."

"The DNA evidence is definitely the most significant," Kulta said.

"Thanks," Kannas muttered. "Crime scene investigation. Work with a purpose!"

Kulta spoke up. "I think we should take Saarnikangas into custody and start the interrogations. He'll talk. Maybe not right away, but he's in so deep that he'll have to say something."

"My thoughts exactly," Joutsamo added.

Takamäki looked at Suhonen.

"I don't think he did it," Suhonen pronounced. "And even if he did, it wasn't because of the debt. Yesterday I went to shake him up a bit, and right afterwards he left to meet a certain Ilari Lydman. Then, right away, a livid Lydman went out of his way to make a call on a landline. Those actions don't indicate that debt was the motive."

"I'm not arguing with that," Joutsamo added. "This could very well be a contract hit, but we'll know more when we get him to talk. If he doesn't talk, then that's his own fault. He'll get life."

Takamäki nodded. "Suhonen, bring him in."

* * *

Markus Markkanen reached the entrance of the warehouse grounds and opened the padlock on the chain link gate. The lock was new, but the fence was falling apart. Rust had eaten through the coating on the steel.

Maybe the Kouvola industrial district was too crowded for this type of job, but nobody would pay attention. The section he had rented was tucked away on the perimeter.

Markkanen drove inside, leaving the gate open. The warehouse was clad in corrugated sheet metal, and was large enough that a semi truck could fit inside.

He left his car behind the building and walked the grounds. Not much to check out: a few worn-out tires and a stack of pallets.

The gate key also fit the lock for the warehouse and he opened the door. The building was long, cold and empty, designed expressly for unloading cargo. He snapped on the lights.

The semi would have enough room to back up to a loading dock in the rear. From there, a ramp descended to ground level. The goods would be quickly transferred from the shipping container to a truck or van. The smaller vehicles had a separate entrance. When a van was full, another would take its place. The forklift in the corner of the building would speed things up considerably.

Along the wall were a tall stack of cardboard boxes and some plastic pallets with Russian text. Those were the rubber gloves.

He tried the forklift, which started easily. Everything was in order. He glanced at the clock: 10:40 A.M. The buyer's vehicles would be there at 10:50 and the first semi at 11:00. If everything went smoothly, the loading and unloading would take less than an hour.

Markkanen checked the holster on the small of his back again. The gun was still there.

* * *

Takamäki was sitting in his office, sifting through piles of email. It seemed like the Ministry of Interior had gone nuts. Every week, a new flood of directives on criminal investigations arrived. Narcotics was to blame, of course. Some of their officers had allegedly used rogue investigative methods, which had been making headlines for a year. The case was still pending. Takamäki couldn't help thinking that on paper things were simpler. Out on the streets, things were different. Maybe the desk jockeys ought to spend more time working undercover before judging others, he thought.

The Ministry's new position was that all crimes should be solved according to strict standard protocols. The laws governing police investigations, interrogations and operations were also being reformed. It would be interesting to see what came of it. One thing was clear: it was almost impossible for the new rules to be any more complicated than they already were.

Takamäki wondered if he'd done the right thing ordering Saarnikangas' arrest. If the man didn't cooperate, he'd be convicted of murder with the evidence they already had. In court, his silence would be taken as an admission of guilt. If he was innocent, he had every reason to clear his name. They'd give him every opportunity to do that.

On the other hand, Saarnikangas might take the rap to protect somebody else. In that instance, despite getting a conviction, the killer would go free.

But Takamäki believed Saarnikangas would talk. After all, this was the same guy who had told Suhonen about the body in the first place.

His phone rang.

"Hello." The caller's number was displayed as "unknown."

"Hi. Sanna Römpötti here," said a woman's voice.

Takamäki would have recognized her voice anyway. She was a veteran crime reporter for Channel 3 TV news.

"What now?"

"Don't steal my questions."

"Huh?"

"I'll ask the questions," she laughed.

Takamäki was quiet for a moment. "But aren't the detectives supposed to ask the questions first?"

"True. So what's new?" Römpötti went ahead with her interview.

"What's new... Actually, not much," he said. Under no circumstances would it make sense to talk about the Eriksson case at this sensitive stage. Broadcasting it would only complicate matters further.

"Nothing?" she pried in a voice that suggested she knew better.

"Nothing that I can talk about or that would interest TV reporters."

"Well, I heard you found a body."

Takamäki swore to himself. "We find bodies every day. The population of Helsinki isn't getting any younger."

"I mean a homicide victim."

Takamäki wasn't sure how much she knew. So far, she was just baiting him with questions.

"Like I said, nothing that I can talk about or that would interest TV reporters."

"How do you know what interests us? Besides, we're not just TV news anymore, We're on the internet in real-time," she said, more aggressively.

"I see."

"Listen, Kari. You've been investigating this murder since the beginning of the week, which means it's pretty interesting. If it was a routine case, you would have announced it right away."

"Sorry," he said bluntly. "No Scoop of the Year this time."

"So you're declining to comment."

"What's there to comment about?"

Römpötti was silent for a moment. "Well, I guess I'll just put it on the website then."

"Put what?"

"Check our website in five minutes," she said and hung up.

Damn. How in the hell had she found out about the case already? That would be almost impossible to answer. Journalists had their sources and dozens of people knew about Eriksson's murder.

Competition for internet news had changed the relationship between the police and the media. Now journalists demanded every crumb of information immediately, and more often than not they published it the moment they heard it. There was a time when Takamäki could have asked her to call back in the afternoon and they could have dealt with the issue like grown-ups. Now, Römpötti was in a rush to get the story online before somebody beat her to it.

One thing was for sure, some details of the case were about to become public. Now Takamäki had to consider its impact on the investigation.

CHAPTER 18
KOUVOLA WAREHOUSE
THURSDAY, 10:58 A.M.

The Russian truck driver was a pro: He backed the trailer into the warehouse, hopped out of the cab and ducked behind the corner to smoke a cigarette. The system was simple. The driver disappears so he never sees what goes in or comes out of the truck. The second semi was idling nearby, waiting its turn.

Markus Markkanen only knew Jormanainen—the buyer—by his last name and he knew it wasn't real. The bearded man was in his fifties and wore a ragged brown leather jacket. Markkanen knew the man had received a suspended sentence for fraudulent invoicing of construction companies.

Jormanainen had brought along a couple helpers.

"Makle, Axeli, and Rahkis, let's move."

A guy in a windbreaker and a baseball cap dragged himself to his feet and slowly swung open the container doors. A younger fellow with copious amounts of gel in his hair started the forklift. The third, a bald man smoking a cigar, sat on the back bumper of an empty cleaning company truck.

"Didn't you clowns hear me? Get to work!"

The TV sets were arranged lengthwise in special racks. Helmet-hair forked the first rack of ten sets out and paused on the loading dock while Jormanainen jotted down the screen sizes from the cardboard boxes.

From the first group, all ten were 70 inch TVs. Markkanen remembered seeing in the newspaper that these top-end electronics had a suggested retail price of between 8,000 and 15,000 euros.

The forklift driver transferred the TVs to the smaller truck.

The TVs in the second rack were all 50-inchers and Jormanainen wrote them down in his pad.

The forklift driver knew his stuff and the truck filled quickly. It had room for 35 sets. The bald guy hopped into the driver's seat and drove off. The guy in the windbreaker backed up a second identical truck into the building. They emptied the rest of the container into it. All together, the container had held twenty 70- and forty 50-inchers.

The forklift driver filled the semi with rubber gloves from the loading dock. That phase of the operation had taken twenty minutes.

They unloaded the second semi just as quickly and packed it full of rubber gloves. Baldie and the guy in the windbreaker had both left with their second loads. Once the semi was gone, Jormanainen sent helmet-hair packing and pulled a fat stack of cash out of the breast pocket of his jacket.

He looked at his list. In total, there were 115 televisions.

"OK," he said. "By my count, we had forty-five 70-inch units and seventy 50-inch units. The price was eight grand a piece for the 70-inchers, and the 50-inchers are four grand apiece."

Markkanen nodded and did the math in his head: the 70-inchers would come to €360,000 and the 50-

inchers would be €280,000. So all together, €640,000.

Jormanainen glanced at Markkanen. "But we could just agree that there were only thirty-five 70-inchers and sixty 50-inchers."

"And?" Markkanen asked.

"A bonus for you and me. I'll buy 'em from you—off the record—for half-price."

"A con on a con, huh?" Markkanen grinned.

"Whatever, but we have to account for the side deal separately. Nobody really knows exactly how many units were in those crates, just as long as the numbers match up roughly."

Markkanen nodded. "And your pals didn't count 'em?"

"No. They're from Kotka. They don't teach math over there. Quite a bunch, by the way. I told 'em to dress normal today. Nothing goofy or anything like that. And what do they do? Come here looking like the cast of *Sopranos*…"

He looked back at his notepad and counted, "35 times 8…then 60 times 4…so 280 plus 240 makes 520."

"I thought they didn't teach math in Kotka."

"I'm from the burbs," the man smiled. "So let's settle the official part first."

He took out a wad of money. Bundles of purple €500 notes were bound together with rubber bands. "Each bundle is ten grand, so twenty bills in each."

Markkanen nodded and kept a tally as Jormanainen counted off the bills. After about ten minutes of counting, Jormanainen evened up the stack and handed it to Markkanen.

"OK?"

"OK," Markkanen said, shoving the bundles of cash into his breast pocket. The pocket strained at the seams.

"Now for Santa's share. Ten 70-inchers at four grand a pop, and ten 50-inchers at two grand each. According to my suburban math, that makes sixty Gs, right?"

Markkanen nodded and Jormanainen counted off sixty-thousand more.

"We good?"

"Yup," Markkanen answered.

"That's it then," Jormanainen said. Without another word, he was on his way.

Markkanen waited a couple minutes and checked his gun again. The foursome could be waiting outside the warehouse door.

He checked around the warehouse one more time. There was no sign that they had even been there. He turned off the lights and opened the front door warily. Nobody. Markkanen locked the door and circled around to his car.

He grabbed a plastic bag from the passenger foot well, thrust Lindström's money inside, and kept his own share in his pocket.

After driving through the gate he got out to lock it up. That took thirty seconds.

He glanced at his watch: 11:59 A.M. Thanks to Jormanainen's shrewdness, his hourly wages were much more than he expected. With sixty Gs on top of the ten he'd get from Lindström, the job had turned out to be pretty lucrative. A construction worker would have to work a few years to earn the same pay.

Satisfied, Markkanen turned on the radio and drove off.

Anna Joutsamo poked her head into Takamäki's office. "It's on the radio now too."

"Yup," Takamäki nodded. "A couple of Römpötti's cohorts have already called."

"What'd you tell 'em?"

"Same thing I told Römpötti. No comment. I can't deny it, since I'd be lying in their faces, but I can't admit it either."

Joutsamo scratched her head. "But if you don't deny it, they'll consider it an admission."

Takamäki had Römpötti's article pulled up on his screen. The headline was striking: "Helsinki VCU Investigates Underworld Hit." The article itself was quite short: "The Helsinki Violent Crimes Unit is investigating a murder that occurred earlier this week. A body was discovered in northern Helsinki. Detective Lieutenant Kari Takamäki of the Helsinki VCU declined to comment. The murder appears to have resulted from a dispute between two criminal organizations."

Based on the article, Römpötti didn't seem to know much about the investigation. On the other hand, she could be protecting her source by being intentionally vague.

A number of VCU detectives, Forensics, the Financial Crimes Unit officers and the staff of the Medical Examiner's office all knew something about the case. Who in the world had squealed? And with all the talk that flies in the police cafeteria, who would ever know? It was a pity, but nothing to cry about.

Takamäki wasn't interested in how much Römpötti or anyone else knew about the case. Now he was focused on how to use the media for the benefit of the investigation.

"Any ideas?" Takamäki asked. Joutsamo leaned against the door frame and shrugged.

"Alright. I think we should release a photo of Eriksson and ask the public to notify the police if they have any information. Let's say he was murdered, but no other details. Römpötti used 'northern Helsinki' and that's close enough," Takamäki said.

"But a name and a photo?" Joutsamo hesitated.

"Yup. Otherwise it'll be too ambiguous. That should also allow us to find out more about Eriksson's friends and activities."

"But if the media has a name they'll dig up his record."

"Does that matter?"

"Probably not, since we didn't get any leads from the fraud cases anyway."

"Maybe someone else will find something," Takamäki said. "I'll send out a press release at three. Before then, make sure a Police Pastor or somebody from our team goes to tell the family and the girl who filed the report…what was her name again?"

"Kristiina Nyholm."

Takamäki reflected for a moment.

"What is it?" Joutsamo asked.

"This is a long shot, but find out if this Kristiina is related to Jouko Nyholm from Customs."

"What makes you suspect that?"

Takamäki looked Joutsamo in the eyes. "Just the last name. Nothing more."

* * *

Markkanen had been driving for about a half an hour, when his phone alerted him to an incoming text. The message was from Lydman, and was concise: "3."

Markkanen cursed.

He had heard the news on the radio, but there was no reason to panic. Lydman seemed ruffled. The message meant that Markkanen should call Lydman on his #3 phone. With a new pre-paid SIM card, he'd be using a brand new number, and any calls made with it would be secure. The cops couldn't tap it in real-time.

A sign reading "The Baron" in cursive directed him to a gas station, actually more of a tourist trap. Markkanen didn't need any of their coffee, gas, food, books, magazines, playgrounds or tourist trash, nor any of their other services. He pulled the Beamer into a snowy parking space and stepped out to get his phones from the trunk. He had some half-dozen cell phones, and the same number of SIM cards. He had written a number on several of them, in the event that he needed a secure line himself. Lindström also had a few of these secure phones in his apartment.

Switching phones was the criminal's way of combating the Finnish police, experts in phone tapping. Phone-tap warrants were easy to obtain. Beyond listening for illicit activity, the Police also used the cell phones to track down associations between criminals by monitoring who they called. The cops could listen in on previously unknown criminals, and continually extend their knowledge of crime networks. By using an uncompromised phone and a brand-new SIM card, Markkanen would get a completely new phone number and eliminate the chance that the police could listen in.

Markkanen installed one of the new SIM cards into an old Nokia 3310. The battery was dead, so he got back in the car and plugged it into the cigarette lighter. The number to Lydman's #3 phone was written on the keypad and he dialed. It rang three times before Lydman answered.

"Fuck," said Ilari Lydman in an icy voice.

"What's up?"

"You been listening to the radio or surfing the web?"

"I heard it on the radio," Markkanen said coolly.

"Fuck."

"You're like a broken hip-hop record. What's your problem?"

"They found Eriksson!"

Markkanen watched a family get out of their car. The kids were jumping around, elated to be outside.

"So what? We're ready for it. Nothing to worry about. If someone goes down for this, it'll be your buddy. There's nothing for us to worry about. You know, we've set the stage. The note about the debt and what not. So, take it easy…"

"I ain't worried about Juha, but that Korpela is another story."

"The Skull?"

"Yeah him. He threatened me with the scissors. He thinks we're putting him away for life."

Tony Korpela was a real head case who had done time for a brutal scissor murder. But Lydman had used one word that Markkanen didn't like.

"What do you mean 'we?'" he menaced. If Lydman had done his job correctly, the Skulls shouldn't know anything about him.

"Yes, we. Korpela said he checked around and found out that this extends beyond me. He mentioned your name."

"You didn't tell him?"

"No."

Liar, Markkanen thought, but understood Lydman's concern. The Skulls were good at keeping their end of the bargain, but when things went bad, it was likely you would wind up on the wrong end.

"What did he say exactly?"

"I didn't tape it!" Lydman snapped, then calmed down. "He cussed like the devil and said we didn't keep our end of the deal. He wished you and me the best in hell, blustered on about revenge, then demanded money."

"How much?"

"Hundred grand."

"No!"

"Apparently that's the standard penalty for contract violation," Lydman said.

"Really."

Lydman paused. "So, you gonna pay?"

"Where would I get that kind of money?" he said, glancing at the plastic bag on the floor.

It contained many times that sum. He thought of another alternative: he had seventy grand in his pocket...maybe he could scrape together another thirty, but... Shit!

Eriksson had been asking for it; he had become too arrogant. Markkanen could have tolerated his crowing and the fact that the kid had passed him up in Lindström's organization, but the blackmail was the last straw. Somehow, the brat had figured out that Markkanen was embezzling money from Lindström, and had threatened to rat on him. In the end, the decision had been easy. Eriksson had stepped, or rather, had tried to step on the wrong man's toes.

Markkanen had lured Lydman into the scheme by claiming that Eriksson was a Customs nark. He was amused that in the end, Eriksson did actually have a Customs connection. Lydman had an in with the Skulls, and had arranged a hit man for 25 Gs. Lydman had also thought of a convenient sacrificial lamb for the murder: Juha Saarnikangas. Juha had been paid to get rid of the body. If Eriksson vanished for good, they'd be in the clear. And if Saarnikangas failed, he would take the heat. The hit man wouldn't talk, Lydman wouldn't talk and neither would he.

Now the hit man was worried for no reason, unless he was trying to rake in more money. Or was Lydman trying to stiff him? He wouldn't dare.

"Listen," Markkanen said. "It's water under the bridge. Nothing has changed, so take it easy."

"Are you gonna pay him?"

"I can negotiate with them."

Lydman laughed. "Good luck with that."

Markkanen considered his options. He didn't want to irritate or provoke Lydman. The man was trustworthy, but unpredictable in his own way. "I'll take care of it. Don't worry."

"Good, but I'm going to Thailand for a couple weeks."

"What?"

"I bought a last-minute ticket. I'm leaving tomorrow night… Maybe things will settle down."

Stupid, Markkanen thought. Running scared. He answered in a calm voice, "OK. That might be a good idea, but first set up a meeting between Saarnikangas and me. I still need him."

"For what?"

"It's better if you don't know," Markkanen said.

"Guess so."

"But go talk to him in person; his phone could be tapped. Tell him to be at the Corner Pub at eight o'clock tonight."

"The Corner Pub at eight," Lydman repeated. "OK, I'll do it, but then I'll be gone a couple weeks. In the meantime, clear things up with the Skulls. This is your mess."

"Of course," Markkanen assured him. He asked for a number for the hit man and Lydman gave it to him, but pointed out that the line wasn't secure. Lydman said that he and Korpela used a special code in case the phones were tapped. Markkanen was to suggest a meeting at the Ruskeasuo Teboil, but it would actually take place in the parking lot of the Tali Bowling alley.

Markkanen hung up and started the car. He'd have time to think on the way to Helsinki.

Before hitting the road, he called his wife. He directed her to take Eetu and leave town for a few days. She seemed confused but agreed to it. She was to take all the money out of hiding, pick up the boy from school and sign in at the Turku Caribia Spa-Hotel under her maiden name. At least the boy would have something to do there. Markkanen promised to be in touch by Sunday evening at the latest.

Taking risks with the Skulls was a bad idea.

* * *

Suhonen was sitting in the police cafeteria, forking macaroni hot dish into his mouth. The lunch room was half-full and Suhonen was alone at a table for four. He had eaten a salad for starters, and was glad to have something healthy under his belt.

Takamäki had ordered him to arrest Saarnikangas, but he was in no hurry. According to the tracking device, Juha's van was still parked in Pihlajamäki, and Lydman's Mazda hadn't moved either. Of course, they could have walked or taken a taxi somewhere, but more than likely, both were relaxing at home. Neither was the type to ride the bus.

The hot dish was good, or maybe Suhonen was just hungry.

He should really bring Saarnikangas in after lunch. Lydman could wait till after Juha's interrogations. Suhonen didn't think he would talk, though. The guy was a survivor who knew better than to squeal on his employers. On the other hand, Saarnikangas wouldn't do life for no reason.

His phone rang on his belt.

He pulled it out and swallowed a mouthful of macaroni. It was the Warden of the Helsinki Prison.

"Hey, Ainola here," the man rasped. "Do you have a minute?"

"Never a spare minute around here, but go ahead."

"You guys cracking a pretty tough case over there, huh?" It was more a statement than a question.

"Something like that."

"Well, that's what I'm calling about. Some of our guards heard from the inmates that this Eriksson could have been a Customs informant."

"Okay," Suhonen remarked. As a formality, he asked, "How reliable is this?"

"Just a rumor, but I thought it might be useful."

"Thanks for the tip," Suhonen replied and took another bite of macaroni.

Ainola paused for a moment. "There's something else. The guy you visited earlier in the week... Eero Salmela?"

"What about him?" Suhonen mumbled.

"Are you eating?"

"Yeah—go on."

"This might not be anything, but if you're interested in the guy, you should know his connections. His drug-running partner Jorma Raitio ended up in the infirmary. Supposedly, he fell down the stairs, but the doctor suspected his knee was busted with a pipe."

"Badly?"

"It'll need a few surgeries, and even then it might not fully recover. But here's the interesting thing. According to the same rumors, the Skulls were behind the assault, and Salmela ordered it."

Suhonen put his fork down. "So Salmela hired out a hit?"

"Yeah. In his defense, Raitio probably threatened him first."

What in the world had Salmela gotten mixed up in now? He was a thief, but he shouldn't have anything to do with the Skulls. Suhonen thought about Salmela's words back at the prison, about someone else getting his back.

"How well does he get along with the Skulls?"

"Not sure. Well enough that they carried out his hit."

CHAPTER 19
POLICE HEADQUARTERS,
PASILA, HELSINKI
THURSDAY, 1:20 P.M.

Anna Joutsamo stepped into Lieutenant Takamäki's office, but lingered in the doorway.

"Yes?" Takamäki looked up from his desk.

"Suhonen's sitting there at his desk reading emails."

"And?"

Joutsamo crossed her arms. "Well, I thought he was supposed to bring Saarnikangas in for questioning."

"Oh. Why don't you say something to him?"

Joutsamo narrowed her eyes. "He takes orders from you."

"But you're running the case."

"Listen, Kari. I don't want any dramas or power struggles."

Takamäki grinned. "So you're passing the buck to me."

"You're the one with the bigger paycheck."

Takamäki got up and followed Joutsamo out. The detectives' squad room was a few steps further down the hall. Joutsamo went in first and Takamäki turned to Kohonen, who was sitting at her computer.

"Kirsi, what's the status on the phone records?"

"No hits yet."

Takamäki nodded. Sifting through the phone list was almost as unbearable as watching hours of surveillance video. Looking for a particular number in a file was relatively easy—matching numbers across various files was more complicated. Computer programs were a big help, but everything had to be double-checked by hand. Pre-paid numbers muddied the investigation even further.

"What about the tap?"

"Kafka's team is on it, but nothing so far. All the phones have gone quiet."

Mikko Kulta was in the far corner behind his computer, looking like a fourth grader who didn't want to be called upon by the teacher. He had probably been playing internet computer games, as Solitaire and Mine Sweeper weren't on police computers.

"How's it going?" Takamäki asked, turning to Suhonen.

"Pretty good," Suhonen responded, without looking up from the screen. Takamäki noticed he was going through his email.

"And Saarnikangas?"

Suhonen glanced at his cell phone. "His van is at his apartment in Pihlajamäki. I presume he is too."

"You gonna bring him in?"

"As soon as I have some time. I figured I'd apply to become the OSHA representative for the Helsinki Police Force.

"Huh?" Takamäki grunted.

Suhonen turned to look at him. "Yeah. I'd be able to monitor everyone's overtime hours."

"I see," Takamäki paused and added dryly: "C'mon now."

"Hey," Suhonen said, addressing Joutsamo too. "I'm gonna bring him in, but now that the case is public, let's wait a couple hours and see what happens. Saarnikangas knows we're watching him, so he's not gonna use his phone. Yesterday he went to meet Lydman and I'd like to see where else he's gonna go...or if Lydman goes with. "

Joutsamo cut in. "As long as he's not silenced permanently."

"Anyone for coffee?" Suhonen asked. "I can put some on."

Joutsamo looked at Takamäki.

"I'll have some," said the Lieutenant. "Tea for Joutsamo."

* * *

Kalevi Lindström answered the door quickly.

"Come in," he said. The businessman had on grey pants and a matching sweater.

Markus Markkanen had left his car on Tehdas Street, where snow had covered the vehicles, but the cobblestone street was still slushy.

Outside, a streetcar rumbled past. In his left hand, Markkanen was holding a plastic bag, which appeared to contain a book.

"How'd it go?" Lindström asked.

"Good. No problems," he said, closing the door behind him.

"How many were there?"

Markkanen handed him the bag, and Lindström opened it eagerly.

"There's 560,000 euros. There were thirty-five 70-inch units and sixty 50-inch units," he said calmly.

Lindström walked into the library and poured the bundles of cash onto an oak table. He took one and started counting the bills.

"There's twenty bills in every bundle. Ten thousand each," Markkanen added. Lindström seemed satisfied with the numbers.

He went through the bills one at a time and arranged them in piles of 100,000 euros. Markkanen stood quietly by the door. The counting took a good ten minutes. Only once did Lindström count a pile a second time.

"Good," he said, then took one bundle and handed it to Markkanen. "Well done."

Markkanen slipped the money into the breast pocket of his coat.

"That's the good news."

"What do you mean?" Lindström asked.

Clearly he hadn't been watching or listening to the news.

"Eriksson's been killed."

"What? When?" Lindström barked.

"I don't know the details. I heard it on the news. He was found dead somewhere in North Helsinki earlier in the week."

"Who did this?" Lindström stammered, scraping the money into the bag, as though it were in danger.

"That's a good question," Markkanen said stiffly. "I don't know. I don't know how it happened either."

Lindström looked Markkanen in the eyes. "Does this have anything to do with...uhh, my businesses or did Jerry have issues of his own?"

"That's what I wanted to ask you."

"I don't have any problems, at least not that I'm aware of."

"Have we stepped on someone's toes?"

"Not to my knowledge," Lindström assured him.

"Then we shouldn't have any problems, unless someone's trying to come after us. Could Eriksson have pissed someone off...or conned 'em?"

"No, no. I don't think so. He wouldn't dare."

"What about the Russians?" Markkanen asked. He didn't know much about that part of the business, but it was safe to say that they were behind much of the trafficking and tax fraud, since the majority of their shipments ended up in Russia.

Lindström thought about it. "They've never told me about any problems... No, no, no. Everything's OK on that front."

"Those crates that stayed in Finland aren't..."

Lindström cackled. "Skimmed off the top? No, they're part of the deal. It's completely legitimate."

Interesting racket, Markkanen thought. Apparently, Lindström was paid in kind.

"Well, it could be that Eriksson had some personal problems. In any case, we'll have to keep our eyes open. If something happens, let me know right away. I'll ask around."

Lindström nodded, his forehead knit. "Okay...alright."

Markkanen looked at Lindström, now a tense and worried man. Was this his Achilles heel, then? On the business end, Lindström was a tough cookie, but when it came to the rough stuff, he started to crack.

* * *

Suhonen's unmarked Peugeot was sitting at a red light near Police Headquarters. He was waiting to turn onto Veturinkatu toward Hartwall Arena, if only the light would change. The snow had made a mess of traffic.

His phone was charging on his lap. Two red dots flashed on the display, both in motion. They moved sluggishly, but even so, Suhonen had checked out a car from the police garage.

In the passenger's seat lay an SLR camera with a telephoto lens.

The dot for Saarnikangas' van had started to move about a minute before the one for Lydman's Mazda. Suhonen had checked the phone tap, but there had been no activity. Unless their simultaneous departures were coincidental, Lydman and Saarnikangas were obviously using some other phone line or messaging system. Suhonen tried to remember if he had seen a computer in Saarnikangas' apartment. He wasn't sure.

It looked like Saarnikangas was getting onto Beltway One, heading west. Lydman had turned north onto Mannerheiminkatu. Soon, he'd be on the Hämeenlinna Highway.

The lights turned green and Suhonen made a right. Traffic was jammed up on the south side of the massive Hartwall Arena. He had a roof light in the glove box, but he didn't want to use it.

Ten minutes later, Suhonen reached the north end of Veturinkatu. The dots began to overlap at the end of Pakila, near Central Park. Suhonen knew there was a parking lot next to the warming house and trail access, but he doubted they'd be going for a hike or a ski. From Helsinki Central Park, one could hike 600 miles of trails due north, all the way to the fells of Lapland. The lot was busy enough not to attract attention, yet remote enough for a private meeting.

Suhonen guessed he was about ten minutes away.

As Lydman shifted his weight to his left, the wet gravel in the parking lot grated beneath the snow.

"Now listen," he said, opening the zipper of his black coat.

"The answer is no," Saarnikangas said. He kept his hands in the pockets of his army jacket.

About fifty cars were in the parking lot. Lydman's Mazda and Saarnikangas' van were on the eastern end, away from the others. Nearby were a small hockey arena and a huge hill that had been built from garbage and compost.

"You don't even know what I'm gonna say."

"Still, I ain't agreeing to anything. Nothing."

"Fuck, then it's your time," Lydman growled and slipped his right hand inside his jacket. "Here and now."

Petrified, Saarnikangas took a step back. He didn't doubt for a moment that Lydman was carrying.

"Should I do it right here or you wanna go lie in the ditch? That'd be easier for me."

Saarnikangas looked around, but nobody had noticed his plight. Should he call for help?

"Listen, listen…" he stammered. "Take it easy, alright?"

"I'll take it easy when you stop dicking around and start listening," Lydman snarled. He kept his hand inside his jacket.

"Okay, okay."

"Number one. Yesterday at the Corner Pub you said some cop had been asking about Eriksson. Has he or anyone else been in contact with you again?"

Saarnikangas shook his head. "No. I've been in my pad all day long. Nothing."

"Good. The news said they found the body a couple days ago. If they knew something, they would've arrested you. So they're probably just looking for background info on Eriksson and you just happened to know him somewhat."

"Somewhat." Saarnikangas repeated.

"Number two," Lydman continued. "There's no reason to panic here. We planned this so that nobody gets caught. If one of us happens to get arrested for some reason, the deal is that nobody will say a word. Nothing. Answer every question with 'no comment.'"

"No comment."

"What? You fucking with me?"

"No-o. Just practicing," Saarnikangas forced a grin.

"The ditch is right over there."

"There's no need."

"You know if this goes to court, the record will show every word that was said in the interrogations and in court. Who said what and who didn't comment. People read that stuff."

Saarnikangas nodded.

Lydman went on. "Number three, and this is the last. Today at eight o'clock, you're gonna meet someone at the Corner Pub. He has a job for you, and you'll do it like a good boy."

"Who?"

"His first name is Markus. He's about six-two and two-hundred twenty pounds."

Saarnikangas knew that, aside from the name, those features would fit about fifty percent of the customers.

"What is this job?"

"He'll tell you then."

"Oh, one of these? I dunno. I don't want to get mixed up in anything else. Ever since I cleaned up my act, everything's gone to hell."

Lydman looked at the miserable junkie.

"Listen, once you've taken care of this, you can join a monastery for all I care."

Saarnikangas imagined a future of long, lonely days behind protective walls, but he wasn't picturing a monastery.

He paused. "By the way, one more thing…"

* * *

As he entered the parking lot, Suhonen spotted Saarnikangas' van and two men talking next to it. He swung the Peugeot behind an SUV about 60-70 yards off.

There was no time to lose. He grabbed the camera and a small plastic bag and got out of the car. The SUV provided enough cover that the men wouldn't notice him. He dug a loose-fitting brown vest out of the bag and pulled it on. On the back, large block letters spelled out, "Bird Photographer." The same text appeared on the front. The vest gave him an excuse to take photos just about anywhere.

Suhonen circled the SUV and pointed the camera towards Saarnikangas' van. The image in the viewfinder was fuzzy until the automatic focus kicked in. The lighting was a bit dark, but the quality of the lens and the additional reflected light from the snow helped. He zoomed in and snapped a half-dozen photos on rapid-fire. Suhonen had a good perspective; their profiles were clear enough that he could easily recognize both Saarnikangas and Lydman.

He crouched down and looked at the pictures on the LCD. Good enough.

Suhonen heard footsteps behind him and glanced around. A woman in her forties with walking poles and a blue wind suit was approaching. She aimed her key fob at the SUV to unlock the doors, then froze when she noticed Suhonen crouching next to her car.

He turned slowly and whispered, "Shhh... There's an Olive-backed Pipit in the thicket to your left. Really rare."

The woman stiffened and Suhonen raised his camera. He snapped a few photos of the bushes and glanced at the screen for good measure. He gave her the thumbs up and whispered, "Anthus Hodgsoni. Really rare in Finland."

The woman said nothing, climbed into the SUV, locked the doors and sped away. Suhonen rose and swung back into his car.

He started the Peugeot and headed toward the Pakila Teboil gas station. There he'd have time for a cup of coffee before the next phase.

The coffee at the Pakila Teboil had been exceptionally good. Suhonen had barely managed to down a cup before the dots on his cell phone started to move again. The meeting between Saarnikangas and Lydman had lasted about fifteen minutes.

Now Suhonen had photographs that the men would have to explain during their interrogations, as well as in court. Of course, he would have rather heard what they said or even recorded it, but he hadn't had time. Had they had advance warning of the location that might have been possible as well.

Audio surveillance presented its own problems. Unwanted noise sources near the device could spoil the whole operation. Suhonen recalled how a full day's work by ten cops was once wasted when a bus driver picked the wrong spot to take his break and left the engine idling.

Now Suhonen was sitting in his car in the parking lot outside Saarnikangas' apartment building. He had predicted correctly that Saarnikangas would return home, and had left while Juha was still at the parking lot. Suhonen had kept his eye on the glowing dot, which had stayed a few minutes behind him.

Saarnikangas was a minute away from the parking lot. Suhonen flicked a switch and the wipers cleared the slush off the windshield.

It was quiet. Only a few people were out walking their dogs. A wet snow had blanketed the cars in the parking lot and the darkening landscape reminded him of Christmas, though it was only November. Hopefully, they'd have a white Christmas this year, Suhonen thought. Probably not, if the last few years were any guide.

The street lights came on, only a dim glow at first. They took a few minutes to warm up.

He watched as Saarnikangas' van rounded the neighboring restaurant and crept into the parking lot. The headlights blinded him, and he couldn't make out the driver.

The Ducato swung into an open space three places down from Suhonen. He got out and walked up to Saarnikangas, who was locking his van with a key.

"Hello," the detective said, making Saarnikangas jump.

He recovered quickly. "What the hell!"

"Right on."

"Huh?"

"You're in a hot spot."

Juha forced a laugh. "Hey, I was just gonna call you. Good timing."

"Really."

"Should we go up to my place?" Juha asked, taking a step towards the stairs at the entrance.

Suhonen grabbed Saarnikangas by the shoulder. "Should we go down to the station?"

"Don't start... Shit!"

Suhonen looked him straight in the eyes. "Juha. You're a peewee player, but now you're in the rink with the pros. You know how that'll end up?"

Juha nodded. "Yeah. Lotsa pucks in my own net."

"At least you understand."

Saarnikangas glanced at the entrance again, then dropped his gaze to the snow-covered ground. "The recognition of truth is the beginning of wisdom."

"Paasikivi. No art history this time?" Suhonen grinned at the famous quote from Finland's first cold-war President. Paasikivi had outlined much of Finland's new foreign policy, which was akin to standing in the middle of a seesaw, balancing the demands of the Soviets and the West.

Saarnikangas chuckled. "I took political history along with my art studies… But that Paasikivi quote isn't too far off, nor is your more modern peewee analogy."

Suhonen was glad that Juha was talking and allowed him to continue.

"Back in the '50s, Finland was that peewee player that had to choose between the East and West teams in a world championship game…kind of like me now…the East hoped to link Finland to the 'peace movement.' Finland consented, but not really."

"What are you talking about?" Suhonen muttered.

"Listen."

Suhonen relented, he was in no hurry.

"So…according to Paasikivi, in a crisis, it made sense for Finland to be on the Soviet side. It wasn't based on any belief in or hope of a Soviet victory, just plain strategy. So had the cold war gotten hot, Finland would've been on the Soviet side. Why? If the Soviet Union had won, Finland would've been on the winning side. In a draw, Finland would've continued to be a Soviet neighbor. But had the West won, Finland eventually would have been able to slink back into the winners' circle."

"Cold war power politics," Suhonen said.

Saarnikangas smiled, "I know how the real cold war ended, now I just need to figure out who's East and who's West."

"You know, Juha, that reminds me of Spain. Once in my younger days, we were on a drinking trip in Torremolinos. After three days in a beach-front cantina, I had quite a hangover. The weather was fantastic, but I just felt like hanging out under the canopy of the terrace bar. Well, that took care of the hangover quickly. But there was a sign in Spanish on the wall of the bar, and for some reason I just had to figure out what it said. The grey-whiskered bartender translated it for me and I still remember it."

Saarnikangas looked at Suhonen. "Well?"

"Talking about the bulls isn't the same as being in the ring."

"Yea-ah," Saarnikangas said, amused. "Better that than 'Drink sangria in moderation.'"

Suhonen was annoyed. "Enough bullshit. Let's go down to the station. You're under arrest on suspicion of murder."

"Don't I even get my one phone call?"

"Nope. You've been watching too much American TV," said Suhonen bluntly. Saarnikangas' jokes fell flat.

"But…"

"Game over."

"If the game's over, can't we have a rematch?"

Suhonen looked at the druggie. He was no killer, but he knew more than he was willing to say.

Joutsamo wouldn't care one way or the other. She would pry all she could out of the guy.

"Let's go. No more games. I don't have cuffs with me, but I can have a cruiser here in four minutes. Either that or nice and easy in my car."

Suhonen fished his cell phone out of his jacket pocket.

Saarnikangas knew he wasn't kidding around. "Okay, Suhonen. Listen to me. I didn't shoot him. I'm not a killer. Hey, I'm the one that called you about it…"

Suhonen pushed a button on his phone and raised it to his ear. "Suhonen from VCU. I need a unit out here to take someone to Pasila… Yeah. In Pihlajamäki, the apartments by Vuolukivi… I've got him, but we need transport to Pasila… Right… Thanks." Suhonen put the phone back in his pocket.

"Shit," Saarnikangas shrieked. "I didn't kill him!"

"You have four minutes. Enlighten me, but without the history lesson."

"Don't you believe me? If I did it, there's no way in hell I would have told you about the body."

"Never heard that before," Suhonen sneered, glancing at his phone.

"That's not funny," Juha said.

"I'm a cop, not a comedian."

Saarnikangas paused for a second. The East or the West? Who would win? It made no difference. He was out of time. He had to resolve the immediate crisis first, just as Paasikivi would have done.

"Three and a half," Suhonen said.

"I was there a while after he was shot," he said in a defeated tone. "But I didn't shoot nobody. It was some guy wearing a ski mask. I was supposed to get rid of the body, but I couldn't do it."

Suhonen let him talk, though he had plenty of questions.

"I'm not cut out for that. I was confused. The killer gave me the gun and told me to get rid of it along with the body. I thought about dropping the corpse in the sea or chopping it up, but I just ran. I drove north in a panic—I had to gas up at the Parkano ABC. Then I decided to go back. Somewhere around Valkeakoski I remembered I still had the gun. I got off the highway, pulled up to some dark cabin on a lake, wiped the fingerprints off the gun and threw it as far as I could. I went back to the garage, but I couldn't think of what to do... How much time do I have?"

"Ninety seconds."

"What else do you need?"

"Who gave you the job?"

"A guy named Lydman. When he called me, he didn't say what the job was. I owed him some money and I figured I'd have to take someone's drugs from point A to point B."

Suhonen nodded. Saarnikangas seemed to be telling the truth.

"What kind of gun?"

"I don't know the make...some kind of .22."

"Where exactly was this cabin?"

Saarnikangas laughed. "Hey, I was all mixed up."

"One minute."

"If you're going to Tampere, it's where you turn off to Turku."

"Highway Nine?"

"Probably. It's on the way to the prison. After the interchange you take a right at the intersection and then head back towards the highway. The most I can tell you is that the cabin had white walls and a dark

197

roof. You could see the highway from the dock; I saw a big semi cruise by. Hey, Suhonen. You believe me?"

"Thirty seconds. I can hear the cruiser coming up the block."

"I don't know anything more."

"Who was the killer?"

"I don't know. He was wearing blue overalls and a ski mask. He mumbled something about a Customs nark, but I didn't hear anything else... Hey, the cruiser... I need to talk to you about something."

Suhonen nodded and took his phone out of his pocket. He pushed the red button again and talked into a dead mic, "Suhonen from the VCU again... Yeah, that transport from Vuolukivi... Right, that's it. Well, we just happened to have a couple homicide guys in the area, so you don't need to bother with the cruiser... Yeah, cancel it."

The trick worked. Saarnikangas looked like a twelve-year-old boy who just scored a game-tying goal with seconds to go in the third period. The game wasn't over after all; it was headed for overtime.

"Good," Juha went on, smiling. "I think you'll be interested. I want you to take care of something for me."

They talked for another ten minutes.

Afterwards, Suhonen got back in his car and Saarnikangas headed for the stairs. In the car, Suhonen took his phone and called Joutsamo.

"Hey," Suhonen said.

"Where are you?"

Suhonen glanced at the bleak apartment buildings. "Around town."

"Well?"

"Couple things. First, get the surveillance tape from the Pakila Teboil, from, say, around ten o'clock the night of the murder. We should be able to find Saarnikangas on it. Second, get the Parkano ABC's surveillance tape from Monday night to Tuesday morning."

"What?"

"Listen to what I'm telling you!"

"Okay," Joutsamo eased up. "The footage from Teboil and Parkano. What are we looking for in Parkano?"

"Saarnikangas' white van. He said he was there on the night of the murder. I don't know the exact time."

"Okay."

A light turned on in the window of Saarnikangas' apartment. Suhonen started the car.

"Third, tell the Valkeakoski Fire Department to go for a swim."

"What are they looking for and where?"

"The murder weapon should be at the bottom of a lake near the highway," Suhonen said, and described the location.

Joutsamo paused briefly before continuing. He assumed she was taking notes.

"Suhonen," Joutsamo said in a serious tone. "Did you arrest him?"

"No."

"Why not?"

"Right now, he's more use to us on the street than in jail," he said. Suhonen couldn't put Juha in a cell now, not after he had coughed up the truth.

"Is that so."

"Yup."

"Where'd you get all this? Saarnikangas, or what?"

"I heard it through the grapevine," Suhonen crooned.

"That's not funny. Are you coming back in?"

"At some point, yeah. I have to see what happens." Saarnikangas was the key, but there were still a few more doors Suhonen wanted to try.

"You'll have to explain this to Takamäki then."

"Don't worry. You take care of the surveillance tapes and look for the gun." Suhonen hung up the phone and took out another. He reserved a room in the Katajanokka Hotel under the name, "Suikkanen."

Suhonen backed out of the parking space and glanced up.

Saarnikangas was standing in the window.

CHAPTER 21
CORNER PUB, KALLIO, HELSINKI
THURSDAY, 7:55 P.M.

It was standing room only in the Corner Pub. In years past, the pub would have reeked of smoke, but now it smelled only of snow-dampened clothing and booze. Most of the customers were men. A few were sitting alone at round tables, the extra chairs having been slid away to other tables.

A television that hung from the ceiling was showing the Eurosport channel: men soared off a ski jump in 60-second intervals.

Suhonen stepped inside and shook the snow off his jacket. He elbowed his way to the bar and ordered a beer.

The undercover detective scanned the bar. He knew what the man looked like. Back at headquarters, he had checked his mug shot from the database. He had used a computer in Narcotics so he wouldn't run into Joutsamo. She would have wanted an explanation, but Suhonen wasn't in the mood, nor did he have the time. Time would tell if this would go anywhere. If not, he'd have to arrest Saarnikangas.

He didn't find the guy in the front of the bar, though he saw two wanted men sitting under the TV. Though Suhonen knew their faces, he couldn't recall their names. The pair was suspected of a string of car break-ins. Maybe tonight they were downing their profits.

Suhonen wandered off towards the rear. He noticed a few familiar faces, but not the one he was looking for. Markus Markkanen was big enough to stand out, even in this crowd. Suhonen didn't know him, nor had he ever met him. Based on the database, "Bogeyman" Markkanen was last released from prison at the beginning of the decade. He had done time for assault and battery and aggravated assault.

Markkanen didn't show up in the organized crime intelligence database, so he wasn't known to belong to any of the gangs. Either he had lived a clean life the past few years, or managed to avoid getting caught.

Suhonen sipped his beer at the bar. Saarnikangas had told him about Lydman's orders, that Juha was supposed to meet Markkanen here, and that Markkanen might be involved in Eriksson's murder. He could even be the shooter, Saarnikangas had suggested. Based on his record, Suhonen figured it was more likely Markkanen was the shooter than the organizer.

Saarnikangas and Markkanen had never met, but even so, Suhonen couldn't pretend to be Juha. He'd be Suikkanen, an ex-con. Anyone at the Corner Pub who was vaguely familiar knew him by that name.

His beer mug was getting lighter and he was starting to feel the adrenaline. He wasn't sure what would happen tonight—he was only after intel. Saarnikangas hadn't known what the job was about. Suhonen wanted to find that out, as well as Markkanen's role in the case.

* * *

Anna Joutsamo stopped by her boss's office. It had been a long day, but those happened when the case called for it.

"I got the pics," she said, and showed him some letter-sized color prints. The quality wasn't much but Saarnikangas was recognizable at the front door of the Pakila Teboil. He had arrived at 9:49 P.M. and left at 10:03; the camera behind the register had recorded him sitting alone at a table. The pictures from the Parkano ABC showed him fueling up in the wee hours of the morning.

"Good. More nails in his coffin," Takamäki said. "What about the weapon?"

"The lake isn't frozen yet, so the Fire Department will search for it tonight. Kulta's on his way to monitor the operation."

"Good... By the way, did you find anything on Nyholm? Any connection?" Takamäki asked.

"They're father and daughter. The dad has an unblemished career at Customs and the girl has no record. Could it just be a coincidence that the girl falls in love with a crook?" she wondered. "Or maybe some kind of rebellion against a straight-laced dad."

"You don't think the girl could have anything to do with Eriksson's murder?"

"You mean that the Dad could've killed her boyfriend?"

Takamäki looked out the window. "Or Kristiina, wasn't that her name, had a former boyfriend—a jealous type?"

"In my conversations with her, she never mentioned any conflicts or dramas like that."

"Just thinking out loud. We don't know whether Saarnikangas knew Eriksson's girlfriend."

"No. I didn't mention Saarnikangas and neither did she."

"A woman is always a good motive," Takamäki said.

Joutsamo was still standing in the door. "By the way, has Suhonen called you?"

Takamäki shook his head. "Has he called you?"

"No. And no sign of Saarnikangas. Should I take a couple S.W.A.T. guys and pay a visit to Pihlajamäki?"

Takamäki rubbed his face. It was worn. The case had been going full-bore for three days. He could use a sauna, two beers, and a long night's sleep. Joutsamo had bags under her eyes.

"No. Suhonen got the tip about the pictures and we might find the weapon in the lake. Saarnikangas isn't going anywhere. Let's take him down when the time is right."

Joutsamo crossed her arms. "Sure would be nice if Suhonen would tell us what he's up to."

Takamäki shrugged. "You gonna be here much longer?"

"Should I?"

"Nope, as long as there's nothing urgent. I'll help Kohonen with the phone taps, but it doesn't look like we'll find anything there."

"These prepaid phones seem to indicate a professional hit."

"It's odd that a junkie like Saarnikangas would get mixed up in a professional job like this. He's more the type you'd find dead in the bathroom of a downtown bar."

"Exactly the same thing Suhonen is wondering."

* * *

A man slapped Suhonen hard on the shoulder; the impact nearly made him drop his mug. "Damned if it ain't Suikkanen," he bellowed.

Suhonen recognized the voice and dropped into a boxer's crouch. He kept his mug in his left hand and swung a playful right hook, stopping just short of the man's fat belly.

"Waltsu, you fat hog," Suhonen grinned. The man grinned back with a broad, bearded face. He wore a tattered denim jacket.

"Suikkanen, you're still quick as a hippo and sharp as Dumbo."

They bumped their mugs. "You're almost empty there," Waltsu growled and shouted at a skinny weasel-faced guy standing in front of the bar, "Hey pal, one more for Suikkanen. It's on me."

"Yeah, yeah. Like you'll pay," the weasel muttered. Nevertheless, he ordered a beer from the barkeep and fished three euros out of his pocket.

Suhonen gave the man a quick nod of thanks and turned back to Waltsu, making sure he could still see the door. "Come on now, I've been to the gym a couple times at least."

"Ha! In the pen, you mean?"

Suhonen laughed. "Nah, I've managed to stay out this time. At least so far."

"Right, just seems like I haven't seen much of you."

The weasel handed the beer to Suhonen and glowered at Waltsu.

"Thanks," said Suhonen, and raised his mug.

"Forget it," Waltsu said and lowered his voice. "You heard of anything going down? You know, anything where a guy could earn a little cash?"

Suhonen knew that unemployment checks and welfare benefits weren't enough to fund a constant stream of liquor. In his time, Waltsu had owned an excavator and operated a variety of businesses around the country. His divorce had cost him the firm. Waltsu didn't really miss his excavator, but the wife even less. Now he brokered small gigs: matching thieves to lucrative targets, and getting a small cut of the action.

"Dunno," Suhonen answered.

"You wouldn't happen to be setting up a company? I have a couple clean guys. You can have their names for two hundred."

"Do I look like I'd start up a company?" Suhonen said. Suikkanen was no boss man. He was more the type to operate quietly in the background.

"No, but you never know nowadays. With globalization and all, it's become trendy to have your own business."

The entrance door swung open. In came the plump "Princess" from the other night.

Waltsu noticed her too. "Oh damn. Here she comes again."

"Who, Princess?"

"What, you know her?" Waltsu asked.

"Nah. Just know of her. Doesn't everybody?"

"Steer clear of her," he groaned.

The weasel had abruptly disappeared from the bar.

The crowd parted and Princess waddled straight toward Suhonen and Waltsu. The bearded man took a couple steps backwards. "Sorry, Suikkanen. Gotta go."

"Waltsu, stop!" the woman snarled and he froze.

Suhonen dodged the perfume-drenched royalty and glanced at the door. At the same time, a tall man in a blue sports jacket entered. It seemed like he was looking for someone. Markkanen, Suhonen guessed.

He wasn't going to rush right over; he wanted to eyeball the guy first. It was possible Markkanen wasn't alone. A single glance could reveal an accomplice.

Princess was chewing out Waltsu and the weasel smirked to himself. Suhonen took a swig of his beer. Markkanen glanced at his phone and Suhonen decided that now was the time.

He weaved through the crowd towards Markkanen. The big man saw him coming in his leatherjacket.

"Hi," Suhonen said. "You're Markkanen?"

"Maybe. Who are you?"

"We're supposed to meet."

He looked at Suhonen with surprise. "You're not Saarnikangas."

"No. But Juha asked me to come."

Suhonen watched him tense up. He seemed nervous and looked around the room. Perhaps he suspected that Saarnikangas had set a trap.

"What the hell is this?"

Suhonen smiled. "Hey, I don't know anything. I'm a friend of Juha's and he asked me to come. I was supposed to meet this Markkanen, and he described someone who looks like you. So here I am."

Markkanen eyed Suhonen carefully.

"Well, get us a table and we can talk."

"A table?"

"You know, one of those things you sit at?"

Suhonen would have smiled, but Suikkanen just scowled.

The cop turned and surveyed the tables in the room. The table where the two wanted men were sitting was the most promising, and he steered over to it. Their beers had been empty for a while and neither had got up to fetch more.

"Fellas," he said coolly.

Neither one answered.

"Here's the deal. I need your table. I'll give you twenty for it."

The men looked at Suhonen, who smiled initially, then abruptly scowled.

"Thirty," the younger one said, though his hesitation revealed that twenty would suffice.

"Punks," Suhonen muttered and dropped a twenty on the table. "You can buy three beers a piece with that."

The younger one took the money and glanced at his friend. They got up. "Sil vous plait."

"You fucking with me?" Suhonen barked.

"No, no," the guy said, grabbing his jacket off the chair. "It's just French. It means…"

"Get lost."

The pair slunk into the crowd and Suhonen waved to Markkanen, who had a beer in each hand.

"You loaded or something?" Markkanen asked, taking a seat. He set one of the beers in front of Suhonen.

"Not really. I just don't know anyone around here and sometimes it's better to do things the easy way."

Markkanen sipped his beer. "At least we're sitting."

"The end justifies the means."

"Works for me. What's your name?"

"Suikkanen," he stated, and took a hard swig of beer in true Suikkanen style.

"Suikkanen? You got a first name?"

Suhonen grinned and took another gulp. They kept their voices low enough that nobody sitting nearby could hear them over the din. "Sure, but I save that for the judge. Barely remember it. Always gone by Suikkanen."

"You from up north?"

Suhonen wrinkled his brow. "Hell no. Lahti, man."

Markkanen grinned. "Soccer or Hockey?"

"Street Boxing," he stated flatly.

Suhonen was really from Lahti; he wouldn't think of saying anything else. He could fool people pretending to be Suikkanen, but only if he could handle the details.

"Okay."

"So what the hell are all these questions about?" said Suhonen abruptly. "I thought you had some business to talk about."

"I gotta know who I'm working with," Markkanen grumbled. "I was expecting Juha and I got Suikkanen. I know him but I don't know you. I need some background."

"Well, alright," said Suhonen, understanding the man's angle. Suhonen knew that Saarnikangas was a stranger to Markkanen, but the big man was pretending to be on a first-name basis with him. Suhonen was also pleased that Markkanen seemed interested in Suikkanen's services, maybe even a little excited.

"First off," Markkanen continued. "How do you know Juha?"

"I don't really know him. I know of him. He's a worthless junkie and I couldn't care less about him."

Markkanen raised his eyebrows.

"But," Suhonen went on. "I knew his dad. Cell mates. Before he died, he asked me to look after his kid. We didn't see each other for probably ten years. Then last spring I ran into him. He hit me up for money, but I know where that would've gone, so I said no. I figured his pop didn't mean I should support his smack habit. I gave him my number so he could call if he needed something for real."

"Did he say he's in trouble?"

"Is he?" Suhonen asked, but regretted his haste. Suikkanen would have said casually that Juha's always in trouble.

"Nah," Markkanen answered, assessing him from the other side of the table.

"How much does this pay?" Suhonen steered the conversation away from Saarnikangas.

Markkanen scratched the back of his neck. "We'll talk about that later."

"Uh-uh. I need to know if it's worth my time," he switched to arrogance as a tactic.

Markkanen's lips were smiling, but his eyes were hard.

"Sure it is."

"If you say so."

"Did you come all the way from Lahti?"

"Yup," Suhonen nodded. He wasn't driving, so he could drink the beers necessary for the role.

"Where you staying?"

Suhonen smiled broadly. "Juha said I'd be able to make enough money to pay for a hotel room. So I thought, since I'm coming to Helsinki and all, I may as well relive some memories over at Hotel Katajanokka."

"The brig hotel?"

One of Finland's oldest prisons had been turned into a Best Western hotel with a penitentiary theme. The hotel had been completed in '07, with remodeled rooms, but the corridors still had prison bars. The "Skatta" had a long history. The first prison at the site had opened in 1749, and the oldest portions of the present building dated back to the 1830s.

"I just had to. Maybe I could expense it, you know." Suhonen said, downing the last of his beer.

"I ain't paying for extra expenses, but the total will cover it. Let's go outside. There's something I wanna tell you."

Markkanen led the way out the door and Suhonen wondered what this was about. The big man had enough assaults on his record that they could be headed for a fight. But based on the conversation, that was unlikely, at least for now.

It was snowing harder now, and a wall of falling flakes beneath the glow of the streetlights split Helsinki Avenue in two. The pub across the street was no longer visible.

There was still no bouncer at the door. Suhonen wondered if it was intentional, or if Lydman had skipped his shift. But he could find out later.

Two inches of wet snow covered the sidewalk, and after the first few steps it started to soak into their pant legs. The men walked eastward along the largely deserted road.

Markkanen stopped. "Listen, Suikkanen. You seem tough enough, but I'm gonna need a sample of your work."

Suhonen kept quiet.

"Right now, the street looks empty, but once we round that corner, someone's bound to come along."

"And?"

"Well, you claimed you were a boxer in Lahti. Three punches for the first chump that comes along and the job is yours."

"Huh?"

"Yep. You'll beat the shit out of the first person you see. If it's some gang of ten heavies, we can skip them, but anything else goes. Don't hurt 'em too bad, just a few good hits. After that, the job is yours.

Suhonen stared at Markkanen. "In Lahti, there was always a reason. We didn't just beat up anybody."

"You got a reason now. The job is easy and pays three grand, but I wanna see if you have what it takes."

Suhonen wondered if Markkanen suspected he was a cop. This was the classic test for smoking out a rat. A cop could blow through a red light or dabble in illicit activities, but you weren't supposed to steal, much less harm anyone.

"What the hell," said Suhonen and strode down the street. "It matter if it's a chick or a kid?"

"Nope," Markkanen answered and held back about ten yards before following along.

Shit, Suhonen thought. He couldn't beat up anyone, not even by faking it. He couldn't go that far. His Glock was tucked behind the waistband of his jeans. Maybe he could pick a fight, lure Markkanen closer, then arrest him. He could bust Markkanen for inciting an aggravated assault, and the guy would do time. But the trial would be a damn nightmare, and the media would be all over it. Claims of provocation would fly, and one way or another, Suhonen would end up in the dispatch center, answering 911 calls. Nothing wrong with a desk job; he just wasn't ready for that yet.

He reached the corner, looked around and spotted a shadowy figure on the other side of the street, maybe fifty yards off. He couldn't tell if it was a man or woman, but it was clearly coming towards him. It would be thirty seconds max before they met.

Suhonen glanced back at Markkanen, who nodded. He had noticed the person too, then.

I can't beat up anybody, Suhonen thought. What if he just pushed them over and pulled a few fake punches. But that wouldn't work. Whoever it was would panic, and Markkanen would be able to tell from his reaction that Suhonen wasn't serious.

He had to arrest Markkanen. Suhonen stepped onto the crosswalk and noticed a cruiser coming down the street. The driver slammed on the brakes and the car went into a slide, stopping a few yards behind the crosswalk.

Suhonen bent over and scooped up a snowball. The distance was only a few yards, and he hurled it at the driver's side window of the police car.

He took a couple steps closer.

The door opened, and out stepped a stocky-looking cop. Suhonen didn't like the idea of scuffling with this guy.

"You got a problem?" the cop asked, reaching for his nightstick.

The distance was only a couple yards now, and Suhonen recognized the cop. He knew Markkanen was watching from afar, so he ducked into a boxer's pose. The cop raised his nightstick to striking position.

"You need help?" Suhonen heard the partner calling from inside the cruiser.

Suhonen couldn't shout. If he did, the cop wouldn't hear a thing he said once the adrenaline hit his brain. He started shadow boxing by the side of the cruiser and whispered just loud enough that only the cop could hear.

"Tero Partio," he began. The cop looked confused. Suhonen kept jabbing at the air. "Suhonen from the VCU."

Partio kept his baton raised. "Yeah, I recognize you. You better calm down here."

Suhonen kept shadow boxing. "Good. Don't worry, just play along. I need your help."

Partio waved his baton. "Huh?"

"No worries. I'm gonna shout now, and we'll go from there."

Officer Esa Nieminen had stepped out of the passenger side door, but so far had stayed behind the car. Partio started to catch on and ordered Nieminen to stay calm.

"FAGGOT!" Suhonen shouted, loud enough for Markkanen to hear. He threw a jab, clearly short. "WHAT! YOU SCARED?!"

Partio answered in a commanding voice. "Calm down! Lie down on the ground. Now!"

Suhonen grinned and whispered. "That's right, let's play some more. I'll explain later. I have to... YOU FUCKING PIG... hit you three times. Just like in police training: straight left, right hook, left hook... You'll swing the baton, but miss... Then fall down."

"ON THE GROUND, NOW!" Partio bellowed.

Nieminen had come around to the front of the car and pulled out his nightstick. His right hand was on the butt of his pistol.

"Give me a little head start and a vague description to dispatch... Ready?"

Suhonen lunged forward and threw a straight left. It glanced off Partio's arm and the baton swung past Suhonen's head. Suhonen landed two solid hooks into Partio's stomach. They weren't very hard, but sharp enough that he felt the man's flak jacket on his knuckles.

Partio grunted and dropped to his knees. Suhonen took a couple steps back and took off running.

"Stop!" Nieminen shouted, taking a few hesitant steps after him. The distance was only about five yards.

"Esa," Partio wheezed, doubled over and looking up at his partner. "Help!"

Suhonen was already on the sidewalk, heading up the hill. Nieminen didn't know whether to help his partner or give chase.

Partio reached out his right hand and grabbed Nieminen's left ankle. The cop slipped and fell onto the pavement. His Glock fell out of his grip, but didn't go off.

Nieminen rose to a kneeling position and stared at Partio, eyes wide.

"You hurt? Did he have a knife?"

"Everything's OK, no knife, but…" he managed to say, still holding onto Nieminen. Suhonen and another man were already twenty yards ahead.

"I'll take care of this. Those guys are so dead," Nieminen snarled. He jerked himself free of Partio's grip and his heel accidentally struck Partio in the cheek. The officer recoiled in pain.

Partio watched the two men slipping up the street. Nieminen ran behind by about thirty yards. Goddammit, Partio thought, and picked Nieminen's snow-covered Glock from the ground.

Suhonen heard someone shouting from behind, "STOP! POLICE! STOP RIGHT THERE!"

Apparently, Partio's sidekick hadn't caught on. They'd have to make tracks, fast.

Markkanen came abreast of him and jerked him into an alley to the right. Finally, their shoes had traction.

"Fuck! Really stupid, but damn brilliant, too," Markkanen seemed impressed. He pushed Suhonen further into the alley and waited near the entrance. He pulled a bandana over his face and tugged his stocking cap down over his eyebrows. "Now it's my turn," he hissed, crouching down. "Here comes the other one."

Suhonen looked on, bewildered.

Unaware of the danger, Nieminen came around the corner and Markkanen jerked him into the alley. The force knocked him to the ground a couple yards from the sidewalk. His nightstick clattered onto the pavement. Markkanen sat on the officer's chest, and pressed a knife to his throat.

Oh shit, Suhonen thought, approaching the pair from behind.

"So you're some tough street cop, huh?" Markkanen rasped, pushing the thin-bladed stiletto against his neck. One small movement and it would sink through the skin. Deep.

The cop lay motionless under Markkanen's weight.

"No, you're no street cop," he hissed.

Nieminen didn't respond.

"You're a milk-lipped little shit, go back to the academy."

Suhonen watched Nieminen's eyes widen and he took his Glock out of the waistband of his jeans. He aimed it at the back of Markkanen's head and tapped him on the shoulder with the other hand.

"We gotta go," Suhonen said, his voice tight. Was Markkanen insane?

He didn't look up, but kept his eyes fixed on Nieminen, cackling. "You had your fun. Now it's my turn. Why shouldn't I butcher this pig?" he growled, pressing the knife deeper. A faint line of blood appeared on Nieminen's neck.

Suhonen saw the movement and nearly pulled the trigger.

"We have to go," Suhonen hissed. "Now!"

The cop tried to wriggle out from beneath Markkanen's knife, looking as though he'd throw up any moment. Suhonen kept his gun trained on Markkanen's head, grabbed his collar from behind, and jerked hard.

"Now!"

Markkanen got up and folded the blade back into its handle. Suhonen stayed behind him and thrust the Glock back into the waistband of his pants.

The cop was still lying on the ground.

Markkanen smiled excitedly, eyeing a grave-looking Suhonen. "This reminds me of my younger days…follow me," he said and dashed down the alley.

Suhonen glanced back at the officer lying on the pavement. He wasn't moving, but had no serious wounds. The cop would be OK, he thought and bolted after Markkanen.

Kallio was a labyrinth of courtyards, cellars and attics, through which they navigated to get from one block to another. Beneath the streets was also a network of service tunnels and parking ramps which helped to throw off anyone in pursuit.

Sergeant Partio hurried up the street, afraid he'd find his partner cuffing the two or somehow blowing Suhonen's operation.

The cop reached the corner of the alley and peered carefully around it. He glimpsed Nieminen immediately, sitting with his back against the wall. Otherwise, the alley was empty.

Partio bent down next to the sobbing Nieminen. "You okay?"

"Yeah. I'm not hurt."

"What in the world were you doing?"

"I went after 'em, but one of 'em tackled me and put a knife to my throat. Think I was scared?"

Partio stared at his partner. "Why didn't you obey my orders? I told you to stay with me."

"But that guy hit you."

"He didn't hit me."

Nieminen looked up and Partio offered him a hand. He took it, and the older officer hauled him to his feet.

"It was an act," Partio explained. "That was Suhonen...he's on a case. For some reason he had to prove he was tough."

"Huh?"

"He whispered to me before I took the punches. It was nothing. Just play-acting."

Nieminen rubbed his neck and felt the tender spot. "Play-acting?"

Partio nodded. "If I give you an order, you gotta obey. Don't even think about running off on your own."

Nieminen went weak in the knees and he grabbed onto his partner for support. "If that was play-acting, then he's in with a pretty rough company."

Partio smiled. "Undercover ops are kind of odd sometimes, but we cooperate when we can."

They walked slowly down the hill toward the cruiser at the intersection.

"How we gonna report this?" Nieminen asked.

"What do you think?"

"Attempted murder, that's what I think."

Partio roared with laughter. "Nonsense. The whole thing was an act. Suhonen wasn't serious, nothing could have happened."

"No?"

"No."

"Whatever you say." Nieminen shook his head.

"Try to see it from Suhonen's perspective. What does he need?"

"Don't know. Lots of meds?"

Partio laughed again. "Anyone who enrolls in the Academy could use some meds. We gotta play along with him, so we'll need some units out here quick. If someone actually hit me, all of Kallio would be blue and white."

"So we're gonna report it?" Nieminen asked.

The pair had made it back to the car and Partio climbed into the driver's seat. He flicked on the cherries, but left the siren alone. "Not exactly. We'll call for half a dozen units to look for a 'drunk driver.' The night's young enough that there should be plenty of idle units about."

"You mean call in a fraudulent report?"

"It's no fraud, we're just giving Suhonen a little extra breathing room. Life isn't always so black and white."

Nieminen turned on the passenger's side interior light, flipped down the sun visor and opened the mirror. He craned his neck, looking for the thin red stripe left by the knife.

Partio threw the car into gear and turned towards Brahe Field. He glanced at his partner. "Ugly looking scratch. Where'd you get that?"

"Hard to say," he said, pausing, "Must have nicked myself shaving."

Partio smiled.

CHAPTER 22
NYHOLM'S TOWNHOUSE,
NORTH HELSINKI
THURSDAY, 11:33 P.M.

Jouko Nyholm was sitting on his sofa with a cognac in his hand. The flat screen was showing late night news. The Customs Inspector didn't care about NATO relations—he just stared blankly at the screen.

His wife was out and about somewhere. Nyholm couldn't decide whether to go to a bar or go to sleep.

The living room was on the lower level. Though fifteen years ago the interior would have been stylish, it had deteriorated along with the owners' marriage.

The door opened. Was she home already, he wondered. It wasn't like her. When the wife went out, it was usually for the evening, or even all night.

He glanced at the door: it was Kristiina. Laundry day, he thought before noticing her pained expression.

"What's wrong?" Nyholm asked.

The girl's blond hair was tangled and her eyes puffy. She was still crying, but managed the words, "He's dead."

Nyholm rose and hesitated, wondering if he should hug her. He hadn't done that for at least five years.

"Who's dead?"

She sobbed. "Jerry... My boyfriend..."

She was still wearing her long, pale overcoat. Her hands rested limply against her hips. She began to sob again.

"There, there," Nyholm said. He didn't hug her. Instead, he laid his hand on her shoulder. He tried to remember how he used to comfort her when she was younger—he would have taken her into his lap and combed his fingers through her soft, blonde hair.

He helped her out of her jacket and hung it. "Slip off your shoes; let's go into the kitchen."

She did as he told and shuffled over to the table.

Nyholm pulled up a brown wooden chair for her, and Kristiina sat stiffly. He took the chair on the end and they sat side by side.

"I must look terrible," she said, covering her face in her hands. The sobbing started again.

"Don't... Please, don't cry, Kristiina," Nyholm said, not knowing what else to say. He got up and plodded over to the coffee table, downed the rest of his cognac, then refilled his glass from the bottle on the table. On a whim, he brought the bottle back into the kitchen, took a glass from the cupboard and poured a generous shot for his daughter.

He returned to the table and set the glass in front of her. "Have some of this. It'll help."

Nyholm didn't think it would actually help, but when the burn of the alcohol hit her mouth, she'd think of something else for a moment.

"What is it?" she asked, then downed it without waiting, spluttering a little.

"What happened?" Nyholm asked.

Either the cognac or the sympathy worked: she calmed down, though her breathing was still intense.

"That lady cop came by today and told me Jerry was murdered... He was my boyfriend."

"What was...or how did...uh, do you know why?"

Kristiina blew her nose. "They didn't say..."

"Was Jerry's last name Eriksson?" Nyholm asked.

Kristiina looked startled. "Yeah. Do you know him?"

"No, not really. But I did know who he was."

"How? From work?"

Nyholm shook his head. "You should stay here tonight." He paused before saying, "I know how hard this is for you... But, can I ask you a question?"

"What?"

"How'd the police know to notify you when the two of you weren't married?"

"W-well, I went to file a missing persons report this morning."

Damn, Nyholm thought.

"Have another cognac," he said, and the daughter held out her glass. This time he poured her a double. Nyholm readily emptied his own and poured himself another stiff one.

He reflected on his predicament: only a miracle would keep the cops from figuring out their father-daughter relationship.

There would be questions, that much was certain. He'd have to frame his answers so the truth wouldn't be revealed.

* * *

Suhonen was sitting on the edge of the hotel bed; Markkanen leaned back in the armchair.

"At least it's bigger than a prison cell." Markkanen admired the creamy interior of the

223

Katajanokka Best Western. The traces of a cell could still be seen in the arch of the roof and the shape of the windows. The old pen was shut down in '02, when new lodging for the inmates opened up twenty miles to the north. The new maximum security prison was supposed to be escape-proof, but that had already been proven wrong.

It was a fine testament to government bureaucracy that the new prison had been commissioned in 1977, but the construction wasn't completed for another twenty-five years.

"I've spent some time here" Suhonen explained. "Grim place. Filthy, dilapidated, plus you had to shit in a bucket..." Despite its reputation for modern technology, Finland still had prisons where each cell sported a bucket for nightly needs.

"C'mon, Suikkanen, when's the last time you felt comfortable in the slammer?" Markkanen smirked.

"...But at least now the peephole looks outward," Suhonen went on. Though peepholes in the former cells had looked inward, the prisoners would often smear the lens with toothpaste.

Earlier that day, Suhonen had reserved a room at the hotel for just this type of situation. He had picked up the key card in the evening and tossed a gym bag of clothes into the room.

The pair had navigated a maze of courtyards and emerged at the Central Fire Station. From there, they had headed toward the Kallio Church. They had seen a half-dozen squad cars with flashing cherries, but had managed to board a bus downtown without incident.

From downtown, they had walked the rest of the way to the hotel: about half a mile. Though Suhonen had wanted to call Partio to talk about what happened, that wasn't possible. He was particularly worried about Nieminen's reaction to a knife at his throat. Suhonen wondered if he should have intervened earlier. The situation had escalated too far, but he couldn't have anticipated all the potential risks. He worried that shit would hit the fan over the incident.

"Well, enough shitting around," said Suhonen, wondering if there was another test in store. "You said there was an easy three grand for me to earn."

Markkanen's manner became serious.

"Right, a real simple job."

"Shoot."

"There's a garage on Tehdas Street with a Mercedes inside. It belongs to someone who needs to learn to pay his debts."

"Who?"

"I figured you'd know better than to ask a question like that."

Suikkanen let out a nervous laugh and forced his lips into a smile. "I didn't pass ninth grade."

"The streets should've taught you."

Suhonen looked annoyed. "So what about this garage?"

"You're gonna put a pig's head on the hood."

Suhonen let out a genuine laugh. "What...?"

"A pig's head."

"Where am I gonna get that?"

Markkanen grinned. "For three grand, I think you can figure it out."

"And just set it on the hood of the Mercedes, huh?"

Markkanen nodded.

Suhonen shook his head doubtfully. "Why don't you do it yourself? What's the catch?"

"A security camera by the garage door, plus another inside. There's no way to avoid being taped."

"And you can't afford to be seen, even in a ski mask?"

"Exactly."

"Tonight?"

"Yup."

Suhonen still looked doubtful. "Without wheels, where am I gonna get a pig's head at this hour?"

Markkanen smiled. "I'll sell you one for a grand."

"Huh?"

"I need my cut, too."

Suhonen gazed at the smiling Markkanen, wondering if there was a bigger fish behind the "Bogeyman." The thug stood up, drawn to the refrigerator. He dug out a miniature whiskey bottle for himself and offered another to Suhonen.

"Not now."

Markkanen took a glass from the minibar and emptied the bottle into it. He grinned and raised his glass.

"Welcome to the team."

* * *

It was just past 1:00 A.M. The old 300-Series Beamer was exactly where Markkanen had said it would be: on Tehdas Street near the Russian Embassy. Suhonen keyed the plate number into his phone and slipped on a pair of gloves.

He lifted a hockey bag out of the trunk and glanced quickly inside. A streetcar rumbled past. Only a few people were about, and nobody seemed interested in a man looking through his trunk. In the hockey bag was a black trash bag, and inside it, a wrinkled pig's head. The stench was nauseating.

Suhonen smirked and grabbed the bag. He slammed the trunk shut, circled the car for a few seconds, then installed a tracking device. This car, too, would be tracked by satellite.

Suhonen hurried ahead. The walk was several hundred yards.

His black ski mask was still rolled up, looking like an ordinary knit hat. Suhonen had taken an old grey jacket from the closet and passed up the mirror. The hockey bag swung from his shoulder and he hoped he wouldn't run into any cruisers. If he were on patrol and saw a character looking like himself, he'd have some questions to ask.

Markkanen had given him directions. The courtyard gate wouldn't be a problem, since he'd received the code. He was to go through the gate, and the garage would be the third on the right. Suhonen entered the code and slipped inside. He left the gate ajar, so that from the outside it looked closed.

The buildings in South Helsinki seemed closed off, but they had surprisingly spacious courtyards. The apartments circled the yard like fortress walls.

Suhonen pulled the ski mask over his face. He fumbled a little, looking for the eye holes.

The courtyard was divided by fences. Lights gleamed from several of the windows. Only two dim yellow lamps hung from the wall, but darkness didn't bother Suhonen. Markkanen had told him the security camera would be at the other end, on the roof of the row of garages. Suhonen kept his gaze down; no sense in showing the camera any more than was necessary.

The wooden double doors of the garage were painted red, and they opened outward from the middle. Suhonen wondered if there was an alarm. Even if there were, the security guards wouldn't be there for several minutes. The right-hand door had an old lock. It would've taken him thirty seconds to pick the lock, but the door felt a bit loose. He took out a piece of rigid double-bent wire and eased it between the doors. There was no deadbolt and the latch slipped easily aside. Opening the door took two seconds.

Suhonen crept inside, closed the door behind him and flicked on a small flashlight. The garage was larger than he had imagined: it held two cars. The next door opened into the same area, the parking spaces separated by chicken wire. The neighboring car was a maroon BMW, but Suhonen was interested in the silver-colored Mercedes next to it. It was a 500-Series luxury model, though several years old.

Suhonen checked the plate number and memorized it. He hesitated for a moment, then opened the hockey bag, hauled out the reeking pig's head, and set it just behind the hood ornament. He smirked and picked up the empty bag from the floor.

The courtyard was empty and Suhonen eased the door shut behind him. He slipped back out through the gate and closed that as well.

Turning onto Tehdas Street, he headed back toward the Russian Embassy. The street was quiet, which suited him just fine. He'd put the hockey bag back where he found it, in the trunk of the Beamer.

* * *

Takamäki woke to a ringing phone. He saw that his wife had also been awakened from the way she rolled over. He glanced at the red numbers on his alarm clock: 2:02 A.M.

The phone was charging on the nightstand and he picked it up and got out of bed. It rang again before he made it out of the bedroom. The call was from an unknown number.

"Hello," Takamäki answered, descending the stairs.

"Sorry for calling in the middle of the night," said a man's voice. "But it says here that I'm supposed to notify you."

"About what?" asked Takamäki. He had walked into the hallway and was looking out the window. The ground was still white, but road conditions seemed to be improving. The townhouse complex was quiet.

"Right, sorry. This is Saarelainen from the Border Guard at the Helsinki Airport," he introduced himself. "We have a man who just went through passport control, and we've been directed to notify you if he tries to leave the country."

Takamäki was puzzled. He didn't remember making any such request.

"Who are we talking about?" Takamäki asked, as though he had made several such requests.

"Ilari Petteri Lydman," the official said and read off the social security number.

Takamäki wondered if Joutsamo had filed this request. Or maybe Suhonen.

"Where's he going?"

"He's on the 3:20 to Bangkok."

Takamäki rubbed his face. His brain was sluggish after having been wrenched from sleep. Lydman and

Saarnikangas were somehow connected. Right, and it was Suhonen who suspected Lydman's involvement.

Why was Lydman going to Thailand? Had he planned the trip in advance or was he on the run?

"So," the border guard continued. "What should we do? Let him on the plane?"

"Does Lydman know he's been flagged?"

"No. The official at passport control let him through, then notified us. He won't go anywhere from the transit hall, especially since there aren't any other departures before the Bangkok flight."

Takamäki was still thinking. Thailand wasn't a problem per se, since their extradition process worked with Finland. On the other hand, Lydman could get to just about any place in the world from the Bangkok airport. That could pose a problem, especially if he held a second passport.

"Uhh," Takamäki hesitated. "I'll have to consult with my investigators. Can you give me your number, and I'll call you back?"

The border guard gave him the number. As soon as the call ended, Takamäki made another. This number was on speed dial, and the phone rang three times before someone answered.

"Suhonen," drawled a groggy voice.

"Did I wake you?"

"Uh-huh."

"Good. I was just woken up, too. Did you file a request with the Border Guard to have them notify me if Lydman leaves the country?"

"Yeah... Uhh, yes," Suhonen said, a little more clearly now. "I forgot to tell you last night."

"On what basis?" Takamäki asked, though he knew the question was useless.

"I thought Lydman might be a key player. By the way, I filed the same request for Saarnikangas. Is Lydman going somewhere?"

"Yeah. The 3:20 flight to Bangkok."

He heard a muffled rustling on the other end. Takamäki guessed that Suhonen was looking at the clock on his phone.

"So he's waiting to board his flight right now," Takamäki offered.

Suhonen figured the Lieutenant wanted his input on whether Lydman should be let on the plane or not. He was torn: Lydman's significance to the case had lessened now that they had Markkanen in their sights. On the other hand, Lydman was about to fly halfway around the world, and wouldn't be missed if he was sitting in jail. They could keep him a while before word got out.

"I think we should bring him in."

"Do we have grounds for that?"

"Well, he's been seen with Saarnikangas a couple times in the past few days, so at least Joutsamo can question him about that."

"Should we bring Saarnikangas in at the same time?"

Suhonen thought for a second. "That's an option, of course, but maybe not yet. Let's see what happens tomorrow, at least."

"How'd it go last night? Anything new?"

"Not really. Trying to make heads or tails of it all. " Suhonen replied.

"Listen, Suhonen. Up till now this has been your case, but we need to talk about how to move forward."

"Yeah," Suhonen said. "Of course, of course."

"Especially now that we're arresting Lydman. At this point, he'll be charged with murder, right?"

"Yeah, looks like accessory to murder to me," Suhonen said. "That'll give us some ammo for the interrogations."

"Okay, I'll ask the Border Guard to take him into custody and we'll bring him to Pasila in the morning. We'll have a meeting first thing at nine, then."

"Alright."

"Well," Takamäki smirked. "Try to get a few winks over there in the middle of that Kallio ruckus."

"I'll try." Suhonen hung up and buried his head in the lush hotel pillows.

**FRIDAY
NOVEMBER 28**

CHAPTER 23
LINDSTRÖM'S APARTMENT,
TEHDAS STREET, HELSINKI
FRIDAY, 8:40 A.M.

Kalevi Lindström heard the doorbell. He set his coffee down on the table and strolled to the door in his robe. He still had to do his morning workout. The trainer wasn't due till nine, but maybe she was early.

He looked out the peephole, recognized the man standing outside and opened the door warily.

"Morning," said the sixty-something man. His grey suit matched his hair. Von Marzen lived upstairs.

The man's expression was dour. "I have something to tell you, neighbor."

He spoke decent Finnish with a German accent. Lindström knew he had moved to Finland in the '80s and studied Finnish as an adult.

"What is it?"

"Somebody broke into our garage."

"What'd they take?"

"Didn't take nothing. But they did something on your side."

"What are you talking about?"

"Nothing on my side, but your car... ehhh... schwein..." he groped for the words, "had pig head on the hood."

"What? A pig's head?" Lindström looked incredulous. He wanted to ask why, but Von Marzen wouldn't know.

"Right. A pig's head. But not to worry. I called police about the break-in and told them about the schwein."

Lindström ran his hands over his face. Eriksson dead, and now this. Clearly a warning. It couldn't be anything else. What was happening? He ought to call Markkanen. Maybe he could shed some light on the situation. Who the hell was behind this?

* * *

Suhonen was perplexed. What was going on here?

At headquarters, he had checked the plate numbers for Markkanen's BMW and the Mercedes in the garage. They were owned by different companies, but the owner turned out to be the same person. Suhonen's colleagues in the Financial Crimes Unit said the guy was some shady lawyer. The similarities didn't end there, though. Two junkies, well-known to the police, sat on the boards of both firms.

Why in the world was Markkanen's Beamer registered under the same owner as the pig's head Mercedes?

The connection got him thinking and he considered the various possibilities.

With one phone call, he identified the driver of the Mercedes. The building super said that Kalevi Lindström owned the garage, and that he also lived in the building.

Lindström's name didn't turn up in any police records. Nothing on the web either, nor in any business journal archives. Apparently, they weren't dealing with a major industrialist.

A former criminal with a violent streak and an apparently wealthy sixty-year-old man were at odds, but somehow in cahoots as well. Their backgrounds revealed common denominators, such as the shared car ownership. And how was Eriksson mixed up in this?

Suhonen was aching for coffee and decided to brew a pot.

It would have to wait. The GPS system in his phone alerted him that the green dot had begun to move. Green was for Markkanen.

* * *

"A pig's head?" Markus Markkanen looked baffled. "Why?"

"I'm wondering the same thing," Lindström responded.

The men were sitting in Lindström's sumptuous library. Lindström had cancelled with his trainer and summoned Markkanen for a meeting.

"It's definitely a threat. Somebody thinks you're shit. I remember this one guy back in the '90s. We used to put dried pigs' ears through his mail slot," Markkanen went on. "They were just pet food, but the message was clear: you're worthless."

"But, why?" Lindström wondered.

Markkanen could smell the old man's fear. Lindström wasn't used to playing hardball. That was good.

"Somebody wants something from you."

"But what?"

Markkanen looked out the window, brooding.

"It's gotta have something to do with Eriksson. He must've been involved in something or pissed off someone. And what's worse for you...or us, is that they've connected the dots from Eriksson upward to you."

"How?"

Idiot, Markkanen thought. You should have thought of that when you hired that kid to do my job. Of course, he had the in with Customs, but loyalty should be respected. I shouldn't have been humiliated like that.

Markkanen watched two little boys cross the street. It made him think of his own family. He had called his wife in Turku the night before. Everything was going well at the spa and the boy was happy to have an extra vacation. He had even made a new friend.

He turned away from the window and looked Lindström in the eyes.

"I don't know. This is strange."

Lindström stood up. "What should we do, then?"

"I'll ask around some more and see who's behind this, but after that we have two choices."

"And those would be..."

"Either we take action or we pay up."

"Violence or money?" Lindström summarized.

Markkanen nodded. "Well, there's always the third way, but that doesn't apply here."

"What?"

"Sex. Somehow, I doubt the enemy is interested in either of us like that."

Lindström smirked. "That'd probably be the easiest alternative."

Markkanen looked at his boss, not sure if he was joking.

Lindström settled back into his armchair. "I got a message from the Russians. In three days' time, a shipment of washing machines will be arriving in Kotka."

"Washing machines?"

Lindström nodded. "Yes. Several hundred. The entire shipment is headed straight for the border, and the buyers want to know if the goods are being tracked."

Markkanen picked a handwritten note off the table that showed the details of the shipment.

"Soo-o. The name of the ship is M/S Gambrini," Markkanen said. "These are all going straight through?"

"Like I said, directly to Russia. If they make it through Finland as some kind of junk, the Russian authorities won't be interested either. It's all about taxes. Or evading taxes, rather."

"How much do they make?"

Lindström shook his head. "It doesn't matter. That's their business; we're just here to help."

Markkanen nodded. He was glad that Lindström was speaking more openly about the scheme.

"Okay. So you're sure there's no trouble with the Russians?"

"Yes. If there were, they'd have contacted me directly. Our problems have nothing to do with them. The Russians are reliable partners, and we have open lines of communication."

"You know...back to Eriksson," Markkanen said. It was time to throw more fuel on the fire. "The more I think about this, the clearer it becomes. Given what happened to him, it looks like the Skulls have been sicced on us."

"The Skulls? Why?" Lindström looked puzzled.

"You'd have to ask Eriksson. It just reeks of a professional hit and that's what the Skulls do."

"Then why was the body found? Looks to me like they messed up."

Markkanen shook his head. "Could be, but I'll find out more. Maybe someone got a whiff of your business."

"And is trying to cut in?"

"Or take over."

Lindström stared at Markkanen for a long time, then shook his head. "Maybe."

"The danger here is that if the enemy thinks they didn't get a big enough share or payoff, they'll rat us out to the cops for revenge."

"But wouldn't that connect them to the murder?"

Markkanen laughed. "Of course not, the tip would be anonymous, and would focus on the Customs stuff. You'd...we'd get busted and someone else would scoop up the business."

"What should I do?"

"Like I said. Either take care of it with money, or play hardball. Both have their risks."

Lindström seemed to be thinking. "Indeed."

"Are you protected well enough? I don't wanna know anything about it, but if the cops bust through that door, is the money safe?"

Lindström tried to smile, but his eyes darted toward a painting on the back wall. Markkanen caught the movement and guessed the safe was behind the painting. There probably wouldn't be that much money, though there might be some info on his other assets.

Lindström chuckled dryly, his manner serious. "Listen, find out who's behind this and let me handle the business side. Let's both stick to what we know."

Dressed in new police-issue green overalls, Lydman sat in the dreary, windowless interrogation room, his bald head hung low.

Joutsamo read off Lydman's ID into the microphone. The video camera sat in the back corner, so Lydman could see it. He had declined counsel. At this stage, getting a lawyer might seem like an admission of guilt.

"What can you tell us about Jerry Eriksson's murder?"

"No comment."

"What were you doing between last Monday evening and Tuesday morning?"

"No comment."

Joutsamo was not surprised by his answers. She and Kulta had picked him up from the airport detention cell, and he had said nothing on the way back to Pasila.

"Why were you going to Thailand?"

"No comment."

"Why don't you want to answer the questions?"

"No comment."

At this point, Joutsamo wouldn't reveal that they had connected Saarnikangas to the case, and Lydman to Saarnikangas. If Lydman wanted to share any relevant information, he'd volunteer it of his own accord.

He was on their turf now and his "no comment" strategy suited them just fine. It would only be further grounds for his arrest and continued detention. In upcoming interrogations, Joutsamo would gradually reveal more about how he'd been connected to Saarnikangas, slowly breaking down Lydman's protective armor.

She was sure Lydman would talk. It might take a few weeks or even a month. He would talk, though. Well, maybe.

"Can you tell us anything about Jerry Eriksson's death?"

"No comment."

Joutsamo ended the interrogation.

* * *

Eero Salmela was in the cellblock kitchenette, plugging in the coffee maker. The window opened onto the empty prison yard.

The kitchen boasted a refrigerator, a microwave oven and a sink. The range had been removed after someone accused of narking got their palms fried on the burner.

Salmela measured the coffee carefully. Two cups would be plenty. He'd drink both himself.

The majority of inmates in his cellblock were employed in the license plate factory or in other workshops. Some were still trying to finish their education, but Salmela wasn't interested in working. His days were spent loafing, reading and filling out crossword puzzles.

Salmela turned on the coffee maker and heard footsteps in the corridor. Curiosity got the better of him and he peeked out. Someone was standing at the door to his cell.

"What's up?" Salmela asked.

An enormous man covered in tattoos turned to face him. Salmela recognized him as one of Larsson's gorillas. He stared at Salmela without speaking. The tattooed gorilla moved towards him and Salmela considered his choices. He couldn't get out; he was trapped in the kitchen. Maybe he could use the wooden chair as a weapon. The gorilla grinned.

"You're having a visitor today."

"Huh?" was all that Salmela managed.

"A visitor. Get it?"

Salmela bobbed his head. Of course he understood.

"Good. Talk with him, then tell Larsson what he wants. Immediately. If he has any requests, figure out a code."

"A code," Salmela repeated.

"Right," the gorilla went on. "So we can let him know over the phone whether we agree or not."

"Okay," Salmela said and the messenger left.

The coffee maker gurgled and Salmela wondered what it all meant. Apparently, he had become a messenger for the Skulls.

* * *

"Strange," Mikko Kulta remarked.

"What?" Kirsi Kohonen asked. Joutsamo and Suhonen were there too, seated at the VCU conference table. The meeting was due to begin soon, but they were waiting for the boss.

"Just happened to see this report about a pig's head found in a downtown garage."

"A pig's head?" Kohonen marveled.

"Who wants coffee?" Suhonen asked, getting up.

"Yeah. Someone broke into a garage on Tehdas Street and dropped a real pig's head on the hood of a car. It was a shared garage and the neighbor filed a complaint."

"Whose car was it?" Kohonen went on.

"Don't know. I didn't get to the end yet."

Suhonen was getting the coffeemaker going when Takamäki stepped in. The Lieutenant was wearing a suit coat but no tie.

"Mornin'," Takamäki grunted, and took his seat at the head of the table. He glanced at the timelines on the wall. Apparently, nothing new had come up.

"Okay," the Lieutenant said. "Let's go around the table and figure out where we're at. Anna?"

"We've made the first arrest in the case," Joutsamo began. "Lydman was taken into custody at the airport trying to leave for Bangkok. At this point, he's suspected of murder. Our case against him isn't very strong, but in my opinion, we can detain him on the grounds that he answered all our questions with 'no comment.' Even so, the evidence is pretty thin so far. Our suspicion is primarily based on the fact that he met with Saarnikangas a couple of times after the murder. On Saarnikangas' end, we've confirmed his story with security camera footage. He was at the Teboil on the night of the murder, and we also found pictures of him at the Parkano ABC. Seems like Saarnikangas has been telling Suhonen the truth. Mikko has the details from Valkeakoski."

Takamäki continued around. "What's new over there?"

"What's ever new over there? Friggin' cold and wet. But the Fire Department divers fished out the murder weapon for us. It took until two in the morning, but they finally found it about thirty yards from the shore. So well within throwing distance. It's a .22 caliber pistol and it's at the lab now; I haven't heard from them yet. The local police are scouring the beach and the area around the cabin. The soil wasn't the right consistency to hold tire tracks or foot prints. The owner of the cabin is apparently not connected to the case in any way. I spoke to him last night and seems he hasn't been there since the beginning of September."

"Kirsi, anything new on the phone front?"

"Surveillance is still quiet—no traffic at all. I did manage to get through the phone records. We got a cell number from Lydman, but it didn't match any numbers on the lists. Apparently, the perps have used so many single-use phones that it's impossible to track them."

"Or they could have used a CB radio," Kulta interjected.

"Possible," Takamäki said. "So the evidence is still leaning strongly toward Saarnikangas. He was linked to the crime scene with forensic evidence, and furthermore, we found a possible murder weapon based on his story."

Joutsamo was nodding.

"Where is Saarnikangas now?"

Suhonen glanced at his cell phone. "His van's still at his apartment in Pihlajamäki; I would assume he's there too."

"Assume?" Joutsamo asked.

"That's what I said."

"Since we have Lydman, we should bring Saarnikangas in, too. Let's get the two of 'em tangled up in their own stories. Can we assume he'll go on record?"

"That I don't know," Suhonen said.

"Did you make any progress last night?" Takamäki asked.

"Well, a little. As far as I can tell, Saarnikangas is on the bottom rung. Next up is Lydman, and then one step further is this Markus Markkanen."

"Who's that?" Takamäki asked.

"Not a major player. He's been a low- to mid-level violent offender. Goes by the nickname 'Bogeyman', which says a lot. Various beatings and debt collections, but recently he's been clean. Not even a speeding ticket…"

"Uhh," Joutsamo interrupted. "I have to ask… How'd you know this Markkanen is involved?"

Suhonen looked her in the eyes. "I met him last night."

"And he confessed to you?"

"Well, no. But don't interrupt," said Suhonen. He had decided in advance what he would disclose, and how. "So… Markkanen is above Lydman, but the ladder doesn't stop there. A businessman named Kalevi Lindström is also involved."

"Hey, wasn't that…" Kulta blurted out.

Suhonen nodded. "Exactly. Last night, someone threatened this Lindström with a pig's head on the hood of his Mercedes."

"Who would threaten him, and why?" Kulta asked.

"Weeell," Suhonen spun his words. "From what I know, Markkanen is probably behind it, but he's also associated with Lindström. For example, both their cars are registered under the same owner. Also, Markkanen is at Lindström's apartment on Tehdas Street right now."

"How do you know that?" Joutsamo asked.

"I was there watching when Markkanen went in," Suhonen said, glad that they had passed up the pig's head without any nosy questions. "I put his car under GPS surveillance."

Takamäki cut in. "So Markkanen's playing games behind Lindström's back."

"That's what I'd say, but we have no hard evidence. This isn't stuff that I could, for example, take to court."

"So, how do you think Eriksson is mixed up in this?"

"That I don't know, but Anna can figure it out."

Joutsamo cracked up.

Suhonen went on, "We still don't know who pulled the trigger. Saarnikangas doesn't know. If he did, he'd have told me."

"Okay," said Takamäki, trusting Suhonen. "Lindström is clearly a new lead. Let's follow that. So dig up his and Bogeyman's rap sheets, backgrounds, and known associates. We'll put their phones and internet connections under surveillance immediately. Once we get a little further, we'll consider bugging the apartment."

"What about Saarnikangas?" Joutsamo asked, looking at Suhonen. "Just let him go free, or what?"

"I think we should take him in," Suhonen said coolly, and stood up.

"Wha…?" Joutsamo was stunned.

"He did his job and led us further down the trail. Bring him in. No need for the Bear Squad—you'll find him there in Pihlajamäki."

"Where you going?"

Suhonen smiled. "Coffee…it's ready. Anyone else want some?"

* * *

Markkanen tossed a paper cup full of coffee into the trash at the corner of Tehdas and Kapteeni Streets.

"What?" Lindström asked.

"Disgusting piss."

Lindström shrugged. He had ordered Markkanen to come along on his morning walk. Since he'd been forced to cancel with the personal trainer, he had to make his own exercise. Markkanen didn't have to walk the whole distance; he was permitted to stop for a few phone calls.

The men stopped at the same corner where, eleven years earlier, Steen Christensen had executed two policemen. The chilling murders had shaken the whole country. The convict had escaped from a Danish prison and made his way to Helsinki. In the middle of the night, he robbed a few hundred euros from a hotel cashier. On foot, Christensen was stopped by a patrol car. The Dane somehow surprised the two policemen, made them kneel, and shot them execution style. This led to a massive manhunt before Christensen was finally apprehended two days later, 100 kilometers north of Helsinki.

Lindström was wearing a blue tracksuit, and Markkanen a leather jacket.

"The Skulls were behind Eriksson's murder." Markkanen said.

"Where'd you get that information?"

"A prison source. Better if you don't know the details."

Lindström gazed up the street. The parking spaces were all full, but few people were out in the bleak grey November air.

"They wouldn't initiate something like that on their own. So who?"

"No, they wouldn't. A felon from Lahti named Suikkanen took out the contract. Now the Skulls want a hundred grand to switch sides."

"A hundred grand?"

"If you ask me, it's worth it. We'd be back in business, problem-free. Otherwise they'll stick with Suikkanen."

A cold gust of wind rushed down the street. Lindström had worked up a light sweat that had begun to cool. He pulled his blue stocking cap down a bit further.

"Can't you take care of this?" Lindström suggested.

"I can take care of Suikkanen, but I need some backing to go up against the Skulls. That would cost a lot more than a hundred Gs."

"I'll have to think about it."

"They want an answer today. Visiting hours at the prison end at 2:15. We have to decide by then, otherwise it could get ugly."

"Who's this Suikkanen?" Lindström asked, beginning to run in place.

"I don't know him. I've been told he's some gangster from Lahti. He's been running booze and cigarette rackets. But we can't start a war against the Skulls. We can take care of Suikkanen later, as long as we resolve the immediate danger."

"How'd Suikkanen know about Eriksson?"

Markkanen shrugged.

"What about the next shipment? Did you call the Customs guy?"

"Yes," Markkanen said, telling the truth this time. "He was a little worried, but apparently we have the green light. They had nothing on the ship."

"Good. I'll call if I need you," Lindström said, and trotted off towards home.

Markkanen watched him jog away, his shoes scuffing the ground. Geezer. How could someone so stupid be so rich. There was something wrong with that.

* * *

Jouko Nyholm was sitting at his desk at the Board of Customs. The morning had been bearable, but now sweat began to bead up beneath the inspector's collar.

Markkanen's call had violated the email protocol they had agreed on. Once again, he was told to sift through confidential Customs intelligence on some ship and its cargo. This time, Nyholm hadn't dared, since all computer searches were archived and could be easily retrieved.

He was convinced the police were onto him. The connection from Eriksson to his daughter, and then on to him was too obvious. Chances were, his phone was already tapped and his computer activities were under surveillance. He struggled to remember what words he had used with Markkanen. Could they reveal the entire scheme?

Now he'd have to lay low. He had told Markkanen that the coast was clear. And maybe it was, but Nyholm wasn't sure. Ships and their cargoes were continually analyzed, right up to the point of arrival.

How could he get out of this? To begin with, he had to calm down and give the impression that everything was fine. Why the hell had he come to work? He should've just called in sick; that would've been easiest. The flu or something.

"Hello."

The low voice startled Nyholm. It was Snellman; he hadn't even heard any footsteps.

Nyholm spun around in his chair and tried to smile. No sound escaped his lips.

"What's wrong?" Snellman asked. "Something bothering you?"

He coughed. "The flu has me on the ropes."

"Hmm, well, don't leave just yet. That detective lieutenant called to say he's coming to ask about something again. He wouldn't say what it was over the phone. I might need you, so take two aspirin and sweat it out."

Nyholm's throat was so constricted he nearly threw up.

CHAPTER 24
HELSINKI PRISON
FRIDAY, 1:10 P.M.

Eero Salmela sat in the visitors' area of the prison compound, waiting. He was alone, apart from the blue-uniformed guard who had escorted him out of the cell block. The guard stood by the wall.

The large, long room contained half a dozen tables fitted with low plexi-glass dividers. The tables had two—sometimes three—plastic chairs bolted to either side.

Most of the room was below ground level. The windows were high up on the walls, so that their bottom frames reached just above grade.

Salmela had already been waiting for five minutes. He glanced at the brawny guard, who was staring blankly at the opposite wall. He pitied the guard: someday he would get out of here, but the guard's job tied him to this shit pen for life.

The door opened, and a second guard brought in a big man wearing a leather jacket. The man's demeanor was confident, yet somehow uncertain. Salmela had never met him, but he could see immediately that the man had done time before. He wasn't surprised.

The guard led the visitor to the table. "You both know the rules. No contact, no matter how much you love each other. If you want that, you need to apply for a family room." Then he withdrew to the wall.

The big man sat on the chair. "How long you in for?" he asked, trying to appear sympathetic.

"What's it to you?" Salmela rasped. The noise level in the visiting room was always at a whisper. Nobody wanted to be heard by the next table, and even less by the guards. "I'm not counting anyway… What do you want?"

The man squinted his eyes. "Shit, you want me to go?"

"Whatever. Doesn't matter to me."

He remained silent, looking at Salmela. "Name?"

"What's yours?" Salmela shot back. In case the guards asked, both the visitor and the prisoner needed to know each other's names.

"Markkanen."

"Salmela."

Markkanen nodded. "Okay. I'll keep this short. Tell Larsson I need Korpela again. Everything's under control, no problems. I'll take care of the money and the other demands."

Salmela nodded, reflecting. For Larsson, that might be enough, but he wanted to know more. The guy clearly didn't know who or what rank he was dealing with. "How much?"

"Same as before."

"Not enough," Salmela said. If he was to negotiate on the Skulls' behalf, he might as well act the part. Nothing was ever enough for them.

"What do you mean 'not enough?' A deal is a deal."

Salmela wanted more background on this deal, even if it wasn't very smart.

"C'mon. You need help—we do that, but it don't come free. Thirty percent more."

"What?" Markkanen groaned.

Salmela's face was rigid. He tried to guess at what Larsson might demand. Money for sure, but the Skulls couldn't send an assassin after just anybody. Larsson would definitely be interested in the target.

"You heard me."

"Okay. Thirty."

Salmela accepted the offer. "Someone's gonna call you on the cell today. If he asks about your bro, then it's a go. But if he asks about your sister, no deal."

"Understood."

"You sure? Girls usually say no, so that's a refusal."

"Nice code."

"One more question: who's the target?"

"What's it to you?"

"Don't be stupid. Loyalty is all that matters in here."

Markkanen sized up Salmela. Who was this guy? He'd made the contact through the usual channels, so there was no reason to doubt the guy was representing the Skulls. Something was not quite right, though. Most messengers just rattled off information, but this guy was negotiating. Maybe this Salmela was some kind of lieutenant or something, though Markkanen didn't know much about the Skulls' hierarchy.

"Well, okay," he began. "A guy from Lahti named Suikkanen. He thinks he's something else, but he's not. I don't want him around no more."

Salmela tried to seem indifferent. "What's he look like?"

"Early forties. Wears a leather jacket and has a long rap sheet. Short, dark hair."

Salmela nodded. Aside from Suhonen's alias, he didn't know any other Suikkanens who'd match that description. What had his old friend gotten mixed up in now?

* * *

Suikkanen was a convenient pawn, Markkanen thought. Very convenient.

It was nearly 1:30 P.M., and the Corner Pub was beginning to fill up in honor of Friday. It probably had more to do with the fact that their beer was the cheapest on the street today.

Suikkanen brought the coffees and sat down on the other side of a table pock-marked with cigarette burns.

Suhonen and Markkanen leaned in closer. They kept their voices to a murmur.

"Did the Mercedes guy pay up?"

"No," Markkanen said. "He laughed in my face and said he'd save the pig's head for Christmas."

Suhonen sipped his coffee. "Should we try again, maybe a bit more persuasively?" He clenched his fist.

Fool, but a gift from heaven, Markkanen thought. "That's what I was thinking, though it won't do me any good if you just beat him up in the street."

"You want the money, right?"

"Precisely. The guy lives in the same complex where the garage is. There's a safe in his apartment with cash in it. Not sure how much—I just know he's loaded."

"So whaddya want me to do?" Suhonen asked.

"Simple. Go to his apartment, make him open the safe, and bring me the money. I'll collect my debt and the rest is yours."

"Just leftovers?"

"Five grand no matter what, of course."

Suhonen raked his fingers through his hair. "I don't know. What kind of guy is this?"

"Name's Kalevi Lindström. He's a businessman selling black market goods to Russia. He runs a tight shop, but otherwise he's soft. You shouldn't have any problems."

Suhonen narrowed his eyes. "Why don't you do it yourself?"

"I can't jeopardize the relationship. We're in the middle of a couple deals."

"Okay," Suhonen said, hardening again. "How far do you want this to go?"

"Just rough him up a little—that should be enough. He's weak."

Markkanen was sure Lindström wouldn't open the safe without a fight. Might even die first.

His plan was beginning to look better and better. Suikkanen would take care of Lindström, and the Skulls would off Suikkanen. And even if Lindström didn't die, he'd certainly end up in the hospital for a stretch. Suikkanen had what it takes. Shit, he even beat up a cop. In any case, the old power struggles would cease, and Markkanen would be firmly second in command, maybe even in Lindström's shoes. That gave him another idea: might it be better if he saved Lindström's life?

Eriksson had wormed his way into his job with deceit and lies. Now he would do the same. His hand was just a little heavier.

"When?" Suhonen asked.

"Today. It's urgent. He'll be at home from three o'clock onward. Be there at four." He took a piece of paper out of his pocket and began to sketch a floor plan of the apartment.

Suhonen was at a loss. It was obvious Markkanen was after Lindström's money. But what would be the best course of action? Suhonen didn't have enough evidence yet to arrest him for incitement. He would actually need to carry out the attack.

* * *

The enormous Skull escorted Eero Salmela to Tapani Larsson's cell door, then stood guard outside. Larsson had been resting on the bottom bunk, but now he sat up. He was wearing a sleeveless T-shirt, and his tattooed biceps bulged in full view.

Various pin-up girls decorated the walls. Salmela recognized the blonde: she had appeared in a few low-budget domestic porn flicks. He remembered hearing that Larsson had dated this Sara at one point. In any case, he was glad he'd remembered it. It'd be a bad idea to crack jokes about the guy's girlfriend.

"So what'd Markkanen want?"

"He said he wants to use Korpela again. Apparently everything's under control, no worries."

The gangster sneered. "Yeah, right. The dick fucks it up, then refuses to pay for it."

"I wouldn't know about that."

"What did he offer?"

"Same as before, but I thought…"

"You thought?" Larsson snapped. "You ain't supposed to think, just deliver the damn message."

Salmela continued, unruffled. "I thought the old rate was low, so I got thirty percent more."

Larsson broke out laughing. "Damn good thinking." But his expression hardened immediately. "Who is it?"

"Wasn't sure if I should ask, but I did anyway. A forty-something small-timer from Lahti...goes by Suikkanen."

Larsson's face tightened. "Suikkanen? Fuck me, I know that guy."

Salmela was dumbfounded. Had Suhonen tried to infiltrate the Skulls as Suikkanen? He stayed quiet, waiting to see if Larsson would say anything more.

Spit flew from the gangster's mouth. "That Suikkanen's a fucking cop. He's an undercover pig."

Larsson turned to a narrow bookshelf and slid out a paperback with a red cover. He shook some photos out of the pages and riffled through them. When he found the right one, he handed it to Salmela. "Look for yourself."

The photograph showed the front of the Pasila Headquarters. Suhonen was descending the stairs at the entrance, chatting with another man. Salmela recognized him as Lieutenant Takamäki.

"The one with the leather jacket is Suikkanen," Larsson continued. "He landed me in here last summer."

"Don't know him."

Larsson's gaze was hard. "Good. Better stay away from him."

"Anyway, back to Markkanen. I said we would...or you would contact him by phone. If he's asked about his brother, the answer is yes. If about his sister, then it's a no."

"Hell yeah, we'll do it," Larsson said, and whistled. The hall guard stepped inside. "Get word to Korpela that we'll take Markkanen's job. Tell him to do it right—that Suikkanen's a cop. But don't tell Markkanen that we know that—he could be in with them. We might have to bump him, too… Also, get Korpela on the phone. I want to talk to Tony myself."

Interesting, Salmela thought. The Skulls had stashed away an illegal cell phone, which Larsson could use to stay in touch with the outside.

"Anything else?" Salmela asked.

"No," Larsson said. "Get lost."

Salmela got up and stepped into the corridor. His cell block was one level up. The doors to the stairwells weren't locked during the day. Now he had to warn his old friend Suhonen about the Skulls' plan. He'd need phone authorization immediately, or he'd have to get word out some other way.

As he climbed the staircase, a blue-uniformed guard approached from the opposite direction. Salmela had just squeezed past the lout when he heard a voice from behind, "Hey Salmela…"

Suddenly, he felt a crushing impact in his right leg. The pain in his knee shot through his entire body, and his leg buckled beneath him. Salmela tumbled onto his side and hit the stairs.

The guard was still standing a bit further down. "Raitio wanted to send his regards to you and your knee."

Salmela caught sight of a raised hand. It came down hard, then everything went black.

The nightstick hit Salmela just above his left ear.

The guard glanced around. The stairwell was quiet, no witnesses. He pulled out his radio and reported that an inmate had either been assaulted or fallen down the stairs. Unable to haul the unconscious victim to the infirmary alone, he requested assistance.

A dreary voice on the other end asked if there was any sign of the perpetrator. The guard said no; he had just found the victim in the stairwell.

A thin stream of blood trickled out of Salmela's ear and ran down his neck.

* * *

Markus Markkanen passed the Helsinki Ice Arena and stayed right at the "Y" intersection. Behind the arena were the Olympic Stadium, host of the 1952 summer games, and a smaller soccer stadium. He was satisfied. Someone had called him to ask about his brother, so Suikkanen's fate was sealed. Lindström had taken the bait, as had Suikkanen.

His stomach growled and he glanced at the dashboard clock. He could go for some food. He took a right turn onto Urheilukatu, then a quick left. A former gas station had become a McDonald's years earlier.

There was a line for the drive-thru, so Markkanen swung the Beamer into a parking space in front of a hedge. He'd get through quicker if he went inside for his meal. Maybe he'd eat in, too.

The Rock 'n' Roll themed interior was actually kind of fun; it reminded him of his youthful fascination with James Dean.

Markkanen was already at the door when one of his phones rang. It was his wife.

"Hey," he answered softly. "How's it going?"

"How are you?" she said, sounding a bit tense.

"What's wrong?"

"Nothing. We've been swimming, swimming and swimming, but…"

"But what?"

She hesitated a moment. "This is a little strange. Lindström called and asked me the same kind of questions you might ask. How's it going and what not."

Damn, Markkanen thought. What was Lindström doing calling his wife?

"What did he want?"

"Nothing, really. He was very friendly. Asked me if we needed any money or anything. Just to chat."

"Did he ask where you were?"

"Well, uhh…yes."

Markkanen groaned. "You didn't tell him, did you?"

"Well, of course I told him. What else could I say?"

"Stupid."

"Don't get mad, Markus. It just slipped out somehow."

"Well, pack your stuff and leave town."

"To go where?"

"I don't know. Why don't you go to Tampere. I'll meet you there tomorrow, if I can make it. Check in at the Lynx Hotel."

"I'm sorry," she said.

Markkanen hung up and considered what this meant. Lindström shouldn't have any reason to talk to Riikka.

His hunger had faded, and he walked back to the car.

Fucking Lindström.

CHAPTER 25
POLICE HEADQUARTERS,
PASILA, HELSINKI
FRIDAY, 2:40 P.M.

Suhonen walked into Takamäki's office. The Lieutenant was seated at his computer.

"You have a sec?" Suhonen asked, closing the door behind him.

Takamäki looked up when he heard the door close. Apparently this was something important or sensitive.

"I was about to head over to Customs, but it can wait. Go ahead."

"I have a situation… It's a little complicated."

"How so?"

Suhonen told him about going undercover to meet Markkanen and about his orders to rob Lindström at his apartment in an hour. Takamäki listened quietly.

"What do you think I should do?" Suhonen asked finally.

"You know you can't go through with it."

"It could mean a breakthrough," Suhonen said. "We're already pretty far along."

"Yeah, you're right. Sometimes we end up in situations where the law is unclear, and the lawyers are no help either. But this situation is obvious, armed robbery is way past the grey area. Think what could happen if something went wrong."

Suhonen nodded. "Well, yeah. In principle, I agree. It *is* very risky."

Takamäki thought aloud. "Too risky. Do we have any other options?"

"What do you mean?"

"I was thinking we could fake it, but that's pretty damn difficult as well, since Lindström is a potential suspect here. If the target was an outsider, we could consider it."

"That's what I was thinking," Suhonen said.

"Let's look at the benefits. What would we get if you carried out the robbery? You might get a little closer to Markkanen's inner circle, find out more about the case, but I don't see a direct benefit to the investigation. You wouldn't find a smoking gun."

"Probably not. Still, the relationship between the two is interesting. Markkanen knows where Lindström keeps his money, yet he doesn't want to do the job himself. He'd rather pay someone on the outside to do it. Obviously, he wants to maintain a relationship with the guy," Suhonen pointed out.

"And when you combine that with Eriksson's murder, it starts to look like some kind of love-hate triangle."

"Markkanen mentioned that Lindström owed him money," Suhonen recalled. "Maybe Lindström told him to kill Eriksson, and now the guy's refusing to pay."

"Or maybe Markkanen's been playing games behind the boss's back and, for one reason or another, took Eriksson out of the picture."

"Or another possibility is that Eriksson and Markkanen were partners, in which case Lindström could've ordered the hit," Suhonen said.

The men stared at each other in silence.

"Then again, Eriksson might have no connection to them whatsoever," Suhonen added. "We don't know for sure. This is pure speculation."

"Never assume," Takamäki smiled. "But we're in no hurry. Let's just go about our business, and the case will unravel when someone slips up."

Suhonen glanced at the clock on the wall. "Right, no hurry. I'm supposed to be robbing one of our primary suspects in one hour. Oh, and Markkanen mentioned that Lindström does business with the Russians. If someone's digging through his background, that tidbit might be helpful."

"Not sure if anyone's had a chance to do that yet," Takamäki said. "Joutsamo, Kohonen and Kulta apprehended Saarnikangas earlier. He didn't have many warm words for you, or so I heard."

"No surprise there," Suhonen said quietly.

Takamäki turned back to the computer. "I have to send off this email. But about that robbery. Maybe it makes sense for you to go there and just observe, but stay out of the apartment. If Markkanen asks you about it later, just make up some excuse."

"Yeah. That's probably the best move."

* * *

Markus Markkanen was livid. What had possessed the old man to call his wife? He wanted immediate answers. He was driving down Kapteeni Street, having just passed the neo-Gothic red brick facade of St. John's Church. A bus up ahead was moving slowly, but he had no room to pass on the crowded, narrow street. Flanked by stone apartment buildings with quaint shops and cafes, Kapteeni Street led south toward Lindström's apartment.

Damn buses.

One of his phones rang. It was Lindström's line.

The bus inched forward and Markkanen took a deep breath before answering.

"Hel-lo," he said, putting too much emphasis on the last syllable.

"Is this a bad time?"

"No. Go ahead."

"We need to talk."

"About what?"

"I'll tell you when you get here. Is four okay?"

Markkanen was on Vuorimies. He could be there in just a couple minutes, but four o'clock would be even better."

"Four's good. I should make it by then."

"Good," Lindström said. "Everything OK?"

"Yeah. Everything's OK."

The conversation ended. Markkanen pulled up to the corner of Tehdas Street and waited for the cross traffic. Within twenty seconds, he'd decided to call Suikkanen. The robbery would have to wait for another day.

He had just stepped on the gas when he glimpsed a familiar figure rounding the corner. The man wore a leather jacket. A black beanie cap covered his head, which, at least a week ago, had been bald. It was Korpela, the Skull. What was *he* doing here?

Markkanen made a split-second decision. He crossed the intersection and swung a U-turn. Tony Korpela had disappeared around the corner.

The blue Beamer coasted back to the intersection and Markkanen could see the Skull about fifty yards up on the right.

He turned the car round and drove slowly, as if looking for a parking space. Korpela was about twenty yards ahead when Markkanen's heart sank. Damn, what if he's going inside!

The door to Lindström's staircase was about twenty yards off.

Markkanen was still crawling along when a blue taxi pulled up to his back bumper. He was afraid it would honk, attracting Korpela's attention, so he flicked on his right blinker and pulled over as far as possible. He missed the driver's-side mirror of a parked Nissan by about two inches. The taxi zoomed past, but Markkanen kept his eyes on Korpela. The man punched in the door code and disappeared inside.

Markkanen shook his head and switched off his blinker. He hit the gas and sped on towards the South Harbor. Now he had to set up a meeting with Suikkanen. The man's task had just changed.

Jouko Nyholm's foot tapped out an irregular rhythm on the wooden floor. Should he leave? Snellman had told him to stick around because that bastard from Homicide had come for a visit. Takamäki and Snellman had been talking for ten minutes already.

He thought for a moment, then started typing an email. His fingers couldn't find the keys and he constantly had to make corrections. In the email, he requested an inspection for a shipment of toilet paper on the M/S Gambrini, scheduled to arrive in the next few days.

"According to some recent intelligence, the cargo bound for Russia on the M/S Gambrini is not toilet paper; it's washing machines. Please take appropriate action," Nyholm wrote.

He read through the memo one more time. The sentence was sloppy, but the message was clear. He clicked the mouse and off it went to the Customs surveillance manager at the Kotka harbor.

That's it, no more, Nyholm thought.

In his desk drawer was a Customs-issued 9 millimeter Glock. It could end this whole mess.

Takamäki and Snellman were sitting at the large conference table in Snellman's office. Snellman had ordered sweet rolls, but neither was in the mood for pastries.

"It's an interesting link, that's for sure," Snellman said.

Takamäki had just explained Eriksson's connection to Nyholm's daughter.

"But on the other hand," he went on. "None of us are responsible for the decisions of our adult children. Fortunately."

"No, of course not," the Lieutenant answered.

"So," the Assistant Director said, standing up. He stepped behind his desk. "I guess our only choice is to ask Nyholm himself."

"Don't..." Takamäki started to say, but Snellman had already pushed the button for the intercom. He told Nyholm to come over.

"I'm not so sure this is a good idea right now," Takamäki said.

"We need answers, don't we?" Snellman grumbled. "If your suspicions prove misguided, you can rule him out. But Nyholm could know something useful about the victim."

Takamäki didn't believe that for a second. Had he known something, Nyholm would have told them about it a couple of days ago when first asked to look into Eriksson's connections to Customs. Snellman seemed to have some sort of power over Nyholm— maybe it was worth a shot.

They heard a cautious knock on the door.

"Come in," Snellman roared.

Takamäki noticed immediately that something was wrong. Nyholm's hair was messed up and he was trembling. One hand was concealed behind his back.

"What's wrong?" Snellman asked, puzzled.

"Nothing," he answered, wiping his nose with his left hand. His right was still behind his back.

Snellman glanced at Takamäki, who looked equally puzzled.

"Well, listen, Jouko," Snellman said in a gentler tone. "The police have discovered that your daughter was dating this Jerry Eriksson, the guy who was murdered. Do you have anything to say about that?"

Nyholm remained standing, but looked a little calmer.

"Sure, I knew that…of course."

"Well, why didn't you mention it when you were looking into Eriksson's background?" Snellman said quietly.

Takamäki had a sudden image of an exchange between a father and his son, who'd been caught stealing apples.

"I couldn't."

"Why not?"

"I just couldn't. It…it…"

Snellman's gaze hardened. "Just spit it out, man," he snapped. "We don't have all day to listen to your blubbering."

Nyholm's expression went cold and he slowly drew his hand from behind his back. He was holding a black pistol.

Both Takamäki and Snellman flinched.

"Shit Nyholm! What are you doing?" Snellman bellowed.

Nyholm raised the gun and pointed it at the men seated at the table. "Stay where you are. Don't move."

Takamäki felt like getting up, but decided it was better to obey. His own gun was back at Police Headquarters, locked in the bottom drawer of his desk.

Nyholm pressed the gun against his own temple. His expression was stoic.

"Don't do it," Snellman said.

Nyholm turned towards Takamäki. "Eriksson met my daughter last spring and found out what I did for a living. Of course, I checked his record. Her life was messed up already, and there was nothing I could do about it anyway. Then the blackmail started..."

Takamäki listened to the outburst. "What blackmail?"

"Eriksson wanted information on our surveillance ops. They were trafficking electronics, primarily to Russia through Finland. The paperwork always said rubber gloves or toilet paper. All I had to do was tell them whether the shipment was slated for inspection. They paid me for it."

"Mole!" Snellman roared.

The gun didn't waver from his temple. "That's right. I told my wife I was gonna kill him, this Eriksson. When I heard he'd been found dead, I thought I might be a suspect. But the scheme went on. Another guy named Markkanen took Eriksson's place. I don't know if that's his real name, but his number's in my cell phone."

His gaze was still locked on Takamäki. "With that number, you should be able to track him down."

"Who's behind this?"

"Yes, I figured that out too. It took a little effort since they hid the scheme behind fronting companies. You'll find the paperwork in my office. The Finnish side is headed by a man named Kalevi Lindström. The Russian side had several names, but I'm sure there are even bigger bosses behind them. Any other questions?"

Takamäki noted the man's unusual calm.

"That's not necessary," the Lieutenant said quietly. "Shooting yourself won't solve anything."

"Hmph, especially not in my office," Snellman grumbled. "You'd make a terrible mess."

"Be quiet," Takamäki snarled.

Nyholm looked at Takamäki. His finger tightened around the trigger.

"Yes it will."

Takamäki tried again. "Let's just talk about this. You've helped us already, and we need you for the investigation. Your situation's not easy, but it's not that bad either. We have time to talk. Let's work out the issues, one at a time."

Nyholm's trigger finger started to quiver.

"I'm here to listen," Takamäki said again. "Don't."

Nyholm lowered the gun to his side and wept. "I can't do anything…not even this," he said and fell to his knees.

Takamäki bolted out of his chair toward Nyholm, who was shaking and sobbing loudly. The gun was still visible, dangling from the man's hand. Takamäki twisted it free and set it on the coffee table.

Snellman was still sitting in his chair. "Goddamn!"

"You said it."

"Take him to jail."

Takamäki glanced at Nyholm, then took out his cell phone.

"I think we'll send him to the hospital first."

* * *

Suhonen got out of his car. The southern tip of Hernesaari, "Pea Island," wasn't an official parking lot; it was mostly used as a pier for dumping snow into the sea. Only a few decades earlier, Pea Island had actually been an island, but had since been connected to the mainland with landfill. It sported a shipyard, a helicopter port, some office buildings, and of course, a hockey arena.

The wind swept across the bay and the trees on the island of Pihlajasaari were visible less than a kilometer away.

Markkanen had seen Suhonen pull up and he got out of the car.

"Hello," Suhonen said, zipping up his leather jacket.

Markkanen gave a nod, went to the trunk of his car and opened it. Suhonen joined him. Inside the trunk was the same hockey bag he had used for the pig's head. Suhonen guessed it contained something else now, though the nauseating stench remained.

"Well, what now?" Suhonen asked. Markkanen had called him fifteen minutes earlier to say that plans had changed and arranged a meeting in the remote, vacant lot.

"Suikkanen, the situation's changed."

"Huh? You don't want me to swipe the cash?"

"No. The old man wants to meet me at four. I don't know what he wants, maybe to pay up."

"Should I do the job after that?"

"Maybe," Markkanen said. "We'll see how it goes, but I need you to watch my back now."

Suhonen nodded. "Sure, I can do that, as long as the pay's the same."

"This one's only worth a grand."

"What do you mean only a grand?"

"Cuz you're just back-up," Markkanen snapped.

"Two grand."

"Alright," he relented.

Suhonen gave him a hard look. "A grand up front."

Markkanen smiled, but fished out his wallet, counted off ten one-hundred euro notes and handed him the money.

"Happy?"

Suhonen stuffed the cash into his pocket and grinned.

"Let's get to business then."

Markkanen stooped down, pulled the hockey bag out of the trunk and opened it. Inside was a long, skinny black and white bag, intended for junior hockey sticks. On the side, large letters spelled out, "FAT PIPE."

"This is for you," he said, handing the bag to Suhonen. "Just a loan. It's loaded."

Suhonen opened the zipper partway and immediately recognized a Franchi Spas pump-action shotgun. The Italian assault weapon was prized by military and police task forces worldwide. Its magazine could hold eight rounds.

Suhonen looked up at Markkanen. "So, this is where the going gets tough."

"You know how to use it?"

Suhonen had fired a similar weapon in training, but Suikkanen wouldn't have had that opportunity.

"I've used a shotgun, but not this kind."

"It's easy. The safety's next to the trigger. Switch it off. When you pull the pump, the shell goes in. Then pull the trigger. Booom! A manly sound." Markkanen grinned.

"Okay," Suhonen said. "Might as well get the money out of the safe at the same time."

Markkanen looked at Suhonen. "Suikkanen, I don't know what's gonna happen in that apartment, and frankly, I don't like not knowing. But I'm going in there alone, and you can either wait in the car or outside in the yard. Just stay close. He might have help inside."

"If you need me, how do I know when to come in? If I hear gunshots, or what?"

Markkanen grinned. "You'd be too late then."

He dug a small plastic box out of the hockey bag and opened it. Inside were a handful of electronic devices.

"What's this?"

Markkanen took out a box the size of a match-book with a yard-long cord attached to it. He held up the end of the cord. "There's a microphone in here. I'll have this with me."

"This is so James Bond. Where'd you get this stuff?"

"I bought it in London a while back." He grinned, then handed a similar box to Suhonen. This one had an earpiece on the end. "You get the receiver. You'll be able to hear what's happening. The code word is 'cognac.' If I say that, get your ass inside. Is that clear?"

"Cognac," Suhonen chuckled, and pushed the earpiece in place. "Got it."

"Good. I just changed all the batteries, but we'd better make sure they work," he said, taking several steps backwards. "Turn it on. There's a little switch on the side."

Suhonen glanced at his watch: 3:50 P.M.

CHAPTER 27
TEHDAS STREET, HELSINKI
FRIDAY, 4:02 P.M.

Suhonen was sitting in the car, waiting. Luckily, he had found a parking spot just in front of the building. Now he wouldn't have to skulk around in the yard or stairwell, carrying a stick bag. Ten seconds earlier, Markkanen had gone inside without so much as a backward glance.

Suhonen had alerted Takamäki, but the time frame was too tight. There would be no backup at the scene. All patrol units downtown had been notified of a possible police operation on Tehdas Street, but Suhonen didn't want any uniformed officers stumbling in at this delicate stage.

In the earpiece, he could hear Markkanen's footsteps on the stone floor. The device worked surprisingly well, considering the building had thick stone walls. If this had been a police-issue device, the signal would have been breaking up by now.

Suhonen heard the doorbell ring and the door open. He opened the car door and ducked into the stairwell, the bag slung over his shoulder.

* * *

"Come in," the bald man said in a nasal voice, cracking the door open a bit more to see if anyone else was on the landing. He glanced down the empty stairwell, too.

Tony Korpela was wearing a grey sweater and a pair of black Levi's. His tattoos burst out of his shirt sleeves onto the backs of his hands. He was in his thirties, and considerably shorter than Markkanen.

Markkanen knew his rap sheet. Toward the end of the '90s, Tony had been sentenced to thirteen years in prison for "murder with diminished capacity." Had he been judged fully accountable, he'd still be serving life. The murder had been brutal, carried out with a pair of scissors. But according to the District Court, Korpela hadn't fully understood his actions.

Finland's criminal code, like many others, included this intermediate step between "guilty" and "not guilty by reason of insanity." Those "guilty with diminished capacity" received lighter sentences, but still did their time in regular prisons.

Markkanen had read about the murder in a popular true-crime magazine. He had been amazed by Korpela's persistence, and the fact that the scissors hadn't been rendered uselessly dull.

Korpela had never settled into prison life, and ended up in solitary confinement in the Riihimäki Prison. Rarely did "the hole" rehabilitate inmates: it only fed their hatred. Prisoners were isolated in their cells, save for a brief spell outdoors. Showers were few and far between. Markkanen wasn't sure how Korpela had ended up in the Skulls, but that didn't really matter.

Markkanen walked past Korpela, then felt the barrel of a gun at the nape of his neck.

"Just a precaution. You carrying?" the man droned from behind.

"No," Markkanen answered. He wondered how much teasing Korpela had endured as a child for his unusual voice.

Korpela patted him down anyway. He didn't find the transmitter, which was taped high on the inside of his right thigh. The microphone was lodged in his belt buckle.

Markkanen dutifully hung his jacket on the hook, slipped off his shoes and proceeded into the library. Lindström was sitting in an armchair wearing a brown cardigan and holding a fat glass.

"Pour yourself a brandy," Lindström said with a smile.

"No thanks," Markkanen said, thankful that he hadn't offered cognac. Had he done so, Suikkanen would be at the door any second. Markkanen sat down opposite Lindström.

Korpela lingered by the door and Lindström shot him a glance.

"An explanation is probably in order," Lindström said dryly. "We can speak freely. The apartment was scrubbed for bugs this morning."

"You can start by explaining what that Skull is doing here," Markkanen said. He wanted to convey to Suikkanen that there were others in the room.

"Actually, that's where I was going to start. Tony came to pay me a visit this afternoon, and he made an offer I couldn't refuse. We've had a good chat," Lindström said, then sipped his brandy.

"How'd he end up here?" Markkanen wondered in bewilderment.

"I drove," Korpela said coldly.

Markkanen racked his brain. How had he been betrayed? How had the Skulls and Lindström found each other? In any case, the situation was not good.

"Punk," Lindström snorted. "But let's keep this civil. Could you please explain why you had Eriksson killed?"

What the hell was going on here, Markkanen wondered, trying to stay cool. Clearly, the Skulls had switched sides.

Markkanen glanced at Korpela again.

"Yes. We've had some very interesting conversations," Lindström sneered.

Korpela had apparently told him about the murder. No use denying it, then.

"Uhhh, well. Right. I wanted to tell you, but I couldn't. I got wind from a reliable source that Eriksson was cooperating with Customs. He was their informant and so…"

"Don't give me that shit," Lindström hissed. "Eriksson told me he had something on you. He didn't say, or have time to say what it was. So? What was it?"

Markkanen shook his head. "I don't know anything about that."

"Does your wife know?"

"You leave her outta this."

"Should we pick her and the boy up from the spa in Turku? Korpela here would be happy to oblige," Lindström smiled.

Markkanen tried to remain calm. "They don't know anything."

"But you do," Lindström said, pausing for emphasis. "Why did you hire Korpela to kill Eriksson?"

Markkanen said nothing. Korpela had snuck up behind him. He seized Markkanen's arms, jerked them behind the back rest and quickly slapped a pair of cuffs on his wrists.

"Hey, what the hell is this?"

* * *

Suhonen was on the landing one floor below, listening intently. What was going on inside? He heard a familiar metallic sound, but it took him a second to place it: the snip of a scissors.

Korpela and scissors. Of course, Suhonen thought.

Though Markkanen seemed to be in trouble, he hadn't given the code word. Suhonen knew the situation wouldn't improve; should he go in now or would that just cause more problems? He unzipped the bag but didn't take the shotgun out yet.

"Where should we trim first?" said the older man's creaky voice.

"His head seems dispensable," came a nasal laugh and the nervous snipping of scissors.

"Hey, hey… Don't."

Suhonen felt his phone vibrate. It was Takamäki. He pressed the talk button, but said nothing.

"What's going on?" Takamäki asked.

* * *

Lindström sipped his brandy. "Do you understand your position here? It's not very enviable."

Markkanen wondered if he should ask for some cognac—not yet. He wanted to see all of Lindström's cards.

"Eriksson claimed I was embezzling money from you, but it's not true. He was just saying that because I knew he was a snitch for Customs."

"He was no nark. You're the only traitor here."

Korpela worked the scissors impatiently; the metallic sound cut through the room almost constantly now. He looked at Lindström in anticipation.

Lindström nodded. "We'll get to that soon enough. I have some more questions for our Judas here. Who's this Suikkanen?"

For a moment, Markkanen considered how to respond, then remembered that Suikkanen was listening in. He'd have to choose his words carefully or his backup would take off.

"He's a gangster from Lahti."

"What's he want from me?"

"Your money, probably..." The constant snapping of Korpela's scissors was getting on his nerves. "How should I know?" he shrieked abruptly.

"Why do you want him dead? And where'd you get the kind of money to pay for the Skulls?"

Markkanen closed his eyes. There it was. Cognac wouldn't help anymore, unless he could turn the tables and provoke Suikkanen to attack out of rage.

"*You're* the one who wants him dead. Those were *your* orders," Markkanen raised his voice. "And *your* money."

"A gangster from Lahti, huh?" Lindström relished ignoring his lies.

"Yeah."

Lindström stared at his captive, looking pitifully weak in his chair. "What would you say if I told you he's a cop?"

Markkanen's mouth dropped open, but he collected himself quickly. "Naah, that can't be true."

"How so?"

"I saw him beat up an officer a couple days ago. Or was it yesterday."

"The Skulls are positive he's a cop. They have a photo of him coming out of Police Headquarters."

Markkanen closed his eyes again. He remembered the microphone. The nightmare situation had just turned catastrophic.

"You murdered Eriksson and nearly ratted out my business with the Russians. Korpela is in danger of doing life…"

Markkanen didn't say a word. If Suikkanen was a cop, the guy was probably keeled over laughing right now.

"You have any suggestions on how to deal with this?" Lindström asked. "I'm prepared to forget about Eriksson and the money you took, provided we can hand Suikkanen to the Skulls; their number two wants him dead. So where is he?"

At first, Lindström thought Markkanen was gasping for air, but he soon caught on. The man was silently mouthing the same sentence over and over: Open… the… cuffs. Open… the… cuffs.

Lindström was dumbfounded. Why would he do a thing like that, he thought to himself. Was somebody listening in? But they had swept the place for bugs.

Lindström's guard was up, though. He took a pen and paper from the desk and scrawled: Why?

"I ain't saying nothin," Markkanen said aloud, then continued mouthing the words: Open… the… cuffs.

Lindström scribbled an order to Korpela, telling him to open the cuffs. The assassin was confused, but carried out his orders.

Markkanen massaged his wrists, then quickly took the paper and pen from the old man's hand. He wrote: Play along. Suikkanen will be here soon.

Markkanen gave the old man an inquiring look, to be sure he had understood. Lindström nodded expectantly. Korpela watched from the sidelines, still baffled. Suddenly Markkanen started to scream bloody murder.

"Fuuck nooo! Don't kill me! Cognac! Cognac!"

Lindström and Korpela looked at him, both openly shocked now. Markkanen didn't care, and kept screaming in anguish. He pulled down his pants, tore off the transmitter, snatched the scissors out of Korpela's hand and snipped the microphone cord.

"What the hell?" Korpela bleated. "You're wired?"

"Who was listening to us?" Lindström stammered.

"Fucking Suikkanen! I didn't know he was a pig."

Korpela's eyes burned with anger and he pulled a pistol out of his waistband.

"And we talked about..." Lindström was saying. Then, realizing the seriousness of the situation, he spat out a stream of curses.

"Fuuck," Korpela bleated. "I don't even know who to shoot anymore. Damn! Maybe I'll shoot you all. Everybody!"

Korpela pointed the gun at Markkanen, but swung it back to Lindström when he took a couple steps toward the table.

Markkanen seized the opportunity and drove the scissors into Korpela's neck. The gun went off with a sharp bang. He pulled the scissors out and for a few seconds, blood sputtered out of the wound. Lindström and Korpela had fallen to the floor simultaneously.

Suddenly, a loud crash came from the hallway.

Markkanen's hands were sticky with blood. As he wiped his forehead, he realized his face was also spattered with blood. His ears were ringing from the gunshot.

"POLICE! FREEZE!" he heard from the door.

Markkanen tossed the scissors on the floor and raised his hands.

A short gurgle escaped from Korpela's throat, then silence. Lindström lay on the floor, a neat hole in his forehead.

A S.W.A.T. officer in a helmet and heavy flak jacket appeared at the door and pointed an MP5 submachine gun at Markkanen.

"DON'T MOVE!"

"They tried to kill me," Markkanen pleaded. "They tried to kill me. It was self defense! Self defense."

* * *

Suhonen and Takamäki were standing on Tehdas Street. Snow was whirling down from the sky. The stick bag was still slung over Suhonen's shoulder.

Flashing lights reflected off the windows of the surrounding buildings. The paramedics were dawdling in the street, waiting for permission to leave. No customers for them today.

The Bear Squad packed up their gear and drove off. Forensics unrolled a length of blue and white police tape across the entrance. Takamäki opened the door to a large white Mercedes van.

"Hi there… Takamäki," he introduced himself.

The man inside scowled. "Uhh, yep. Mölsä from technical support." He was a small, mousy character with slippers on his feet. The inside of the van was bristling with high-tech devices.

"You get it on tape?"

"Nope, nothing on tape," the man said, "it's on the hard drive. It took a while to scan for the bandwidth, but we got everything from the point when the scissors started snipping."

"Good," Takamäki said.

"But next time, give us some advance warning about this sort of thing, so we can prepare. The van could've easily been in for servicing and we wouldn't have made it here at all."

Takamäki didn't respond. He just nodded as he slid the door shut.

Suhonen was gazing up at the apartment window. The snowflakes felt cold on his face. "You should've let me go in. We might have two less corpses on our hands."

"Safety issue," Takamäki said.

"But didn't we just let two people get killed?"

"Had there been an innocent bystander or a hostage involved, it would've been different. Their deaths aren't your fault, nor will the world miss them."

"Well, yeah. Maybe so," Suhonen said. "It won't miss Eriksson, either, but still we put in a lot of work to solve his murder."

Takamäki nodded, suppressing a grin. A crowd had already begun to gather behind the police tape.

"I'm gonna take off before the TV cameras get here," Suhonen said.

One of the ambulances was double-parked next to his car. Suhonen flashed his badge at the driver. "Can you move so I can get outta here?"

He turned back to Takamäki. "Wanna go out for a couple beers tonight?"

Takamäki shook his head. "Can't. The wife told me to get groceries. Stuck at home."

"Alright. I'll ask Joutsamo," said Suhonen, and slid behind the wheel.

CHAPTER 28
THE BAR AT HOTEL PASILA
FRIDAY, 10:15 P.M.

Suhonen ordered a Strongbow cider from the bartender and walked back to the table. Joutsamo took the glass, smiling. The Pasila Hotel was only about two hundred yards from headquarters and its downstairs bar had become a regular police hangout. Large windows cast the streetlight onto the circular booths along the walls. In the middle of the bar were a few tall tables ringed by bar stools, some still unoccupied.

"Thanks."

Suhonen shrugged. A street car rattled past the hotel.

For over an hour, they had talked about everything but the case. Both were intentionally avoiding it, but finally Joutsamo gave in.

"On the tape, Markkanen said you beat up an officer. What was that all about?"

"Mmm. It was just an act. In order to get on the inside, I had to stage a fight with an officer I happened to know," he tried to sum it up.

"I see. What was his name?"

"Ha!" Suhonen laughed. "Am I the subject of an internal affairs investigation?"

She felt bad for prying and tried to laugh it off, "You have the right to remain silent…"

"Sergeant Tero Partio," Suhonen said. "I don't have anything to hide here. I'd welcome the minister of interior, the ombudsman and the attorney general, the parliament, the president… They can all put me under the scope, but these hands are clean."

Joutsamo took a sip of cider. "Not that I suspected anything. Anyway, the case would've been solved even if we had arrested Saarnikangas right away."

Suhonen wasn't so sure, but he didn't want to argue.

"By the way, Juha was pretty pissed at you during the interrogations."

"No surprise," Suhonen remarked. "I'll go talk to him at some point. He'll calm down once he understands that he'll get out in a few years. He won't get life for his involvement."

"True."

"What about Markkanen?"

"He was stunned and had 'no comment.' We got a search warrant for his apartment, but didn't find much of anything."

"No money either?"

Joutsamo shook her head. "No. His wife and son live there too, but no trace of them."

Suhonen sipped his beer. "Markkanen's prospects are pretty shitty. He killed one of the Skulls' legends. And with his own scissors, too. Then there's the recording from Lindström's apartment…that'll definitely be played at the trial. He'll have a helluva lot of explaining to do. Not in court, but in the pen. Nobody's gonna believe it was his own wire. They'll think it's a cover story invented by the cops to protect their snitch."

"In the pen, he wouldn't survive an hour with the general population," Joutsamo added. "He'll have to apply for protective custody. A life sentence in there is twice as harsh. It's basically solitary confinement."

"Nobody'll have to listen to his bullshit, then," Suhonen said.

Joutsamo paused for a moment. "There's a contract out on you. It's right there on tape."

"Not the first time, nor the last. When that stuff starts to scare me, I'll apply for a desk job. I suppose they'll save one for an old hand like me."

Suhonen remembered something and rummaged through his pockets. "Oh yeah, I got some money."

He set the one-grand wad from Markkanen onto the table.

"Where'd that come from?"

"From Markkanen. For the Lindström gig."

Joutsamo smiled, took the money off the table and stuffed it in her pocket.

Both jumped when they heard Kulta's raspy whisper from behind, "Ooooh! Prostitution. For once, the police are in the right place at the right time. I've always dreamed of this." He shot a cheeky glance at Kirsi Kohonen, who stood next to him.

The redhead jabbed Kulta in the ribs and cut in, "I apologize in advance for Detective Kulta's obscenely large mouth, but may we join you anyway?"

"Guess we're still waiting on his gag order," Joutsamo smirked, and scooted over.